D1498808

Dear Janet,

I hope you enjoy my b

and a little about Brazil!.

Best

(and happy writing!)

Luis Rodrigues

xox

**I was no longer the dashing young man I once was, and I could not protect my niece...**

For one moment, I thought there was going to be a happy ending. I thought they would surrender. But, the next second, the boy with the gray pants standing close to us pulled Mariana violently from her aisle seat. He held her arm with one hand and the revolver with the other. I tried to get up and he pointed the gun right to my forehead.

"You make a move and she dies, Grandpa."

He looked right into my eyes. The reddish circles were inflamed around his pupils. I felt paralyzed and looked at Mariana. She was crying in silence.

"Uncle Fe..."

"Shut up, woman. Don't say anything. You will be quiet, and you are coming with us."

"No!" she said, now looking at him. "Please, no!"

"When we escape from the police, we will let you go."

I tried to get up again. "Please, take me instead of her."

He pointed the gun at me again. "Shut up, Grandpa!"

"Police will shoot us all if we take you. You are old, soon you will be dead anyway."

Felipe Navarra rises from poverty to conquer São Paulo, Brazil, the city he loves. He becomes a radio celebrity in the age of Bossa Nova, classic sambas, and *radionovelas*. On his way to fame and fortune, he falls into a heart-breaking love triangle with his childhood sweetheart and sells his soul to the dark dictatorship that took over Brazil from 1964 to 1985. His rise runs parallel with the city's decent into crime, where the gap between rich and poor gets dangerously wide and no one is really safe...

# KUDOS for *Days of Bossa Nova*

"No passport or time travel machine is necessary to experience life in São Paulo, Brazil, over the past 70 years of political unrest and financial change. Ines Rodrigues's descriptive writing will make you taste the Brazilian coffee and hear the Bossa Nova music, while you join Felipe on his journey from a poverty stricken childhood to a life of wealth and privilege." ~ Eileen Palma, author of *Worth the Weight*

"This multi-layered novel opens a window on Brazil for English speakers. Its humanity is illustrated in the characters of the Navarra family. It also tells the story of São Paulo in the second half of the century, the vibrant music, flavors and smells of the city...the criminality that infected every aspect of life. Rodrigues is a wonderful storyteller." ~ Marlena Maduro Baraf, blogger of the Soy/Somos series on *Huffpost*

"Rodrigues tells an incredible story of hardship, unbridled determination, and the unbreakable spirit of a young man determined to be all that he was capable of, no matter the cost. A marvelous read." ~ Taylor Jones, The Review Team of Taylor Jones & Regan Murphy

"*Days of Bossa Nova* opens a window on the rich, varied, and exotic country of Brazil that few travelers will ever see. We experience through Felipe both extreme hardship and abundant fame and fortune, but the good fortune comes at a price. A thought-provoking and moving story told in a rich and unique voice. I heartily recommend it." ~ Regan Murphy, The Review Team of Taylor Jones & Regan Murphy

# ACKNOWLEDGMENTS

This story had been in my mind for many years when I decided to join a writer's workshop at Sarah Lawrence College in 2010. On the first day of class, as we sat at a round table, two instructors, Patricia Dunn and Jimin Han, gave us a schedule, and we had to present our first fifty pages in a few weeks. I panicked, but they infused me with a magic confidence that just grew over the years under their mentorship. Thank you, Pat and Jimin, for all your guidance. You are the best.

While I was working on this novel, I also found the most wonderful writing group. This book would never have been possible without Ahmed Asif, Marlena Maduro Baraf, Nancy Flanagan, Jacqueline Goldstein, Rebecca Marks, Nan Mutnick, Eileen Palma, and Jessica Rao. You have my eternal gratitude and friendship. Rebecca, a special thank you for introducing me to the Black Opal Books family.

Carmen Hall, thank you for wise words, hugs, Cuban food, and for being such a talented copy editor. Thank you, Plinio Ribeiro Jr., Richard Minfelde, and Marie-Agnés Daumas, you always allow me to be myself, dance, and talk as much as I want. Christine Peckett, thank you for being the first brave person to read a non-edited draft and still believe I had any talent. Susan Kleinman and Preeti Singh, thank you for your constant support and friendship.

During my research in Brazil, I interviewed Mabel Freitas and Dr. Miguel Angelo Boarati. Thank you for your time and precious information. A special mention to Simone Alcantara Freitas and all my longtime friends from São Paulo, partners in navigating the big city.

Thank you to all the staff at Black Opal Books: Lauri, Faith, Jack, Arwen, you are great!

Thank you to The Sarah Lawrence College Writing Institute community for embracing me and giving me so many opportunities to grow.

Many thanks to the O'Connor clan, my amazing in-laws, who provided me with green landscapes, Irish love, and quiet time to do research and write over a few summers.

Thank you to my parents, who never get tired of telling me stories.

My husband David, thank you for being such a hard worker and for taking care of everything on the weekends that I disappeared to write. Thank you for teaching me how to be stronger and appreciate Irish humor. Thank you, Laura and Patrick, just for being yourselves. The three of you have more than what words can express. You have my heart.

# Days of Bossa Nova

## Bossa Nova

## Ines Rodrigues

*A Black Opal Books Publication*

GENRE: HISTORICAL FICTION/HISTORICAL ROMANCE/WOMEN'S FICTION

DAYS OF BOSSA NOVA
Copyright © 2017 by Ines Rodrigues
Cover Design by Fernando Naviskas
All cover art copyright © 2017
All Rights Reserved
Print ISBN: 978-1-626946-77-4

First Publication: MAY 2017

Published by Black Opal Books **http://www.blackopalbooks.com**

# DEDICATION

*To my parents*

Do povo oprimido nas filas, nas vilas, favelas
Da força da grana que ergue e destrói coisas belas
Da feia fumaça que sobe, apagando as estrelas
Eu vejo surgir teus poetas de campos, espaços
Tuas oficinas de florestas, teus deuses da chuva

(From the oppressed people in lines,
in the villages, slums
From the power of money that lifts
and destroys beautiful things
From the ugly smoke that rises, erasing the stars,
I see your poets appear from fields, spaces
Your workshops of forests, your gods of rain.)

Caetano Veloso, "Sampa"

# CHAPTER 1

*São Paulo, Brazil, 2009:*

On the day of my older sister's funeral, my wife gave me an extra dose of diuretic pills, and her mistake saved my life. Nobody died when part of the second floor collapsed, but I am seventy-five years old, and I've been enduring a long parade of physical suffering. How could I run downstairs as fast as the children when the floor, eaten by thousands of termites, cracked and shook like an earthquake?

I was supposed to see the body, but, as there was just one bathroom on the ground floor and I had to use it every ten minutes, we all thought it was safer for me to pay my respects from a distance and sit on the porch.

Termites were the only company Rá had in old age. Eating, chewing, carving their way into the old floors, cabinets, closets, digging sinister tunnels, inch by inch, the insects probably planned to take occupancy when the house was finally left alone. The fall of the second floor during her wake was more dramatic than *carpideiras'* tears—women who were hired in the old times to cry at funerals and make them all more sentimental. First we heard a cracking noise and, suddenly, the wooden planks seemed to be just made of paper as they started to fall

down and apart. People stomped fast down the stairs, before the room came down in a few seconds with the bed
and the corpse. Luckily, there was nobody standing in the
living room right below, as we always congregate in the
kitchen. The termite colony showed the Navarra family
who was the boss and who inherited my sister's house.

*Insects are like the criminals in this city. They rule
and control everything. Thank God, I don't need to go out
and win my bread every day anymore. I remember a time
when leaving the house in the morning had an exciting
taste of discovery: the cold smell of rain, the constant
drizzle in the winter, women wearing black gloves and
skirts, the metallic noise of trams scratching the rails.
Now we have a safety list instilled in our brains: don't
take your debit card in your wallet to avoid being kidnapped; don't wear jewelry; don't drive with the windows opened or, instead of a breeze in your face, you will
face a gun or a knife, your watch and cell phone will be
gone in seconds. Streets are crowded, buses are noisy,
rich people are snobs, and poverty has long lost its dignity.*

"Felipe, Felipe," Rá told me the last time we saw each
other. "Who, between the two of us, is going to close the
family gates?"

After all four of our siblings were dead, the gates were
the only prize we competed with each other for. As I was
not in great shape, my angelic wife Emilia used to see her
more often than I did, and Rá never forgave me.

"I am going to leave all my money to Emilia. She is
the only one who loves me," she said proudly, her brown
eyes opaque by cataracts.

I really couldn't care less about Rá's money. She was
so attached to her coins that they might bring bad luck to
whomever takes them. I'm pretty sure she died in her

bed, scrubbing her thumb and index finger constantly, the sign of counting money in her final hour.

"Auntie Rá was so scared, she didn't even have a husband or a child to pass the money on. She was lonely, the poor thing," my niece Mariana said.

She was always kind. I couldn't care less.

"Mariana, dear, can you bring me two slices of that chocolate cake I saw in the kitchen?"

"You know you shouldn't be eating cake."

"Today is a special day."

After the fall of the house, and after a cleaning crew was called to rescue the dignity of the dead, Rá was taken to the cemetery wake room where she stayed until the time of her funeral. The whole family, not more than twenty souls, remained all night, praying rosaries and sweating under the November humidity. She was buried in the morning after a quick ceremony, and I couldn't wait to go back to my air-conditioned Mercedes once we placed white roses on the fresh tomb. Rá was gone, and I was left to close the gates.

# CHAPTER 2

*Taubaté, State of São Paulo, 1940*:

My strongest memory of my father's death is the new outfit and shoes I got after his funeral. I was six and I had never had new clothes until that day, just hand-me-downs. I don't remember my father's face, just his hair, the color of copper, always cut very short. I know his hair was curly and abundant, because it is like mine, except mine is black as Mother's. He died of typhoid fever but the family always says it was of embarrassment because of his multiple gambling debts. Mother had to pay some of them afterward, but others were forgiven, due to our situation—a thirty-nine-year-old widow with six children and a miserable pension of 250 *réis* a month. It could barely buy all the rice, beans, bananas, and *toucinho* we needed to eat for the same period. So she decided to join her cousin Lorenzo in the city and change our lives forever. She has always been brave and adventurous, and taking us to the unknown didn't seem a big deal at the time, at least for her. We were terrified but we needed clothes for the journey.

She used her last *réis* and her dignity to go to *Armarinhos Garcia,* the haberdasher at *Rua São José.* She bought the whole piece of a striped white and green cotton fabric, thread, and ugly green buttons to match.

"Green is the color of hope!" she said as she stomped into the kitchen that day, the big roll of fabric in her arms, her customary generous smile on her face.

"Probably nobody wanted the green stripes., I bet it was cheaper than the other colors," Rá said behind her back, while we were peeling oranges outside in the backyard. We would never dare say anything like that in front of Mother. She would give us lots of *croques* on the head.

It took her and my sister Maria a week to sew buttoned shirts and long shorts for the boys, just Décio and I. The girls—Maria, Rá, Lana, and Gilda—had the same shirts and matching A-shaped skirts below the knees. We sold the big iron pots and the furniture that was not taken by creditors to my aunt Mariza, who also had become a widow years earlier and lived in my old grandpa's house with her eight kids. With the money, we bought the train tickets, along with three dozen mandarin oranges and plain crusty bread to eat during the trip.

A week prior to our big journey to the city, I was supposed to wear my new clothes. Although they were ready, I was too scared they would be damaged by my siblings. For three days, I saved the parchment paper that came from the bakery. They used to wrap French baguettes in these soft, translucent sheets of paper. They were never large enough to protect the whole loaf of bread, but they kept its freshness and smell. With a few pieces of paper I was able to wrap my shorts and shirt. They looked like fancy packages just out of an upscale shop.

I cleaned the shoes every day with a rag and put them on the top of my wardrobe. These are the first recollections I have of my life in the house where I was born, a *sobrado* with blue large windows facing the church, from where my eyes always tried to reach the sky. Life, as I know it, started in the city, and the *première* smelled of starch and coal from my mother's heavy flat iron preparing our travel outfits.

# CHAPTER 3

*Taubaté, 1941*:

The third class seats were small and very hard—just two wooden planks, one for sitting and the other as a backboard. We got into the train, and I ran aboard first. I wanted to save seats for all of us together. But along the journey, most of the passengers would stand up and walk around the carriages. It was impossible to sit in those torture chairs for more than half an hour. Now, when I think of it, I find the carriages of the poor much more social and lively than the first class, where everybody was sitting comfortably, reading, and just whispering. We were telling jokes, laughing out loud, and sharing the food we could afford to bring.

During our day-long memorable train journey to São Paulo, my sister Maria stared out the window, wiped her tears, and verbally announced her frustration. She had just turned eighteen and had to leave her boyfriend Louis back in Taubaté.

"I will never get married! He was going to propose! I know he was! Now I am in this family trap!"

Every time Maria blew her nose, Mother tightened her lips. She was not taking any of that. If we had been at home, I am sure she would tell Maria to shut up, that she was a fool, and, because of that, she would never get married, and so on. Here, she had to control her temper, and that's why she started to chat with a woman who was standing beside us. Mother stood up and asked how many kids the woman had. Of course, the conversation got boring, but before I stopped paying attention, I heard that she was going to visit her family in São Paulo. She had warm food in aluminum containers and a bag full of bananas.

I kept pulling Mother's arm to show her what I saw outside of the window: little dusty towns, the curvy tracks around the hill, the shape of clouds.

"*Sossega menino,* go to sleep!"

She had no patience for that. Mother always complained I was a chatterbox.

As our journey progressed, I warmed up to the small woman with rosy cheeks who shared her bag of bananas with us. They were *prata,* a quality of banana I had never tasted before: firm, smaller, and not as sweet as the *nanica* we used to have at home. I don't remember how many I ate, but hours later, when we arrived in São Paulo, I had an upset stomach. When my sister Rá asked why, I lied and said the oranges we brought were too ripe and the bread was horrible.

Lana was fifteen at the time and the prettiest of my sisters. She inherited my father's hair color and her shiny curls fell over her shoulders like liquid copper. She was the only one who came up with green eyes, and she stole Mother's full lips. Unlike Maria, Lana was pleasant, spoke softly, and was delighted with the trip and the move, as she dreamed about all the window shopping she would do at *Mappin Stores.* She talked to almost everyone and enjoyed holding the small children around while their mothers took a break. The green striped skirt and blouse Mother sewed looked different on her than on the other Navarra girls. Men turned their heads as she passed, and I've heard my mother telling my aunt that she worried about Lana in the city.

"Can you imagine what's going to be of this one with all those hawks in the city, used to easy women and with no morals? I have to find her a husband very soon."

Lana had different plans. She wanted to find a job as a secretary, not a husband. She saw herself getting dressed up to work every day, wearing long gloves in the winter, and taking the tram downtown, with a good salary to afford better clothes and shoes. A job like that was exactly what Mother feared, as she thought it would deliver her daughter to the hawks. My mother was a woman born in 1901, so she never believed in education or work for her daughters. She encouraged us boys to stay in school, as we would one day need a good job to support a family.

"But why should women have to study?" she questioned. "Elementary school is what we need to add and subtract at the grocery store and read signs in the street, maybe read a magazine or two. Women spend their days going from the stove to the laundry!"

Rá was just a year younger than Maria and both had already quit school for good. They spent their days helping Mother to cook, scrub the floors—"many, many times until they look like a mirror"—and take care of us, until they found their respective husbands. On the train, they sat together, enduring the torture of the hard seats for most of the time. They paid little attention to the images through the windows, passing as fast as a movie—cows dozing in the grass, as oblivious to the world as the two of them were to our trip companions. Maria still cried every now and then, and Rá tried to console her. Rá kept her head down most of the time and refused to eat. Chewing in front of anybody who was not family was embarrassing to Rá, though I never asked the reason for her behavior.

"I am a spinster now, I will never leave this miserable life," Maria cried. "I was so close to getting married!"

Rá, on the other hand, never imagined finding a husband. I don't think she ever had a boyfriend, or sex, or even had thoughts about it. She was always the one who said the wrong things at the wrong time. I thought she was unpleasant and hid behind her abnormal shyness. In my mind, staying away from her was better.

Mother was always scolding her for looking ugly and strange, like a groundhog. "She's like a *marmota*," she used to say, and "*marmota*" became her nickname among us.

Rá was the odd sister, the ugly one. She was the smallest and skinniest, never weighting more than 100 pounds. She had my father's copper hair and freckles all over her body. She was so mortified by her freckles that she never wore short sleeves, even when it was 100 degrees in the shade, during the humid city summers.

"I wanted to be rich just to be able to buy creams and make up, so I could hide this horror. It looks like a disease," she used to say about the freckles.

Half of the family had the same skin, and nobody else gave a second thought about concealing them.

Maria's face was also covered with freckles, and Louis, her boyfriend, used to say she was the most beautiful girl of the *Paraíba Valley*. They were introduced to each other the year before, at the Military Academy Ball, a big "find your own husband" kind of seasonal event in Taubaté. He was the son of a pharmacist who was there with his tenant brother. Louis and Maria started a proper courtship. He visited us every Saturday and Sunday afternoon, sitting on the living room sofa with Maria. My mother used to sit on a chair right in front of them. She invariably brought a plate with fresh pineapple slices as a snack and strategically placed it between the couple.

Mother had also a bowl with raw beans in her hands, and she spent the next hour in silence, threshing them while they talked.

Unable to soften Mother's heart, Louis—who was nice but not particularly good looking or charming—tried to gain our sympathy. He used to bring us caramels in a brown paper bag every time he came to see Maria. But one day, it was probably Decio's tenth birthday, came the most unexpected miracle. He gave a can of condensed milk to each one of us. We had never had it, not even on Christmas Day, when the grocery stores shelves were full of *Leite Moça,* destined to other family's special desserts.

The can was the size of a teacup, round, the label with the standing Nestlè maid—all beauty and European health—holding her bucket. That can was a symbol of foreign lands, their grounds covered with snow, that I would probably never see. Those images were magical in my little mind. We had to use a can opener to pierce the can, and *plop!* The soft custard-like cream would fill the small hole, all its sweetness spreading over the top of the can. The first lick was the best, and its intense sweetness used to make me shiver.

I can see my family on that train very clearly now. Mother laughing loudly, chatting, and all my brothers and sisters dressed elegantly in the same colors, with our small-town concept. We were naïve but hopeful.

I had no idea of what was going on, but now it's so clear how big the challenge was for us, and especially for Mother, who would never admit a failure or a mistake. She was always right and always the boss. Even after we grew up and left the house, we kept this fearful respect for her.

# CHAPTER 4

When the train arrived at *Luz* Station—*Station of Light*—and stopped on the platform, I felt I was part of a fairy tale. While we collected our belongings in the car, Mother was talking about an article she saw in a magazine years before. It was about the *Luz's* history.

"The walls and cast iron decorations are massive! They said in the article that the station was designed by the British and built to make old provincial São Paulo look more dignified."

I thought of the sleepy Taubaté we had just left behind, with cows and stray dogs roaming in the main square, its church bells loudly blessing ordinary life. It didn't prepare us for São Paulo.

Mother kept talking as we waited, slowly getting off the train. She brought up one of her favorite themes, Europe. "My grandparents came from Spain and your father's family as well, Felipe. Our last name, Navarra, is the name of a very important city, as large and beautiful as Madrid!"

We knew it by heart. We also read between the lines that she would give anything to cross the ocean and visit Spain. But it was more for the trip itself, as Mother was a natural traveler. She didn't need to discover the country, as she had it all set in her own imagination from the red sand of the fields in Plazas de Toros de las Ventas to the lace in women's *mantillas* and the meadows in the Parque del Retiro.

"In Madrid they eat *tortillas* for breakfast," she would say sometimes in the morning.

"And what is it, is it sweet?" I asked her as my mouth was watering just to think of a creamy chocolate cake.

"No, it's a potato omelet!'

We finally reached the platform, as long as a road. We almost couldn't see the end of it when the train stopped. It took us almost half an hour to get off. People had loads of luggage crammed in every little space so, when all the packages were pulled out, there was almost no room to move along.

"Let's go, let's go," a woman behind me complained, pushing us.

She turned to a young lady who might be her daughter, and they spoke in a funny language. I couldn't understand a thing. I bet she was complaining about us, as she talked and talked and pointed at me with her chin.

We walked with difficulty around the station, as we had a big travel bag with all our clothes and shoes in it. It was covered in a chess pattern fabric—black, red and white. The rest of our belongings—a few utensils, sheets, blankets, and my mother's collection of images of saints—were all accommodated in a few *trouxas,* the easiest travel bag in history. You just placed a sheet or blanket flat on the floor, put everything you wanted to carry in the middle, and then closed the four ends in two tight knots. Then we carried it as a big bag, remembering not to drag it on the ground. Otherwise, Mother would not be pleased.

"Lift it up, come on. Do you want to leave our stuff along the way?" she yelled at us all the time.

Darkness was falling upon São Paulo when we left the station, and I had my first glimpse at the streets that would be mine forever. The lampposts were too small, and they had a yellow pale light that didn't illuminate anything, but I never thought they had a useful purpose. In my mind, they existed to reflect the constant drizzle, and we would know how hard the rain was just by looking at the drops reflected around the light.

The *Luz* Square had the same elegant Englishness as the Station, and they were created in an effort to beautify the gates of the city a few decades before—brick towers, tall ceilings, dark wooden benches, and mosaics on the floors, like on Roman baths.

The coffee barons made São Paulo a rich city and put it in the map. Before the coffee fever that brought rich farmers to set residences and build sumptuous *casarões*, São Paulo was just a passageway, a high plateau connecting the Atlantic Ocean to the jungle. There were no bridges with golden sculptures, no theaters that imitated buildings from Paris, no *Luz*. The coffee barons, the kings of the coffee empire, could never dream that the immigrants they started to bring here in the 1800s to slave in their coffee farms wouldn't stop coming and would take over the imposing train station with *trouxas*—old fashioned trunks—wonder, and the fierce hope every immigrant brings in the eye.

My ancestors were some of these people who fled poverty from Spain. They ended up in the Paraíba Valley, harvesting the *green gold* until they couldn't move their sore fingers. It took one generation of hardship and ferocious savings until my grandfather could buy his own small piece of land in Taubaté. My father lost it at the gambling table, and there we were again, repeating the saga. This time it was just a train ride away. Displacement runs in the family.

Coffee fever was long over, and the new foreigners didn't go to farms anymore. They stayed in the city. São Paulo was an enormous magnet, and here we were, gazing at the street, in awe, dragging our junk and our ancient travel bag until we saw my uncle Leontino waving from the other side of the road. He would give us shelter for a couple of days.

# CHAPTER 5

D ecio fell ill with the flu on the first week after we arrived. His nose was red as a tomato and he coughed with a sound of death. Mother gave him honey with lemon and the best mattress in uncle's spare room.

At night we could hear her whisper, lying in the darkness, "*Ave Maria Cheia de Graça, o Senhor é Convosco...Ave Maria,* Hail Mary, Full of Grace, the Lord is with You..." praying the Rosary over and over.

It was all she could do. The money we brought with us had to be stretched for a few weeks, and we had to find a decent house to fit all of us. All my siblings—except Decio, Gilda, and I, who were too young—had to find jobs to help with the grocery store and the rent. Spending money at a pharmacy was not on Mother's plans, let alone seeing a doctor.

Almost one week went by and Decio didn't get better. I couldn't understand why Uncle Leontino didn't call a doctor, as our aunts used to do back in Taubaté. That evening I heard Mother talking to Aunt Elisa in the kitchen. I was building a fort with tree branches outside and, as they started their conversation, I stopped piling them up and glued my ears to the back door, trying to breath slowly so they couldn't notice my presence. The evening was quiet and it smelled of pink flowers and wet dirt. There was no breeze to disturb the lemon tree in the backyard.

Mother's voice was heavy. "I know I am more than a burden, but I have nowhere to go, and I am not finding any house. Rents are much more expensive than I imagined and I am always worried that Maria and Rá are not taking good care of Decio. I need a few more days. Please try to understand."

"I do understand, my dear. I was just asking when you are leaving because you don't have a small family, and we have to go on with our lives and take care of our expenses too"

"But I am helping with the food, and I can pay rent if this is the problem."

Mother's voice was now altered. She lost her cool very easily. While I was listening, my tummy started to ache and my muscles became tense. I didn't know the meaning of the word anxious, but I started to picture us on the sidewalk of Santos Dumont Avenue with the rest of our savings, our *trouxas,* and our horrible travel bag with nowhere to go. I even thought about stealing something interesting in Uncle's house and selling it— actually, there was nothing good to sell there—but I knew stealing was not good and, God forbid, imagine if Mother found out! She always said she could accept begging in the streets for food, but never having a criminal in the family. I believed Mother's punishments and harsh words would be much worse than going to jail. It couldn't be as bad as fifty *croques* in the head, sleeping outside for a month, or scrubbing the floors every week until Lent.

"It's not just the money," said Aunt Elisa. "We normally rent that room anyway, but not to seven people. Look at our situation: we have just three children. Suddenly, we have twelve people in the house, and you are all squeezed into one room, sleeping in three old straw mattresses. Listen, I will never let you down, all I was asking was how long you intend to be here. And I want to give you some advice about Decio. My dear, he needs to see a doctor. I don't want my kids, or your other children, to get sick. He has a bad flu."

I pictured my brother losing his life, not to the flu, but to leprosy, like those people Jesus used to heal in the Bible—their skin falling apart, the red scars all over, smelling of putrid organs. My tummy ache got worse. I had to close my eyes tight to make the images go away. What if Decio had it? No, it wouldn't be possible. At church they tell you to pray, and God will come and help you, as Jesus did with the leprosy people. So, given Mother's connection to her Rosary, it absolutely could not happen to us. We were protected, as long as Mother had her purple beads with the silver cross in her hands at bedtime.

Mother was in no position to complain. "Do you know any doctor or a clinic, Elisa?"

"There's a clinic at the end of the road behind the house. It goes all the way up the hill. It's about three kilometers from here. The only way to get there is to take the tram, the hill is too steep for Decio. The clinic belongs to the nuns, and all you will have to pay for is the medicine, if he needs some. I can go tomorrow with you. We have to leave before six in the morning. There's always a line by the door when they open it at eight o'clock. But they give priority to children," Aunt Elisa said. "We can ask Maria and Rá to cook and arrange Leontino's meal to take to work. My girls have to go to school, but they will help later with the little ones too. That's the best I can do."

Mother's voice seemed tired. "You don't need to come with us. Do what you have to do at home. I can take him on my own and the girls will look after the little ones and help you with the cooking. Thank you for everything. I hope, one day, somebody is as good to you as you are being to us."

"You are welcome. Get some rest now. You will need energy for tomorrow. Decio is already asleep and Maria is in the room with him."

"I just need some fresh air," Mother said.

She walked toward the living room window and opened the shutters. I knew she was still upset. She liked to watch the world by the windowsill back in the country-side. That was the only distraction for many people, peering at neighbors' lives. In the midsummer evenings, people used to bring their kitchen chairs to the sidewalk, so they could escape the heat indoors and chat. Here in São Paulo it didn't seem to be the same. People were always busy, always doing things in a hurry.

Mother was quiet at the window, lost in her thoughts. I pulled a chair close to her and climbed on it. She looked at me and immediately made room for one more at the window frame. I didn't dare say a word. It was warm outside. The smell coming from a jasmine bush was overwhelming.

That's when we saw the lady coming down the road, carrying two enormous grocery bags, apparently with lots of trinkets inside. When she came closer, I could see they were pots and pans.

"Mom, why is she carrying her pots and pans?" I asked.

I was so loud it was impossible not to be heard. Mother probably would have given me a disapproving scowl, but the woman responded from the sidewalk before she had the chance.

"I am a cook and I spend all day delivering food," she said. She had a different way of talking, always extending her last words. "Do you want to taste something tomorrow and maybe you can become my customer?" she asked with a smile.

Her voice seemed louder than mine, I thought.

I didn't expect to be heard, so I was suddenly shy.

Mother said, "No, thanks" with a smile so pale she looked more like a sad doll at a dusty shop.

The woman approached our window. "Maria Pagliucca, *muito prazer*." She put one bag on the ground and extended her right hand to Mother.

"Walkyria Navarra, *muito prazer*."

"Are you visiting *Dona* Elisa?"

"I wish it was just a visit. No, we are here to stay, we arrived a few days ago. We are here until we find a house."

"I live at Coroa Street. Two blocks down this road, you turn right, then just three more blocks, and there I am. Wait, are you looking for a house?"

"Any roof I can afford at this point," said Mother with no enthusiasm.

"My next door neighbors are moving and I think the house is not rented yet. It's an old place. It needs some repairs but the owners are honest people. You could talk to them even before they put a sign by the front door. Do you want to take a look? I am going home now, I can show you the house."

If we had been in the city for maybe a year, probably Mother would never have accepted that odd invitation. But she was so desperate that she didn't even stop to think about it. And that small middle-aged woman, with olive skin and brown hair pulled in a tight bun, couldn't be harmful.

"*Por que não?* Why not?" Mother said. "Let me just tell my daughter I am leaving for a moment."

"Can I go with you? Please, Mom, *please!*" I begged.

"You can come, but if you don't behave, you will have no dinner for two days."

The woman's house was a ten-minute walk from Aunt Elisa's. Within those six hundred seconds, we got to know everything about the odd woman's family from the Veneto, in Italy, how they left when the war broke and spread poverty on those hopeless lands.

"São Paulo seems scary at first, but you will find people here very welcoming once you pass the first barrier, believe me," she said.

"They might be welcoming if you have enough money to pay for the roof." Mother obviously couldn't help her grumpiness, even in front of strangers.

We went into Maria Pagliucca's house for a few minutes. She needed to drop her bags and tell her children she was home. I was amazed to see she left a twelve-year-old in charge of her other three children on their own all afternoon while she was delivering food. How wonderful could it be to have the house just for ourselves for some hours every day! Maybe that's the way it was in the city when your mother had to go to work. Exciting!

We left, walked a few yards, and knocked at her neighbor's door. A man in pajama pants and a shirt that looked like old passion fruit skin opened the door. He looked tired and not welcoming.

"Mr. Fontes, *boa noite,* sorry to disturb. I know you are moving and I have somebody who might be interested in the house. Can they take a look? *Por favor*..."

"It's a bit late..." He scratched his baldhead and looked at us. "Can you come back tomorrow?" he asked, looking at Mrs. Pagliucca.

"*Cinco minutinhos*...please," she insisted.

"*Está bem*, but just take a quick look. And don't bother with the mess, I was not expecting anyone."

He didn't even look at us. We entered quietly, stepping softly on the wood floor, being extra careful not to
trip on anything, just trying to be invisible. The living
room was small and the walls screamed for a coat of
paint. The kitchen was twice the size and they had a cozy
wood stove the length of a whole entire wall. The floors
were dirty as a pig hole, made of burned cement. It
seemed the man lived on his own.

"Stay here while we take a look upstairs," my mother
said to me.

I obeyed, but I was afraid of the man who completely
ignored me. As Mother came down with Maria Pagliucca
she inquired about the rent.

"I pay 120 réis a month, but you have to check with
the landlord. He lives two blocks away from here."

"Dona Walkyria will talk to him in the morning.
Thank you so much for letting us in, Seu Fontes."

The man didn't look at us, let alone follow us to the
door. He was sitting at the sofa, glued to the radio,
scratching his right toe, visible from a whole in his black
sock.

The air outside was fresh, and I was relieved to leave
the smell of cabbage and onions behind in the little
house. I wondered if that was the actual smell of the
house and if we would have to get used to that every day
if we moved in.

Mother sighed. "It's too expensive for me. It's almost
my entire pension. I am sorry I accepted your invitation
to come here, put you in all this trouble."

"Don't worry about it. If I were you, I would talk to
the landlord anyway."

"I don't need to embarrass myself. I doubt they will
lower the price for somebody they have never met before,
especially a widow with six children."

"Maybe they will, maybe they can help."

"I don't need their pity."

Maria Pagliucca stayed quiet, and I thought Mother had probably gone too far.

Mother shook her head. "Thank you, anyway, for everything. You are the nicest person we met here since we arrived."

"Well, you now know where I live. Stop by anytime. Our children can play together. By the way, you said your other son is sick? Why don't you take him to get the Friar's Pill?"

"*O, que é isso?*"

"They see people at the convent, behind the train station. You have to get there early, lines are long. Have you ever heard of Friar Octavio?"

"No."

"He was a friar who did *miracoli* in many places around São Paulo," she said. "He created these pills in order to save a woman who was dying in labor. She had a healthy child. Friar Octavio is famous for a lot of other stories! After he died, the other friars in the monastery continued to make the pills and distribute them to people in need. His pills can cure anything."

Mother, who was a big fan of stories of the lives of Saints, and all sorts of miracles, was suddenly amazed. "But how can I get them?"

"You have to go to the Luz Monastery, close to the train station. They distribute his pills there. They are free and anyone can take them. You just have to explain your health problem or maybe take your son with you."

Of course, the hospital was now out of the question, and off we went to Luz Monastery the next morning. I knew Mother would have more faith on the dead friar than on doctors. She always hated doctors and, even decades later, she cursed them every day in her deathbed at Samaritano Hospital.

Decio was weak and we decided to take the tram. What a marvelous adventure! I never forgot the smoothness of this big car rolling on the tracks. I could hear the *dlin dlin* when it stopped to collect and let out different people. Mother let me sit by the window so she could have some peace to look after my brother, who slept all the way. Through the glass, I could see how crowded the streets were in the morning. Men in suits were going to work. Some of them wore hats. They looked like the door-to-door vendors who were so common in our Taubaté. I thought about becoming a salesman when I grew up. I promised I would make a lot of money so I could ride the tram every day and eat bread with lots of butter at lunchtime.

There were few ladies on the street. Two of them, alone and well dressed, wore outfits like the ones my sisters saw in magazines. Most of the women were like Mother. They wore plain dresses or skirts always under-the-knees length. They invariably wore tights and flat shoes, normally black and with heels no taller than one inch. No hats or gloves. No shiny buttons or brooches adorning their chests. These women who wore the boring dresses always carried along children of different ages.

The trip was too short. I was just starting to dream when Mother told me to get ready as we would be getting off on the next stop. It was in front of the big train station, but this time we crossed the road and went to this place that looked like a church. Mother spoke to somebody at the door, and he pointed to a line on the side street. We went there and stood behind another family with four children, one of them a baby in her mother's arms. The mother was a blonde woman, and I stared at her for a long time, as it was very unusual to see hair so yellow that it looked like straw.

Then I realized she spoke to her children in a strange

way. Even if I was hearing it perfectly, I couldn't understand a word.

We were there for a while. Decio was quiet, the proof that he was really sick.

Mother gave us some bread she brought in her grocery bag. I sat at her feet and ate the bread slowly, so it would give me something to do besides looking at people passing by. The sky was cloudy, but the day was hot and humid.

Finally, our time came, and we were directed to a small table. A friar was sitting there.

"*Bom dia!*" he said, his voice as soft as a lullaby.

I felt sleepy.

"Why do you need the pills today, *senhora?*"

"Please help my son, he is very, very sick."

"What are the symptoms?"

"He has been with a temperature for a week, he coughs all the time, mostly at night. It's a scary cough. Do you think it might be tuberculosis?"

"No, I don't think so," he said with a smile, crossing his small and pale fingers over his belly. "Many children have the same symptoms at this time of the year when the season changes from spring to summer. The air gets heavier, you know?"

Mother took a deep breath. "Friar, we are not from here, I just arrived from the countryside a few days ago. And now I think I made a huge mistake, I put my child in danger. He could even die, and it's my fault. I should have stayed at home, that's our place," Mother said, and I saw her eyes fill with water.

Her hands were shaking. I don't remember seeing her like that, even when she used to go to dad's gambling clubs, armed with a broom in her hands, to make him come home. At those times, she was mad but now she was different. She couldn't find an answer within her own box of solutions. And Mother always solved all the problems.

The friar paid attention to all she said without interrupting her. He smelled of Lux soap, the same one Uncle Leontino had in his bathroom. The friar was a small man with pale skin. His gray hair was greasy and carefully combed toward the back of his head. I thought maybe I could become a friar when I grew up. They must make a lot of money to afford nice soap. I was tired of having showers with coconut soap we bought in big bars at the food market, the same soap we used to wash our clothes and the dishes.

He then opened a drawer and took out some envelopes the size of a pillbox. They were actually pieces of parchment paper folded four times, forming a perfect square. When he unfolded them, there were these almost invisible pieces of rolled paper looking like rice grains.

"Mom, is Decio going to eat paper?" I inquired.

Mother didn't even bother to answer in front of the friar. He looked at me with a saint's smile. He gave Mother a few of the squared envelopes, each one containing three pills. They should last a week.

"Make him swallow one pill three times a day. And pray. He will get better soon. Also, don't forget to give him plenty of water. If he doesn't get better in three or four days, come back and see me. Do you have enough food in the house? We give away some bread and soup, as well, on Tuesdays and Thursdays."

"I still can manage the food, but it's good to know we have an option," she said. "Thank you so much, you are very kind."

"God bless you all," said the friar. He turned to me and drew a cross on my forehead with his thumb.

Mother put the pills carefully in her money pocket, and we left. Decio got better in three days.

# CHAPTER 6

When Decio was unbearable again, making my life hell and driving Mother crazy, making noise and running around, she decided it was time to move on. Convinced by Aunt Elisa, who couldn't wait to get rid of us, Mother decided would talk to the grumpy man's landlord.

On Monday morning, she put on her pink Sunday dress and carefully combed her short dark hair, styled as in a picture of Louise Brooks she saw on a magazine years before. Mother was not fat, but she had big bones. When she dressed up, her frame looked even larger. She came back an hour later in tears. She went upstairs, changed the nice dress for a shabby *avental,* and made *café com leite* for everyone. We sat around the kitchen table. Uncle and Aunt were not at home, and our cousins where busy playing at a neighbor's house.

"They can lower the rent to 100 réis a month, but just if we give them six months payment in advance. I don't even have extra for a doctor, let alone 600 réis. Oh, Lord, why did I decide to come to this place? We should go back to Taubaté. I don't even remember how many houses and apartments we have seen since we arrived. We will end up in a *cortiço*," she said and started sobbing like a child, her nose and cheeks turning red and shiny.

I had heard that *cortiços* were horrible places where many families lived like rats, sharing rooms and bathrooms without water or electricity. I got scared.

"Mother, why don't you take your ring to the pound?" Maria asked.

"The ring dad gave her when they got married?" Rá quickly replied. "But that's our inheritance."

"Well, what's the point in keeping something valuable if we are sleeping under the bridge or in the *cortiço*?" Lana said.

"I saved it, regardless of all the debts your father left—so unfair," Mother said.

Decio, Gilda, and I had our drinks quietly. They were too light, more milk than coffee. Mother went upstairs and brought down a lacquered box the size of a bible. Inside, there was her rosary, her prayer book, a few letters, and a small black velvet bag, tied with a string. Mother opened it and took out the ring. The ruby was rectangular, the size of a pea, held by two very small hooks shaped like lion paws. On the sides, there were two almost invisible diamonds. It was an old fashioned piece that fitted perfectly on Mother's long fingers. I saw her wearing that ring a few times when Dad was alive. She put it on slowly and tears rolled down her cheeks. She finished her coffee, stood up, and left us sitting there. Maria and Rá cleaned up, and nobody said a word. Mother always preferred to cry alone.

We moved to our new house in *Coroa* Street one week after she sold the ring. One hundred *réis* would be our rent after the seventh month, and everybody would have to work hard to make ends meet. The old man in pajamas left us two twin beds with straw mattresses in good condition and also the living room set—one leather sofa, two armchairs to match, a dark *jacaranda* coffee table, and a nice *cristaleira*. This one was Mother's favorite part of the deal. *Cristaleiras* were tall cupboards with glass doors, intended to hold all the fine china and crystal, things people normally got as wedding presents. The items were permanently shown in dining rooms as in an exhibit.

If we ever had any crystal glasses or china, they were probably sold before our moving. Mother proudly arranged her unmatched white pottery cups and empty jam jars in the *cristaleira,* and we used it as any other cupboard for many years to come. I was disappointed when I realized the pajama man didn't leave his radio, as it would have been so nice if we could have a big fancy radio so I could listen to my favorite songs.

A few days later, we got a nice surprise. Uncle Leontino, a professional carpenter, arrived on a Saturday morning with a *caminhonete,* his small old truck loaded with a heavy rectangular kitchen table in the back. He and his aide pulled it out of the truck slowly, sweat dripping over their foreheads. It took them more than half an hour to bring it to our kitchen, passing carefully through the narrow doors.

"Walkyria, it's not a perfect table. It's made with demolition wood, there are some imperfections, but it also makes it unique. We made it at the shop. It's our present for you. Good luck in the new house," Uncle Leontino said while he polished the table with a yellow cloth.

Mother was so happy that she invited Uncle and Aunt for dinner that night. After he left with the other man, she realized we didn't have anything special to offer. We had a large bunch of bananas sitting in one of the kitchen corners, rice, and beans. Mother cooked bean soup and banana bread with the last cup of sugar we had on the shelf. She put magic and hope into that meal, and it came up quite delicious. It was the first of thousands of celebrations we would have around that heavy table.

In the end, we drank black coffee and Mother spilled her entire cup by accident on the bare wood. A stain was still visible the next morning, and I asked Mother if she was upset with the mess on the new table.

"No, Felipe, not at all. I think this is a sign of luck."

The coffee mark had the shape of a star.

# CHAPTER 7

*São Paulo, 2008, one year before Rá's death*:

U ncle Fe, are you sure you want to take an hour ride on the bus with me?" my niece Marianna asked. "You can reschedule the doctor until the car comes from the dealer."

"If you were not going to the university, I would not do it, but it will be nice to have your company and to remember old times when I always took the bus around town. We can leave early and you can come to the doctor with me. Then I will call a cab when I am done."

"Why don't we go on the cab together? The bus can get crowded crossing the city in the morning, Uncle Fe. You will be very tired."

"I am not dead. And you will be with me anyway. I haven't taken a bus for such a long time. I sometimes miss the flavor of living in this city, of seeing real people. I get sick of this bubble: condo, garage, car, driver, shopping mall, doctor's office. Let me just have an adventure, Mariana, come on!"

"If it makes you happy."

"Okay," I said. "We will have to take the bus two hours before your classes start."

"It's a deal. I have to go now." Mariana said goodbye

with a laugh, kissed my forehead, and left. Her long brown hair was always tied in the back, and she carried elastic bands around her wrist all the time. Her hair smelled of baby shampoo and family life.

Later, of course, came Emilia. "A man of your age and in your position doesn't need to ride a bus, for God's sake."

"What's the fucking problem?"

"First of all, watch your language. You are getting older and rude! And think about it. Buses are not comfortable or safe. Do you know how many robberies happen in buses nowadays? You just take the bus in this city if you really need it."

"There you go again with your safety, blah, blah, blah. If we think too much about what's safe, we don't go out at all," I said, picking a fight, but I had to confess Emilia was right. Life was getting more dangerous here, but on that day I was in the mood to cross São Paulo on a bus as I did for half of my life. "At least if I die tomorrow I will remember this last ride."

She rolled her eyes, and that was the sign of giving up. She said nothing and left the room, making no noise, as she always did. Emilia walked as she was flying low, a pale woman of small and soft gestures. My voice, instead, was like thunder. I had olive skin and always closed doors with a bang.

I would never give up on the bus ride. It would be fun to do something different with Mariana. She has been a light in my life since she was born twenty-four years ago, the granddaughter of my younger sister Gilda. It's impossible to dislike her, especially when you knew her struggle, coming from a suicidal mother, unhappy grandparents, and an absent father. Taking care of her was my way to make up with my little sister who died so young. And it all came into place, as I never had children of my own. Sometimes I think I should have done more for Gilda while she was still alive and struggling with a miserable existence.

I never thought life would pay me back in such a tragic way. The number 137 crossed the city East-West to the USP Campus, and we were at the bus stop at Rua Augusta, half way to the university, two stops before it got crowded going down Rebouças Avenue and not even a fly could fit in the aisle.

"Mariana, we should take a bottle of water with us, it's a long ride," I said.

We were standing at the bus stop half a block from my apartment.

"Good idea. Let me run to that café and get it quickly."

"No, no, look! We have no more time, the bus is coming."

"We can take the next one."

"Are you crazy? It's going to take almost half an hour. I can't stand here all this time. Let's go without the water, and nobody will die because of that."

"All right then."

It was just after eight in the morning. We got in and, right away, somebody gave us a place on the first row, behind the driver.

"At least people still respect the elderly here," I whispered to Mariana.

The bus ride was still as I remembered: smells of old sweat and sweet Avon perfumes mixed in the squish-squash of the crowd. Many travel all the way standing up, their bodies too close to each other, shaking with the jolts. The journey was punctuated by long detours, in order to reach some forgotten places, everybody being pushed to the left and to the right as the bus advanced on the sharp curves. I was enjoying my seat and the sight of those places, desolated corners of this puzzled city you don't see very often when somebody drives you in a fancy car all the time.

The bus went all the way down Rebouças and reached the long bridge over the river. At the stop, right before the bridge, some people got off.

"Finally, we can breathe here," I whispered again.

Mariana just smiled.

The wheels were starting to move again when five young men got in, rushing at the last moment. They were agitated and there was something wrong with them. As the doors shut, I felt heaviness in the air as if we were in a gas chamber. My mouth got dry.

*Damn it, we should have gotten those bottles of water*, I thought with a bad premonition.

The bus started moving again. The five boys, still standing close to the driver, showed five guns.

"Hey, *bacanas*, nobody moves," one of them yelled. "We want watches, jewelry, money. Don't say nothing or you will die."

His voice was hoarse, as if he hadn't slept for many nights. His eyes were injected with red anger. The bus crowd was disoriented and started to move to the front of the bus as the thieves cut their way toward the back. Mariana held my hand tight. We didn't say anything to each other. A woman was standing close to our seat, and I saw sweat coming down her face. Her mouth was whispering a prayer, "Our Father who art in heaven…"

"Keep calm, keep calm, don't react," Mariana told me, her voice trembling.

She was holding my arm so tight I felt pins and needles in my hands. All I could think was that probably my heart would stop right there, and I would be dead. Who would save Mariana?

Despite the efforts of the crowd to get rid of the

thieves as soon as they got to the next bus stop, when they would probably order the driver to open the doors and escape as a flash, something went wrong. The five men were moving fast and were already coming back to the front of the bus to reach the door, taking everything they could on the way and dropping all people's belongings in a cloth bag that looked like a pillow case.

Suddenly one of them realized a man was dialing the police emergency number from a cell phone. The thief immediately turned and shot the man's hand without a word. The noise echoed like a bomb. Blood, screams, tears, people holding hands. The bus skidded, the driver's hands shaking like Jell-O.

"If someone else calls the cops, this is it," one of the boys said. "Next shot will be on the forehead!"

He was standing not far from Mariana, the gun pointed to the back of the bus.

His eyes were very dark, and he seemed to be looking nowhere. There was a scary emptiness on his face. He was dressed in gray formal pants, Nike sneakers that looked brand new, and a T-shirt with a surfer in the front. His eyes were reddish around the pupils. He seemed happy to be in charge. All the boys' eyes were scarier than the guns they had in their hands. I just prayed for them to go away fast. That's when we heard the sirens.

Four police cars were coming by the end of the bridge. They stopped quickly, screeching tires, blocking the bus passage as in an American movie.

For one moment, I thought there was going to be a happy ending. I thought they would surrender. But, the next second, the boy with the gray pants standing close to us pulled Mariana violently from her aisle seat. He held her arm with one hand and the revolver with the other. I tried to get up and he pointed the gun right to my forehead.

"You make a move and she dies, Grandpa."

He looked right into my eyes. The reddish circles were inflamed around his pupils. I felt paralyzed and looked at Mariana. She was crying in silence.

"Uncle Fe…"

"Shut up, woman. Don't say anything. You will be quiet, and you are coming with us."

"No!" she said, now looking at him. "Please, no!"

"When we escape from the police, we will let you go."

I tried to get up again. "Please, take me instead of her."

He pointed the gun at me again. "Shut up, Grandpa!"

"Police will shoot us all if we take you. You are old, soon you will be dead anyway."

Another boy came from the back with his gun. "Should we take care of Grandpa now?"

The other laughed and Mariana pleaded, "No, no! I will go with you. Please leave him alone."

The second boy looked at me and, for one second, we had the same thought: Shoot? No shoot? But the others called from outside:

"Let's go, let's go, move, move fast, Tião!"

And the beast had a name, Tião.

I heard the screaming outside and I got dizzy. The air escaped from me, as I couldn't see Mariana anymore. I started to find it difficult to breathe. I think I told people to watch over my niece, not let them kill her. I remember something pressing on my chest and then nothing else. I woke up at the hospital with Emilia by my side and a couple of IV tubes stuck into my arms.

"Where is she?" I asked Emilia as I opened my eyes.

"We still don't know," she said. Her eyes were two red and purple puffs, like two small prunes.

"We have to do something."

I started getting up but felt chest pain and a nurse came in at that moment.

"Mr. Navarra, you had an emotional breakdown and have to rest now."

"How can I rest? You don't know what you are talking about! My niece was kidnapped by gangsters."

"You have to get better to be there for her when she comes back," Emilia's voice was a tired whisper.

The nurse was firm, no sweetness. She gave me an injection with such efficiency I got scared. Soon, I felt dizzy but before I fell asleep I remembered the last scenes I heard at the bus before I collapsed. The boys were yelling at the policemen outside.

"We will kill her if you approach, let us go, let us go, son of a bitch, *filho da puta!*" They were angry. They pulled me Mariana as if she was another bag with money. They had a car waiting by the end of the bridge.

When I woke up for the second time, almost twenty-four hours after Mariana was kidnapped from the bus, Emilia told me there was still no news about her. The doctors cleared me to go home, and I almost preferred to stay in hospital. I didn't want to go back home and not find Mariana there. The guilt about not taking the damn taxi was killing me. That Tuesday was supposed to be an ordinary day, when she would get to university in time for a public health conference in the main theater. She also had a haircut scheduled for five o'clock in the afternoon.

# CHAPTER 8

I left the hospital the day after the kidnapping with no news about Mariana. The twenty-minute trip home was a different world from the top of a mountain in the Alps into a war zone with no previous warning: from sterilized corridors and whispers to thousands of car engines, horns, dust, gray smoke, and people, so many loud people.

I never realized São Paulo could be so loud. People can hurt your ears when they talk, when they cheer each other in the street, when they complain, even when they don't say anything. When I got into my car and shut the door, Wilson, my faithful driver, was prompt to say:

"I am very sorry, Seu Felipe. "

"Thanks, Wilson."

He had been our driver for many years and, even if he knew how to be invisible when necessary, he was not being the best silent companion we needed that day. He kept saying that Mariana's face was on the news and the police were all over the case. When we got home, some neighbors and the doormen were waiting at the lobby to sympathize.

It was embarrassing, and, I had to say, annoying.

"She will be okay. We are praying for you," said Anderson, a skinny doorman with slicked hair, wearing white gloves that made him look like a poor version of Michael Jackson.

Everyone had something to say. After five minutes, I was bored to death and couldn't get away that easily, but Emilia saved me:

"Thank you so much for being here, but Felipe is still weak and he needs to rest. We really need to focus now, but we appreciate your kindness."

She kept talking and dispersing the crowd while I turned my ears off and entered the elevator.

"She's been gone for two days," I muttered.

I didn't say anything to Emilia, who could not eat and barely spoke, but I was starting to prepare myself for the worst.

Why were they keeping her for so long? There was no reason. If they wanted a ransom, somebody should have called already. But maybe they wanted to hold the call so we get more desperate and pay quickly when time come. I wondered if I should move some money to my check account."

I was thinking about calling the bank when the elevator went up in a *whoosh*. It always reminded me of a space capsule. But nothing prepared me to open the door after I left the capsule and saw the apartment where we all lived together, this time with no clue of Mariana's destiny. Something hit my stomach, like a twenty-pound stone was just placed in there. I fumbled to get to the sofa, my vision suddenly blurred. My legs were cold and, for a moment, I thought I was dying. I sat down and the bus came to my mind. Why, my God, why had I had the stupid idea of going on that trip? Why we didn't buy the bottle of water we wanted and take the next bus? Why?

A wave of sorrow covered my body as a blanket. I thought about my worst mistakes, the lies I told over the years, or things I never revealed, all the suffering I caused. I was being punished. It had to be that—

"Do you want a cup of tea?" Emilia asked. Her voice was weak, seemed to be disappearing, but still had power to take me away from my dreams and tortures.

"I want strong coffee. No sugar, no milk."

"Good, you can't have too much sugar anyway."

I said nothing and started to think about the next steps. What else could we do that the police and the detectives were not doing? How did we prepare for paying a ransom? Who we should call?

"Emilia, could you bring me a piece of paper, a pen, and the phone?

She came after two minutes with it.

"I have to make a list, a list for our next steps. We can't be sitting here, waiting for her to come back. *Pensa, Emilia, pensa!* Think. Think of all the influential people we might know. I've been in an important business for so many years. We must have something left of it."

"She came with two cups from the kitchen and placed them on the coffee table."

"Where's Rita?" I asked.

"I told her to stay at home for a couple of days."

She sat beside me and we began writing a list of names. We started remembering so many people I had forgotten over the last few years while my health was not at its best, after I retired and felt tired of social life. I couldn't believe I had such a long list of contacts—from people in the media, on TV, and people with connections to the police. Emilia and I started making calls. Each person we called involved a long conversation. Everyone shared how worried they were, and they all offered help. After a few hours of talk, I realized the coffee was still on the table, cold as black ice in a cup. I went to the kitchen to prepare another one when my cell phone rang. Unknown number.

"Hello."

I could hear only a cracking noise of bad connection.

"Yes, hello, hello! Mariana, is that you? Please, don't hang up. Talk to me!"

The person hung up. I was petrified. I had to sit down as my hands were shaking and blood just ran away from my face. I tried to call the unknown number back, just in case but it was not set to receive calls. I was sure there was some connection to Mariana. What should I do?

Emilia was talking on the phone in the living room, and I didn't want to scare her. I took the phone to the laundry room and stood by the window. I thought about a million people, but couldn't call anyone. What if she was calling again? *Stay calm, stay calm. Focus. Breath. One two, one two. Bullshit. Who can relax in a situation like this?* I was cursing, sweating, but kept going with the coffee machine until the phone rang again after two long minutes.

"Hello, it's Felipe. Mariana! Mariana, is that you? Please say something!"

I heard a voice on the other end of the line ask, "Do you accept a call from Osasco?"

"Yes, yes, Mariana?"

I waited for the person to respond, for that annoying sound to end. Sweat started to drip from my forehead. I closed the laundry room door.

"Hello, who's there?"

"Uncle Fe! Uncle Fe, it's me!"

"Mariana! Oh my God, you are alive!"

She started to cry. I could hear sobs and the line being cut off every two seconds.

"Please Mariana, don't go away, where are you?"

"I don't know. Uncle Fe, they left me in the street."

"Where?"

"I don't know."

"Please, ask someone, give me a clue, let me come get you."

Sobs again. I could hear voices close to her. I got nervous.

"Stay with me, please, just give me a clue."

"Hello?"

That was a woman's voice. I could feel the cold blood going up my legs, the trembling in my hands holding the cell phone.

"Who is this?"

"My name is Esther. The girl knocked on my door and talked about kidnappers, bus, she is very confused."

"Please, where are you?"

"I am going to take her to a shop on the corner where I work and you can pick her up there, okay?"

I got angry because I could tell the woman was afraid, she didn't want to get involved, she didn't want Mariana in her own home. "Can you give me the address?" I asked.

"Sure."

The place was very far away, one of the cities around São Paulo, maybe one hour away.

"We will be waiting there until you come. What's your name, sir?"

"Felipe, Felipe Navarra. Thank you very much."

She hung up before I finished.

I ran to the living room, got Emilia, and went downstairs to find our driver in the garage. He was always ready to take us anywhere. In ten minutes, we were on our way. That's when I realized I was still holding the empty cup of coffee in my left hand.

# Chapter 9

I learned how to read and write in the spring of 1942. The school was a couple of blocks from our house, and I was attending classes every day since first grade started in the month of February. Gilda would be going after the next summer but not for long, according to Mother's plans.

"She just needs to learn the basic ABCs. Then she will be able to help me at home or find a suitable job for women, like Rá did at the hospital."

Rá was now a janitor at the Santa Lucia Women's Hospital. It suited her well as it was a quiet and simple environment where she was surrounded by women who were mostly nuns managing the hospital. She didn't need to interact with people since talking and making herself understood was one of her greatest problems. When she was at home, she hated going out and was incapable of even buying groceries on her own. It always made Mother furious:

"Your sister is a shellfish! She's good for nothing!" she barked, going from the living room to the kitchen, holding tight to her broom.

Rá would never confront her, she never had an attitude, and Mother knew it. I am now ashamed of realizing that she secretly liked to humiliate Rá since she always knew there would be no reaction. I think Mother was happy to have Rá around for just one or two weekends a month.

When Uncle Leontino's wife found Rá the job at the hospital, she was hired immediately with no interview, since she was recommended by my aunt, whose word was enough because the lab manager was her brother.

Three days before Rá started to work, we had to get her a few clothes. She only owned two pairs of knee length light brown tights and two dresses, both discolored, with flower prints fading dramatically in the belly area. She had a hand-me-down short coat for winter mornings that was too big for her size and a red wool cardigan with a missing button. She wore one pair of rope sole *alpargatas* in the winter and rubber flip-flops on warm days. She couldn't present herself on her first day of work looking like a peasant.

But how could we get money for new clothes? Mother was still doing odd jobs to add a few coins to my father's meager pension. She helped Maria Pagliucca with the cooking and she cut hair at home. Mother was never trained as a hairdresser. She did it by instinct and was reasonably good at it. Sometimes she would snap a tiny piece of an ear with the hair, but her services were so cheap there was no competition in sight. There was a special chair facing her small vegetable garden in the backyard for the haircuts. Eventually, people would pay her with *dulce de leche* bars, a bag of oranges, or even a live chicken that we kept in the yard until it was good enough for Sunday lunch. These unusual forms of payment were the reasons for our lack of money.

The angels were always on our side, as Mother used to say, pointing at the image of St. Benedict on the kitchen wall. Two days before Rá started the job, we considered borrowing a few dresses from Aunt Elisa when the campaign man knocked on our door. He came in a cart pulled by a sad gray donkey. His name was Oswald, and he was polite. He talked to Mother at the front door for a while, and I couldn't understand very much of what it was about. Mother always liked a good chat, especially with somebody different. I just noticed what he said when he mentioned the riverbanks.

"They will extend the paved roads all the way to this neighborhood. Part of the riverbanks will become cement and they will canalize the streams where the *lavadeiras* work."

*Lavadeiras* were women whose job was to wash clothes together by the stream that run behind *Coroa* Street. There were many of them in São Paulo at the time, mostly *mulatas,* who probably learned the trade with their slave ancestors. They walked the streets as soon as the sun rose, collecting clothes from house to house. They put them all in an enormous *trouxa* and walked tall with the loads on the top of their heads, like a super-sized African turban. I always admired their balance. They had an elegant way of walking, as their heads were always up and their posture was regal as a princess's on the palace steps. After collecting clothes in *Campos Eliseos,* they went back to the river or to the streams and washed everything with coconut soap. They left them to dry in the hot afternoon sun while they had their lunch break, chatting while their kids played around them. I was envious of these kids because I imagined they never went to school, as I had to do every day. Now I know these children never crossed the school gates, as so many other poor kids of my time. We could always see a tiny hand washing cars, pulling carts at the market, or helping a mother who was a maid, slowly learning a trade. These kids never had time for school. They started life with a job.

In the late afternoon the *lavadeiras* walked back home with dry clothes on the top of their heads. I still can remember their sweet smell of soap in the sun. All the clothes were then pressed under heavy coal irons and folded impeccably. Sheets, towels, and linen shirts were ready to be delivered to soft beds, tiled bathrooms, and important men. The next day, the *lavadeiras* woke up with the sun, had black coffee and bread in their kitchens, and prepared for the long walk again, in order to give back the clean and take care of the unclean one more time. Part of their job was to make dirtiness invisible.

"But this will be the end of their business!" exclaimed Mother, her hands over her mouth.

Oswald nodded. "Many women in this area won't be able to support their families. They are mostly single mothers who learned their trade from their own mothers. It's a way of working and keeping their children close by instead of leaving them under the care of older siblings or paid help. We don't know what else to do. My own mother is one of the oldest *lavadeiras* on this part of town. She's been here since the 1920s and she doesn't know any other job."

He talked and talked. I could see Mother was distracted, cooking up something while looking at the cart. Before saying goodbye, Oswald picked up two pieces of folded white fabric and gave them to Mother.

"Of course, I will help you. It will be like a civic duty!" Mother said while she waved goodbye and called "Good luck" once again.

Next thing I saw was Mother filling our biggest bucket with water and Clorox. She bleached the sheets, making them shiny white. She spent the next day sewing two new dresses for Rá. They were both plain, but Mother managed to use a few ribbons here, a couple of old buttons there, and they ended up much better than anything Rá had in her drawers. Later, I asked Mother why the man had given her the fabric.

"It was not fabric. They were sheets for the *lavadeiras* campaign against the stream canalization. They are painting slogans on white sheets some linen shop donated and asking neighbors to hang them in front of their houses to show support."

"But you said you were supporting them."

"I actually am, but I really wanted the free fabric to make Rá's dresses.

"Was it a lie?"

"No. I said I supported them, but I might not have said I was going to put the slogan up."

"What if the man comes back to check?"

"I will tell him the wind blew the sheets away. He may even give us more fabric," Mother said, while opening the top drawer of her dresser. She picked up a small package, wrapped in brown paper and gave it to me with a smile. She had made two pairs of boxers with the scraps for my brother and me. I hugged her tight and forgot about the lie and the *lavadeiras*.

# CHAPTER 10

*São Paulo, 1943*:

Maria turned twenty years old in September of 1943. By then, she was Mother's number one assistant—cooking, cleaning, washing clothes, mending socks and shorts, taking care of us with diligence, while Mother worked on different little jobs to put enough beans in the pot. At the time, when a girl reached this age, her destiny was sealed, as it happened to Antonella Pagliucca, our friend Maria's daughter. She was nineteen and already pregnant with her second child. She had married at sixteen, the same age Mother married my father and started our large family. Some other girls we knew were in the same boat, not even twenty years old and already running a family enterprise with the same diligence Maria had toward us.

"Energy and hope are endless at this time of our lives," Mother used to say, while talking about those girls.

I now realize the weigh these words had on her as she looked back on her own experience with my father, all those years she had to share him with the gambling tables.

After a year of crying and waiting for letters that got

scarce, Maria stopped complaining about her old boy-friend, but there was still no sign of another one.

"I am sure he already has somebody else," she said almost every afternoon after checking the mailbox where there was never anything for her. She was then quiet for the rest of the day. In one of these afternoons, I sat in the kitchen playing with my toothpick soldiers and I noticed she was crying.

"Maria, are you sick?"

"No," she answered without facing me.

"Why you are crying?"

"I am not crying."

"Yes, you are."

"No, I am not."

"Yes, you are."

"*No!* Don't you have anything to do? I need help sweeping outside before dinner.

The last time I saw Maria crying in the kitchen was the day before her twentieth birthday. The next morning Decio, Gilda, and I gave her a newspaper necklace we made ourselves.

She was very emotional and promised us she would wear it for the whole day. "I don't think I will ever have children of my own, but I don't need them, as I am so lucky to have my little brothers and my sister."

She squeezed us all in the same embrace, and I could feel her warm tears on my cheeks. Her brown curly hair smelled like the jasmine in warm evenings and this scent still comforts me.

On that same day, around dinnertime, somebody knocked on the door. I looked through the window and didn't recognize Louis. He seemed even shorter than before, around five feet, five inches, the same height as Maria. His bulldog eyes gave him an older look. His mouth was always on the unhappy face mode, falling down, and, when he smiled, he always seemed to be pretending. Joy was definitely not made to fit his looks.

He was wearing his military uniform. He entered the house and went straight to shake Mother's hand, always respectful, or maybe scared of her, like everybody else. Mother, surprised as everybody else, led him straight to the kitchen table where we were having coffee with corn cake.

He sat there, facing Maria who quickly took off her apron and passed nervous fingers through her hair all the time, hoping her curls were not all over the place. She had a silly smile on her face and didn't say a word. Louis and Maria kept just looking at each other. At that moment, I thought love was quite boring. Louis brought us caramels, as usual, but I was a little disappointed there was no condensed milk in sight. After we finished the cake, Decio, Gilda, and I were told to leave the table and eat the caramels in the backyard watching the chickens peck.

Half hour later, Maria came outside screaming, "I am engaged, I am engaged!"

I guess she wanted the entire neighborhood to know she wouldn't be a spinster, after all.

We hugged and kissed her flushed cheeks. Deep inside, I was not affected, as I felt Louis stealing my sister. She was the one who cared for us, and who would now take her place at home?

In the fall of 1944, my oldest sister was the first to walk down the aisle, wearing the same lace dress Mother wore when she got married. Maria moved back to *Taubaté* and, a few months later, she announced her first pregnancy. I was nine years old, and my own mother was about to become a grandma. I found it very peculiar to be such a young uncle and told everyone at school about it. It brought me some respect for a while, until I found something more exciting during a tram trip downtown.

Mother let me sit by the window, as usual, and, when we were crossing the Ponte Grande over the Tietê, I saw a group of boys walking on the grassy margins of the river. Each one carried a box. All boxes were too big for the kids to hold. And then I saw Antonio, our neighbor, one of Maria Pagliucca's sons, a few years older than me.

Two days later, he passed in front of our house while I was leaving and I asked him about the boxes. " I saw you by the river carrying them. What did you have there?

"Frogs to sell."

"What?"

"Yes, frogs. We hunt them in the riverbanks. There are tons of frogs there at this time of the year."

"But who wants to buy *frogs*?"

"The Italian restaurants at Vila Romana. People eat them."

I felt my stomach churn. "Who eats frogs?"

"In Italy, they are a delicacy. People fry them and the meat is very soft. You don't know anything about good food. In this place, all people eat is rice, beans, and yucca flour. You are all savages."

"I am not a savage! You are stupid!"

We were almost starting a fistfight when Antonio's friend Roberto intervened and threw me at the lion's cage. "Felipe, why don't you try to chase the frogs with us? You can make a lot of money selling them, but before becoming our partner in the business you will have to try one. People in the Italian bar give us some fried *rãs* when we go to make deliveries. You can come with us and we will see if you are good enough to work in our team."

Now it was a question of pride and—most importantly—of money. I thought that I could afford my own condensed milk cans and no frog or smart older boy would jump in my way.

They invited me to a " practice hunt" on the next day after school, and I accepted. It was more difficult than I imagined.

We were five boys: Antonio and I, Roberto, his brother Juca, and a small boy that I had never seen before. He was probably six years old. They gave me a trap they made with old mosquito nets tied to the end of a tree branch in the shape of a little bag. The bag had a small opening and the trick was to get the frog exactly by the opening. Then we had to be fast and hold the opening, so it wouldn't escape. Next step was bringing the victim to the cage and releasing it inside the small space, without letting the frog go. It was not as easy as it seemed.

The frogs are no fools, and it takes a long time to trap one of them into the net. After I did it, I let at least four escape before I reached the cage. Their skin was slippery and disgusting, and it gave me the creeps when my hand touched them, but soon I got used to it, since all I had to do was think about the condensed milk. On that first day, I got just six frogs. We were all covered in mud from the riverbank and we smelled like shit. When the cages were full we walked more than one hour to the *Lapa* district where the Italian bars and small restaurants paid fifty cents for each frog.

They gave me a fried one to eat, and I realized the meat was similar to chicken. I even told Roberto I enjoyed it very much. On that first day, I came back home with two réis. The profit of my two other frogs went to Antonio, my "employer," but I didn't mind. That was my first job and for the next three years, until I was a teenager, I hunted frogs in the muddy riverbank of the Tietê. Soon, I got sick of condensed milk and started to bring things like sweet rolls or an extra pound of sausages home in order to help Mother.

Everything was getting better, life was almost perfect,

and I didn't know anything about the war that was going on in Europe.

Soon, its wave would come down and shake our little remote world. We thought we were so far away from all the tragedy, but we were very close to becoming a part of it.

# CHAPTER 11

*São Paulo, July 1944*:

B efore the Chá Bridge was built, people had to go all the way down to the valley to cross the river and reach the other side of town. It was a long and steep hill with a few paths of red dirt cut into the tall grass. When it rained it was a disaster. Even donkeys fell in the mud."

Mother loved to tell stories she had heard about São Paulo. She was happy on that Friday afternoon when she took me to St. Francis's church to light a candle. The church was beside a famous law school. After church, we crossed the Chá Viaduct to the new downtown, where there was an opera theater and the famous Mappin store.

My sister Lana said that all the rich people of São Paulo could be seen at Mappin on Friday afternoons. "That's when they buy new clothes for the weekend parties and receptions," she explained with an authority acquired from borrowed fashion magazines.

Lana was the prettiest girl I knew, and I thought no one could be more elegant than my sister. She had copper hair carefully styled like Rita Hayworth in *Gilda,* with the soft waves down her shoulders. Her skin was pale with freckles. Freckles ran in half of our family, thanks to my father's Spanish origins, but instead of hiding them like Rá did, Lana simply pretended they didn't exist. She had green eyes, like my father's, and her lips were perfectly heart shaped. Her only problem was always complaining loudly about the lack of money to buy clothes, shoes, gloves, hats, and make up. In her mind, these were investments for her future to find a rich and handsome husband, but Mother never listened to her.

"If you want to buy these *porcarias*, you find a better job and get them with your own money. I won't take food from my kids' mouths to put more rouge on your cheeks. And you better find a husband soon. Any husband!" Mother just yelled often.

Later, I found out that rouge was a powder stuff you put on your face to make people think you have been at the beach, or that you were healthier, with rosy cheeks. Some women in the streets looked like clowns with those pink stains on both sides of their face. I didn't understand why rich men would want a woman painted like such.

We were now crossing the Chá and there was so much to see that I forgot about Lana. It was far busier than I imagined.

"Mom, why is it called Viaduct of Tea? Do people drink tea here?"

"No, I think there was a tea farm here before they build the bridge, that's why it's called that."

Dozens passed by every second. Some people were nicely dressed in suits, ties, and hats. Others had just knee length pants with no shirts, their sweaty torsos shining in the hot afternoon sun. The shirtless people normally carried something heavy, and they had darker skin when compared to the nicely dressed people. Some women wore scarves on their heads or even fancy umbrellas to protect them from the heat, not unusual even in a July winter afternoon. Others were sitting in small booths selling food, and they put just a white handkerchief on the top of their *carapinhas* to avoid baking their brains.

"Come, come, enjoy now while it's warm: *empadas, coxinhas, pastéis* " they all yelled in different tones, directly at the people passing by.

One of them even talked to us. "Hey, you, lady with the little boy, give your son a treat today. I have the best *empanadas* in town."

The delicacies where basically the same: small chicken tarts, chicken fried croquets, and dumplings. The smell of cooked meat and fresh cilantro with garlic filled the air and I thought I could try on Mother's good mood, even if I had very few hopes of having a treat:

"Mom, can I have a *coxinha*?"

Mother kept on walking in silence, as she was not paying attention, but I knew she could hear me.

"Mother. Mother!"

"Not today." She didn't look at me or at the food stall. I stopped walking.

"Please, Mom."

"We can't stop now. I am going to show you the theater."

"I don't want to see any theater. I want a *coxinha*!"

I felt like crying, but I knew that would make things worse with her, as it would change her mood and she would probably yell at me in the middle of the street.

A boy passed by walking fast with a pile of newspapers in his hand. "The latest on the war! The war!" he shouted, waving the folded newspaper with his right hand.

I was distracted, looking at him, when the siren started. It was like a ferocious screaming mouth engulfing everything at once. Suddenly, Mother pulled me with a firm grip that just she could endure. I didn't understand what was going on. Everyone in the street was running somewhere. I didn't see where they all went, but a lot of people just stopped walking and were standing by the walls.

We got into this place with stairs that went down to a basement. There were other people there. They didn't talk to each other that much.

"What is that sound, Mom? Why are we here?" I asked when we stopped.

"It's nothing, just practicing. This is the basement of a big shop," Mother said.

"Practicing for what?"

"It's the war, practicing for an attack."

"Are we going to be attacked? When?"

"We don't even know *if* we will be attacked. We probably won't. But we have to practice just in case. If it happens, we have to find shelter as quickly as possible and the city will be completely dark if it happens during the night. Now *shshsh!*" She put her index finger over her lips and looked at me straight in the eye.

Everybody looked more bored than worried in that shelter. There were two dozen souls in the room and few chairs. We were all standing up, doing nothing. I had no idea we were at war. I just knew there was a war somewhere far away because of the movie trailers. My sister Maria used to take Gilda and me to the movies when she came to visit. Before the movie, there was always news about the war. It was already going on for a couple of years.

And then there was Mother's radio at home—we bought one to pay in twenty-four installments—with the news, which I rarely paid attention to since all I liked about the radio were the songs, Emilinha Borba the Radio Queen and Orlando Silva "*Atire a primeira pedra, aquele que não sofreu por amor.*" I also loved the group Anjos do Inferno, The Hell's Angels, "*Um Vestido de Bolero,*

*lero, lero, lero, já mandei comprar."*). I loved to learn the songs and pretend I was a radio star myself as that's what I wanted to be when I grew up. I had nothing to do among all those people, so I was singing to myself, trying to remember the words for this song, sitting on the floor, when I saw her.

First, I noticed her dreamy black eyes staring at me. She seemed scared. My first thought was what kind of nickname Mother would put on her because of those round, fishy eyes. She was wearing a red plaid skirt, white socks, and a navy shirt with short sleeves—maybe her school uniform. She was looking at me. I was the only child there, and we were apparently the same age. When she realized I was looking back she quickly hid behind her mother's dark green pencil skirt. Her hair was black and straight, like the hair of a Japanese girl. She had it cut below the ears and this gave her a sort of mysterious look, even being just a little girl.

I couldn't stop staring at her, and she stared back, always behind the green skirt. I felt a different happiness just by looking at her, and I realized I could do that for hours without being bored. This was very much against my jumpy nature.

Meanwhile, a man beside us looked at Mother. "How ridiculous is this? What are we doing in Italy, fighting Nazis, and we have the Nazi right there in Rio, at the presidential palace?"

Wrong move. Mother couldn't let it go. She was a great fan of the president Getúlio Vargas. "Why do you think he's a Nazi?" Her voice was already louder than normal.

"Well, everybody knows. Someone who's in power for fourteen years, chasing communists and opponents as hunters' dogs chase foxes can't be anything else."

"But we are fighting the Nazis."

"Well, after our ships where sunk by the Germans and the Americans were putting pressure on us, dumping millions of dollars here, we don't have other option, do we?"

Mother turned her face to the other side. She was quiet for a while. She was impulsive, but on this rare occasion, I now think she didn't feel comfortable picking a fight with a stranger in a provisionary bomb shelter. The man turned to somebody else and started the same blah, blah, blah.

The president was a constant topic of conversation at home. She defended Getúlio's ideas in front of neighbors, friends, and relatives, and she actually was able to make some people change their minds about the gaucho because she was so passionate about him. To Lana's total embarrassment and dismay, Mother had a photo of him beside St. Benedict's image in the kitchen. Her political opinions were never a secret.

"He is the poor people's father. Nobody, nobody, before him thought about us, about making our lives better." Her cheeks even got inflamed red when she talked about his ideas. "Minimum wage, eight hour daily working journey, paid vacations, who else did this? Who else? Tell me!"

That day at the shelter was different. She was probably scared too. We didn't know this side of war. We were released from the shelter after half an hour and came back home, but we were already facing other consequences, like food rationing:

"Who's going to the sugar line this week?" Lana used to ask us every Sunday morning on our way to mass.

"I was there last week and it took me three hours to get that little package of sugar, not even a kilo," Decio said.

"I am not going. Rá has to go next time," Lana said.

"Ha, ha, that's a good joke," Decio replied. "What if

somebody asks her a question while she's on line, and she gets so embarrassed and shy she drops everything on the ground and runs home?"

We all laughed while Rá just kept on walking in front of us.

"I can take the food coupons and go to the line," I said. I thought I was big enough to help.

"Who asked you to join the conversation, *pirralho*?" Decio asked.

"Look who's talking," I said. "Do you think you are that big? Look at yourself in the mirror, clown. You are older but I look smarter and everybody laughs at your red hair. My hair comes from the good side of the family!"

Nobody should ever mention the carrot-colored and curly hair that Decio, Lana, and Rá inherited from my father. Their silly curls didn't go anywhere and they had freckles all over their bodies. At the time, it was almost like a curse, it was unusual, and the unusual was not considered exotic but more like freak stuff. Sometimes people turned their heads on the street to look for a second time. But their expression was not of amazement or admiration, but of pity. That hair color and freckles was almost perceived as a disability.

"I am normal, and you are not, you are not," I sang to Decio, laughing and pointing to my own hair.

Instead of behaving as I expected—running toward me, trying to hit me or stop me—Decio went straight to Mother to complain. He would cry and make a fuss about it. "Felipe called me an aberration! Mom, he's mean," he whined.

"I didn't say that. I don't even know what *aberration* means!" I protested.

She invariably sided with him. He knew that she was on his side all the time. She sensed he was the weak child, the one who would be always in trouble.

And I got *croques* in the head and an extra job: to stay in line that Sunday to exchange the sugar and wheat flour coupons. I was actually happy with it, as it didn't sound like a punishment. We got the food stamps from Social Services because some items became scarce during the war. The larger the family the more coupons we got, but it was never enough. On that day, I ended up getting to the distribution center too late and all the flour was gone. The bakeries were charging a fortune for a loaf. I came back home with a kilo package of brown sugar in my hands and getting prepared for another punishment for being so late and not bringing the flour. Surprisingly, Mother was a bit disappointed but said nothing. She sent me to play outside.

I saw her opening the cupboard in the kitchen and pausing for a minute. All we had was a package of flaky corn flour, the one Mother used to eat with her hot *café com leite,* mixing it in her bowl as people do today with cereal.

She poured the thick flour onto a big plate. "We should mix it with hot water to make it softer."

Lana took the kettle from the wood stove. She held the handle with a kitchen towel and kept it far away from the rest of her body. She looked totally misplaced in the kitchen. She didn't have the natural household abilities Maria used to have.

She poured the boiling water into the mixture. Mother added salt, waited a few minutes, and started kneading again. She suddenly stopped and looked at the cupboard. "Do we still have fennel seeds, the ones we use for making tea?"

Lana took a while searching for a small package, tied with a little black ribbon. There were not even a handful of fennel seeds there, and Mother just dropped it into the mixture.

"Are you sure, Mom?" Lana asked, twisting her nose to one side.

"We need something to give it a kick. It's the best I can think of."

They rolled countless little croquets the size of an index finger. They were all lined up on a tray. Then Mother fried them in hot oil, and she didn't let us taste until they were all ready. She made black coffee. There was no milk that day.

The corn flour cakes were crispy outside and soft inside. A little bit dry but delicious, especially because we could add a little bit of butter as we would have done with the bread rolls from the bakery in other times. Mother discovered a new source of making some pocket change, and our kitchen table became a small corn cake factory until the war ended. Then the old baguettes were back at the local shops and we moved on.

# CHAPTER 12

*São Paulo, 2008*:

Six months passed since the bus robbery, and Mariana didn't seem any better. She was still going to her classes at the university, but she was doing so poorly on her grades that she was considering taking a break. The biggest challenge was facing the journey to school. Crossing the city was a daily hell, as she couldn't even think of driving a car on her own anymore. She got terrified and started shaking and hyperventilating as soon as she landed in the driver's seat. She tried using our driver or take taxis every day, but the streets still made her nervous. She began therapy.

"I tried to take the same bus again and move forward as I wanted to confront it, but every time I got in and sat down, I started to shake, sweat, and feel shortness of breath. Then I had to get off and pull myself together, and I would find myself in a different, probably unknown part of the city, and the fear just got worse." Mariana told me the story many times exactly as she told her therapist. She started to shake all over again just remembering it. "I looked at desolate *botecos,* small bars with two or three people drinking *cafezinhos* in small shot glasses, sometimes eating bread rolls with butter, preparing for their journey through the day. I felt useless to realize I was not able to go through my normal day anymore. I was desperate, I wanted to cry all the time. These scenes that used to make me curious about life in such a diverse place, that made me think of our social differences, that used to make me want to change something, now they make me feel lost and foreign in my own hometown. Everything is a menace."

Mariana invariably ended up calling somebody—Emilia or me—to pick her in an obscure road somewhere between home and the campus. A couple of times I got a cab and went there myself. The battered and small creature I found sitting at a bus stop or terrified inside a café was nothing like my favorite niece.

"I just want to stay home all the time," said Mariana, sitting in our living room.

On that afternoon, I accompanied her to therapy as usual and, to tell you the truth, I think doctors can make you feel worse. This one was a middle-aged woman with round glasses and the stupid habit of giving patients a long hug every time they got in for their hour with her. She had a maternal look, and Mariana didn't like the way she handed her a box of tissues after any difficult question.

"'If you unblock it from your mind, you can start the healing process.' That's what she says to me, Uncle Fe. But I just feel scared of remembering the details."

I hated Dr. Lorenzata, her designer glasses, and her box of soft tissues, but I hoped she could make Mariana talk about what happened during her forty-eight hour ordeal, even if I doubted Mariana could relax in that office full of terracotta and yellow ornaments, looking like a hotel room for business people and smelling of new leather.

After the sessions, we used to come to our apartment

in the Garden District. Rita prepared a *caprese* salad with lots of fresh mozzarella, Mariana's favorite cheese. One afternoon, we had an early dinner sitting at our small table at the balcony looking at the tall buildings of different heights that frame the city sky from all angles. We could see part of *Trianon* park and the long immovable tail of red lights from the cars in the rush hour traffic in *Casa Branca* Lane.

"It looks pretty and exciting when you see all from above," Mariana said, her eyes moving from the crescent moon that was starting to glow and the street life below.

In the neighboring condo, we could see a couple playing tennis on the clay court. They had on white outfits, and their racquets moved fast as experienced tennis players. Darkness was falling quickly and dozens of lights were starting to appear everywhere like fireflies in a dark forest.

"It's a question of point of view," I said. "Listen, darling, we know many people that have been through a lot here—house robberies, bank robberies, traffic light robberies. There are so many ways of being frightened, but if every person who's been through violence here stays at home, the streets would have been empty for a while and the bad guys would own the town. Does it sound fair, Mariana?"

She kept looking outside.

I ate my last piece of tomato and placed my fork and knife on the empty plate. The maid immediately came to clean the table.

"Dessert, seu Felipe? *Cafezinho?*" Rita asked with her soft tone of voice. "Do you want anything, Marianna?"

"Nothing, thanks. Just coffee."

"Two expressos, Rita."

"Right away." Rita left without making noise. Part of her job was to be invisible.

We heard the church bells in silence. It was six o'clock in the afternoon. The *Angelus*. Church bells were less and less common these days. Engines, laughs, loud music in the streets, TVs—these were the city sounds, but nothing meant the passage of time for me like the old calls for prayer, more than any pendulum clock or the sight of myself at the mirror.

# Chapter 13

I'd been living in the Garden District for twenty years now. This neighborhood was the dream of any *paulistano*—tall condos surrounded by clean streets with fine restaurants and a Louis Vuitton shop right on the corner.

There was a heavy gate at the building entrance and security guards to keep the rest of the world away from our pool, gym, and party rooms. You had everything in your own home. You actually didn't need to go out, and who wanted to do it?

It was early in the morning. I went downstairs for my daily walk around the pool. Afterward, it was up the elevator again, and I was at home, sitting in front of my big screen and watching the morning news. Then Rita arrived, part of our *staff*, as we call them now—doormen, maids, security people. We paid for an army of cleaners. There were so many of them in this building, hiding every sprinkle of dust from our view, making life quiet and ordered inside our heavenly safe gates. They were always smiling, efficient, kind.

"Good morning, sir."

"Always my pleasure, sir."

"How are you today, sir?"

If they did something wrong and you reprimanded

them, they bowd their heads as a toddler who'd been bad: "It won't happen again, sir."

Sometimes they called me *doctor*. I knew it was a deference, as to be a doctor in this country meant a lot. So, if someone is supposedly important, why not add *doctor* to the title? I guess this is the ultimate goal to work for forty years and then get old, sick, with high blood pressure, diabetes, thrombosis, and come to a building like this to be called *doctor* without having been to medical school.

The doorman broke the news this morning. "A passenger robbed Lucas, the taxi driver, from the corner. It happened yesterday in the outskirts of the city. He got shot. He was lucky, that's what everybody says. He tried to reach a police station. The thieves realized it and *bang*! He's now at the hospital but he will survive to drive the cab again."

After watching the news and listening to the *blah, blah, blah* of Rita and my wife in the kitchen, I had my morning snack of fruit and black coffee. Sometimes bananas *prata*, if they were in season, or fat slices of mangoes.

Coffee from the coffee machines never tasted the same as the stuff made in Mother's cloth bag percolator. My childhood kitchen always smelled of coffee in the morning. Mother used to wake up around five, still dark in the winter with the endless drizzle outside. I woke up right after her with the *flap flap* of her slippers on the gelid ceramic floor. She always wore a pegnoir. That was what they used to call the warm flannel apron every housewife had in their closet to put over the nightgown in the morning.

You could see a line of women by the doors at Coroa Street, waving at their husbands when they left the house, all wearing the same thing, with one arm busy saying goodbye and the other crossed around their stomach, as if to hide the outfits that should be worn just indoors. Some ladies still had the bobby rollers in their hair.

Mother had no husband to wave to but always woke up hungry and in good spirits. Her first thing was coffee. She filled the biggest saucepan we had with water and the wood stove with logs. While waiting for the water to boil, she had the eight-inch-long cloth bag ready, hanging over the *bule,* our aluminum coffee pot. The bag was attached to a round metal handle and it was white when new. Then it quickly became dark brown because of the coffee mixture that was strained every day through it.

"The darker, the better," Mother used to say. "It absorbs more and more of the coffee taste."

Our bags lasted almost a year, and she just replaced them when they had holes and the coffee came out Turkish style.

By the time the water was boiling, I was already sitting at the big wooden table, the one Uncle Leontino made for us from demolition wood. Mother took the grinded coffee from a can and dropped a few spoons of it into the boiling water. She quickly stirred, took the pan off the heat, and that's when the coziest smell came up: it filled my mind with dreams and my stomach with warmth. After stirring coffee into the water there was a thick black soup and then it was time to pass it through the cloth strainer into the *bule.* It always took the longest five minutes in the world. By this time the milk was being heated in another pan and the thick cream accumulating on the top. When the milk started to boil and rise, Mother took it from the heat and finally poured half black and half white with a spoon of sugar in a cup for me.

When we had bread or bananas, I was the first to feast on them, but sometimes the coffee with warm milk was all we had in the morning. It tasted like Christmas.

# CHAPTER 14

*São Paulo, October, 1945*:

Good afternoon, this is the Reporter Esso. We have breaking news. General Dutra is the new president of Brazil. Getúlio Vargas lost the election. After fifteen years, Getúlio is moving out of the Catete Palace, in Rio de Janeiro."

The trumpets played the march that ended the daily broadcast of *Reporter Esso*, the most popular news program in the country. Everybody was glued to the radio. Mother couldn't believe it. After the news, she sat in the kitchen in silence for a long time. No one dared talking to her about the elections.

Getúlio Vargas left the presidency on October 29, 1945. He promised he would go back to power "in people's arms," and it actually would happen nine years later, but after the war ended there was too much pressure to break his dictatorship. How could we have soldiers fighting against Hitler and have a dictator at home? One who sent Jewish Communists to Germany, people who ended up in concentration camps? Elections couldn't finally be avoided anymore, and General Dutra became the new president. Mother was not pleased. She joined marches against him.

At the time, I was not at all worried about politics. All I thought about was the girl I saw at the shelter months earlier. I had to see her again. After that afternoon, I couldn't erase her dark eyes from my mind. I had dreamed of her many nights. The dream was always the same: I was at a birthday party, playing with my friends, and then somebody approached me.

"Look, that girl is waiting for you, she's there for a long time."

I looked at a corner and I saw her, wearing a miniature of her mother's green skirt, sitting on a table, smiling at me. I walked toward her and, when we got closer, we didn't say a word, we just gave each other a warm and tight embrace.

I always woke up, enveloped in that embrace, and felt a punch in my stomach when I realized it was not real.

I saw her again on the day Getúlio Vargas left the Catete Palace, during the spring floods. Every year between mid-September and Christmas time, it rained almost every day. Our street went up and down, drawing sharp curves along a good portion of the Tietê river, and it became a big swamp at that time. This was a poor immigrant's area and nobody paid too much attention to our suffering during the rainy season. The only way to deal with the water was to lean on your neighbors for temporary shelter, besides good talent for rebuilding and recycling what was left every year. During the floods, part of my usual two miles route to school looked like a deep pond. So I had to make a long detour, going up the hill to Santana and then making a sharp turn and going back to my *Grupo Escolar,* adding a long a circle around my usual path Luckily, our house was sitting on one of the few hilly areas of Coroa Street and we were safe. There was no flooding, though lots of leaks from the ceiling.

At night, I always feared the roof was going to collapse on top of us. There were buckets in the living room, in the kitchen, and in our bedroom. We got used to sleeping with drops falling noisily into the metal buckets, *plop, plop,* all night long. In the bathroom, the leak was on the wall. The water was constantly dripping, like a miniature waterfall, making its tortuous way down the wall as a shine vein swelling the old cement. I used to watch this waterway for a long time when I was sitting on the toilet. I imagined it was a river and I was navigating with a small canoe, rowing fast and then trying to go backward as I approached the floor. I always followed my big imaginary fall with a long scream, and that's when my brother or my sisters came to knock on the door:

"Felipe, shut up and open the door, the bathroom is not only yours, *folgado!*"

I think I was probably the only person in the city who thanked God for the floods on Sunday mass. One morning, when I turned the corner where my detour to school began, I saw a girl with big eyes and braided hair in a red and navy blue school uniform leaving a small yellow house. That was her. I had to stop for a couple of seconds in disbelief. In a city of so many blocks and so many distant neighborhoods, there she was, just fifteen minutes from my own house.

In my innocence and surprise, I had nothing to say. She didn't even know my name and I didn't know hers. When I saw her leaving the house, all I could do was stop and admire. She walked hand in hand with her mother, her tidy brown backpack placed on her shoulders swinging behind her with the pace of her walk. I walked behind them for a while, keeping my distance. They didn't see me. I had no intention to talk to them: what would I say? They would think I was a lunatic or a thief and probably would run away or call the police. Most of all, I was on a cloud just with the sight of her and to know I could see her again and again as I knew where she lived. It made my day and many other days. Of course, the longer way to school became my usual path during the rest of the school year.

Getúlio Vargas had been president since 1930, even before I was born. We had to look at this picture every day at school, and it was obvious to me that he was going to be president until his last breath, like a king.

In October of 1945, it all changed. The country was different and there was freedom and progress in the air. I felt it too. On that spring day, I decided my future. I was going to meet that girl, she was going to be my girlfriend, and we would be married when we grew up.

# Chapter 15

São Paulo, 1946

The radio had been playing "Boogie Woogie na Favela (Boogie Woogie in the Slums)" for months: "Boogie Woogie, the new dance that's part of good neighborhood policy," the lyrics said. Everybody talked about America and how it was cool. After the War, Europe and Japan were destroyed and America was the winner of the world. US news was on papers and magazines almost every day. And music started to mirror the changes. I loved "Boogie Woogie na Favela," and I knew how to sing it by heart.

It was wintertime and the whole neighborhood was busy with the June Street Festivals, honoring the three saints whose birthdays are celebrated during this month: St. Anthony, St. John the Baptist, and St. Peter. During that time, when weekend evenings were colder and foggy, we had a tall bonfire in the fields by the end of our road. Everybody would come, even people who lived in the richer areas. We used to make paper lanterns and light them, sending dozens of gigantic fireflies into the night sky. There were paper flags glued to long strings and hung all over little food stalls. They used to sell corn on the cob, peanut candy, popcorn, hot wine with mulled spices, and my favorite dessert, *curau,* made with grated corn, coconut milk, and sugar. Kids could eat as much as they wanted for free, and this was a real plus. During all my life, I had felt a special wave of happiness during the month of June, and it certainly had to do with the cozy São Paulo winters and the memories of these festivals, especially the one from 1946.

"Ladies and Gentlemen, now comes the moment of truth. The singing contest! Whoever wants to participate please come forward, there will be a guitar player to play along and help you win! Please, come and sing your favorite song!" After the dances around the bonfire, Luca Gentile, the party manager, who was also an informal neighborhood major, announced the singing contest.

We could sing anything we wanted, and there were prizes for the winner. I wanted the cups of Jell-O and flannel shirts they gave us in the end, but mostly I wanted to be noticed. *She* was there with her family, the girl of the dreamy dark eyes. At that point, she certainly knew me. During the past seven months, I had been passing in front of her house on my way to and from school. During the summer, I found all the possible excuses to be in her street.

Six people volunteered to sing. I was among them, preparing my own version of "Boogie Woogie na Favela."

"A nova dança que faz parte da política da boa vizinhança…"

I used to sing it on my way to school, on my way to the club on Thursdays, where I collected tennis balls to help the players and got some money. I used to sing it in the shower, and also before falling asleep at night. But on that cold evening the words didn't come to my mind, as they should. I was nervous. Entire verses escaped from my memory. It made me more insecure standing there, in front of everybody and my normally good voice and tuning became a catastrophic fiasco. I had to stop in the middle of the song. I left without a prize and without impressing the girl. All I wanted was to disappear. I walked home with Decio and Gilda, and I promised myself I would forget her for good, I would never pass in front of her house again because I was the most ridiculous man in the entire universe. Of course, my friends made it difficult for me to overcome my shame:

"There goes the king of radio. Are we having another show tonight, Felipe?"

They made fun of me for at least one month, every single day, as soon as I set foot out of my house.

After a week without seeing her, my heart was heavy as a stone dropped in the ocean. I decided to pass by her house on my way to school for the last time, as a farewell ritual. It was the last day of June and the last day of school before the July winter vacation. I was going to be twelve in August, when I was due to be back to school. Mother had already organized an afternoon job for me as an office boy at a company where Decio did the same work two years earlier. My days of collecting tennis balls, hunting frogs, and delivering newspapers every other Sunday were over. I would soon have a "steady" job and I would go three days a week to the office as soon as I left the *Grupo Escolar*.

I decided to make it a proper goodbye ceremony: I put on my Sunday brown pants, a white shirt, and blue sweater. I shined carefully my only pair of shoes and combed my hair using a secret formula to tame it: wet the palms of my hands with water and mineral oil, rub them together, and spread the mixture over my unruly mane.

It was a beautiful and rare winter day with no drizzle, a cold breeze, blue sky, and sunshine. I walked up the hill and tried to think of other things but her and didn't hum

my ex-favorite song. At that point I decided to give a
break at singing and had no desire to remember the
"Boggie Woogie" lyrics.

I turned around the corner close to her yellow house
and there she was. She had to be outside today! She was
talking to another girl in front of her house. They were
laughing together. Suddenly they said goodbye and the
other girl left as I was approaching the house. I crossed
the road as I was too embarrassed, but when I was in the
middle of the street, I heard her voice for the first time:

"Hey, 'Boogie Woogie' singer! How are you?"

I looked at her, but remained silent, my lips glued,
paralyzed.

"Hey, I am talking to you! Aren't you the singer from
the festival?"

"Well, I think I can't avoid being so good and so famous." I don't know how the funny answer came to my
mind. I was in shock, but she smiled and walked toward
me. My knees started to tremble.

"Hi, I'm Valentina."

She presented me a hand so delicate I thought it could
break it when I shook it. I was dumbfounded, looking at
her, and forgot to say my name.

"I don't remember your name."

"Sorry, I'm Felipe."

"Felipe, do you live around here?"

"Yes, down on Coroa Street."

"Well, it's not exactly around here. Where do you go
to school?"

"Down at the *Grupo.*"

"And do you take this way to school every day? The
*Grupo* is down the main street, close to the river—but I
see you pass by all the time with your school books. This
is not your way to school. Don't tell me! You skip classes?

Oh my God! She had noticed me. I didn't know if I should be happy or embarrassed, but I wanted to look good. *Think fast, Felipe, think fast.* "No! I don't skip classes at all."

"So why do you take this road and make a long detour to go to school?"

"I—I started taking this way during the floods."

"But the floods are over for at least six months. And during the summer you always passed by. There's no school during the summer.

I took a deep breath. "I didn't know you noticed me passing by."

I could not think that fast and I had a horrible feeling that I was not as impressive as I wanted to be. But I never thought this was going to happen, so I never had time to rehearse. *Damn it!*

"Well, this is not a long and busy road. We end up knowing everyone who passes by every day."

"I never thought you could notice somebody like me." Silence. It was better to keep talking. *Think fast, Felipe.* "I like to come this way. I—I like this part of the neighborhood. It's very nice. I like to walk here and imagine myself in one of these nice houses. Our area is not so pretty." Now, that was it. *Felipe, you are so stupid. Now she won't be impressed. Poor and nosy.* What the hell had I ended up saying?

"Well, I don't know your area very well. We never really go down there."

"There's nothing nice there to know about."

She was smart.

"How old are you, Valentina?"

"I am thirteen. Today is my birthday."

"Wow! I chose the right day to meet you! Happy birthday!"

"*I* chose the right day! I said hello, remember?"

"Yes, sorry, it's true. Are you going to have a party?"

"Yes, later. My sisters go to afternoon school, so it has to start after five."

For one moment I thought she was going to invite me to her party, but she didn't. I had to find an excuse quickly to see her again.

"Do you listen to radio?"

"Yes, my mother likes the *radionovelas.*"

"My mom likes them too. Do you like music?"

"Yes, a little. I like the Carnival marches."

"Me too."

Silence.

"Are you going away during the winter vacation?"

"No, are you?"

"No."

"Can I come here sometimes just to say hi?"

"Sure. You can ring the bell. It's okay."

"Really, is it okay with your mother?"

"I think so."

"Okay, I will come next week then, when school is over. I know a lot of songs from the radio. Thank you for letting me in."

"Okay, see you next week."

"Happy birthday again. Thanks."

"You are welcome."

We were both looking down at the ground. I could feel a hot flush on my face, and I was so afraid of looking at her. She lifted her head and smiled. I looked at her but I don't remember if I smiled back. She said goodbye, turned around, and crossed the road back home. I stayed there, motionless for a while, just looking at her silhouette moving farther and farther away. I tried to keep in my mind all the details from our short dialogue so I could replay it over and over in my dreams until the following week would come.

# CHAPTER 16

*São Paulo, 1951*:

Valentina and I became best friends before we held hands for the first time, maybe two years after the day we spoke in front of her house. To my own surprise, I made the first move and took her small hand between mine. It was a Tuesday afternoon after school. We were listening to "A Hora da Peneira" on the radio, sitting on her kitchen floor, drinking chocolate milk, and pretending to help each other with homework. As I held her hand, she didn't say anything, just smiled. She didn't move her hand away.

"I know you like me," she said after a while, "but my parents don't allow me to have a boyfriend until I am sixteen. I don't think you will wait—"

"I think I can wait. It's good to be friends. I don't mind. My days are perfect when you are around. I don't mind, really."

I couldn't even imagine the possibility of not seeing her anymore. Even if we never kissed, at that point, I thought I would be happy just with the possibility of talking to her about anything I liked. I realized on that day that I told her stuff I normally wouldn't tell anyone.

And so we waited. We held hands and we even kissed

when nobody was looking. It was a delight and it was our secret, a stronger bond between us. Valentina was afraid of her parents, but at the same time she was as daring and curious as I was when we were discovering love together.

Now, in 1951, I was officially introduced to her family as a boyfriend. It was not a surprise to her parents who already knew me well. She invited me for Sunday lunch after the twelve o'clock mass. Between the *pasta Bolognese* and the *quindins* her mother prepared for dessert, we told her parents about us, and I officially asked their permission to date her.

"You seem to be a good man, and I just expect decency and respect from you." That was all her father said. No smiles, no hand shaking. He stretched his arm holding the dessert plate. "Two please, Marieta."

Valentina's mother immediately tried to make me feel comfortable and started telling me all about her famous *quindins*. "They take almost a day to get ready and we use sixteen egg yolks for one recipe, but they melt in your mouth. And I grate the fresh coconut myself. You will see the difference from the sweets you buy in the store!"

I ate three *quindins* and paid attention to every detail of their dining room to feel less nervous. Unlike Mother, her parents were relaxed about not having a spotless house. The floors didn't shine as our living room floors did, and there were newspapers scattered over the coffee table. Sometimes there were dirty cups lying there for a whole afternoon before somebody picked them up. I could see some dust on the windowsills too, but their updated and more expensive furniture made everything look much better than in our home.

Suddenly her father started talking again. "Do you like soccer, young man?"

"Yes, I follow it a bit, but I don't play and I have never been to a stadium."

I guess that was my way of telling him I appreciated the national passion, but I was not crazy about it. Afterward, I realized it was unusual to a man of my age to never been to a live soccer match, but I was doing my best.

"We should go one day to the Pacaembu Stadium, I'm sure you will love it."

"I'm sure I will."

I tried to move the conversation to cinema. I mentioned the new movies showing at the Cine Metro, the *premiéres* every Wednesday where I used to go with Valentina, but he was just interested in sports. I declared my passion for radio and the new Bossa Nova music that everybody was talking about, but he seemed to consider it a minor diversion. He said he didn't have time to go to movies. The last movie he saw was *The Martir*, a four-hour Good Friday family program—the story of Jesus and His sacrifice, which was replayed every year in theaters during Easter holiday.

Valentina's mother loved *radionovelas* and Angela Maria songs. While we helped her tidy up the kitchen that Sunday, we talked about *O Direito de Nascer*—The Right to be Born—a tremendous radio hit. I was not crazy about *radionovelas,* but Mother wouldn't miss one chapter at dinner time and the radio was the centerpiece of our kitchen table, so I knew all about Alberto Limonta, the adopted boy who grows up to meet his blood family by chance and falls in love with his cousin.

Her mom was friendlier than Mother would have ever been with any of my sister's boyfriends, but they were similar in one point. They never left the couple alone. There was always somebody watching us, and if we went to the backyard just to hold hands, soon somebody would come along and stay around. Valentina was not upset about it:

"That's the way it has to be. They do the same with my older sister. They talk about honor and decency all the time, but I think it has nothing to do with doing it before getting married."

Valentina was getting more and more a mind of her own. She didn't seem to care about being a girl to marry or a girl for fun. That's how boys labeled them: the ones who let boys touch them everywhere, and the ones who kept themselves for the altar. I never doubted my girl-friend was the marrying type, but sometimes she surprised me. My sisters never talked like that, never questioned the rules. They obeyed, they were afraid of being caught, or—God forbid—getting pregnant.

"If you disgrace our family, you will be sent to the Convent of the Franciscan Sisters and the child goes for adoption! You don't have a father, but you have your honor!" That was Mother's thunderous warning to my sisters, even though I doubted she would be capable of sending a grandchild to adoption.

Of course she would take care of the kid, even if the neighbors and the rest of the family would look at us as an inferior cast forever.

But Valentina? All she talked about was seeing the world and being independent. She was not obsessed about marriage and children, like most of the girls I knew, including my sisters. I guessed she knew all of these ideas of independence were allowed just until the point she settled down. She did a secretarial course, instead of high school, and got her first job as a secretary at the Light Electricity in the month she turned seventeen. When she got the job, she was so happy that I felt jealous. I kept wondering if she would celebrate the same way if I proposed. Also, I couldn't understand why a job could make somebody so thrilled. Jobs were a way to get money and that was all. I started to work as an office boy, delivering letters and documents at the HA paper factory when I was fourteen. There was nothing to celebrate about that. I had to wake up as early as six a.m., walk twenty-five minutes to get there, work all day in and out of the building, and then go to school at evening time to finish up to eighth grade. When I was sixteen, I left school and got a promotion. I started to do office work and didn't need to be in the street all day. Now I had a little more money, and I was not too tired, but my only dream, my real dream, was to work on the radio. Mother would laugh at me when I mentioned that.

"And who's going to give you a job at Radio Record or Radio Tupi? Just if you want to do the cleaning!"

So I decided not to talk about my dream of meeting all the artists and making a living out of it. I once went to Radio Record headquarters, close to the law school, and asked how much they would pay me to be an office boy or even a cleaner. They said they didn't need anybody at that moment, but when they said they just paid 150 hundred *réis* a month, I couldn't even consider it. It was half of what the factory paid me, and Mother would not accept a new job that decreased the amount of beans on our table.

# Chapter 17

*São Paulo, December 1953, Friday evening:*

I never thought I could cry looking at a painting. It was so powerful, so magical," Teresa said. "You have to go and see Guernica, the whole world should see it!"

" Better than Guernica is the building!" Carlos agreed. "The new Pavilhão da Bienal. Man, there's no way to describe it, you just have to go there and see—this big white curvy beauty in the middle of the park—it's amazing, São Paulo never saw such a beautiful piece of architecture!"

Valentina's eyes were luminous as she listened to Carlos and Teresa talking about the International Arts Bienal. "Oh, Felipe, we have to go to the Bienal, we have to see it!"

It was the second one happening in São Paulo and people were so proud. They never thought that our messy city would compete with places in Europe or North America to host such a vanguard art exhibit every two years.

Apparently, it was good. I never gave it a second thought and I never thought Valentina was so interested in this sort of thing. On that Friday night, she was so excited about meeting this couple she knew from work. She picked me up earlier at the paper factory to go downtown and find a spot at the Paribar, another famous place, maybe as famous as Guernica. Her new friends were always there. There was nothing special about the bar with a few tables outside Praça Dom José Gaspar and cozy wicker chairs where people sat for hours smoking and drinking.

Carlos and Teresa went on and on about Pablo Picasso. The couple was a little older than Valentina and me, maybe late late-twenties. He was an English Professor at the state university, and his dream was to live abroad and see all the famous paintings for real. Teresa was a secretary at Light, and she worked with Valentina. Carlos and Teresa were married less than a year ago, and they had a little apartment in Bela Vista, an area between downtown and the south of the city. Teresa wore clothes similar to Valentina, flowered dresses tight on the waist with sandals and ballerina flats. She was a little fat, so everything fitted better on Valentina's tiny waist. Carlos was a little different. In our neighborhood, people would say he was an *efeminado*. He wore light sweaters with turtlenecks and dark pants, but the sweaters were always lime green, intense blue, or even pink. Sometimes he had a blazer over the light sweaters. He never wore buttoned shirts or short sleeves like we did all the time. His hair was curly and messy, a bit too long, and he didn't bother to put some Brylcreem on or even to comb it. He seemed to like his disheveled and wild look. He had a lightly superior air when he spoke, arrogant, always trying to make a statement. He annoyed me a little but I figured we were not supposed to see them all the time.

On that day at the Paribar, after they exhausted the painting's theme, they took us to a *cantina*, an Italian small restaurant, close to their apartment. The area is still a traditional Italian neighborhood, but became very touristy later. At the time, Bexiga, as it's still known, was poor, with ancient little houses, many *cortiços*, and great homemade food. We ended up at the back of Signora Luisa's house. She was a strong Neapolitan woman with big green eyes and gray hair held in a tight bun, reminding me of Maria Pagliucca. She always spoke in what I thought was Italian, but Carlos explained it was her dialect. He always knew everything.

Her business was simple, and I kept going back there for many years until she died and the restaurant disappeared. She cooked two appetizers, one main pasta course, and two desserts as the daily menu. She had six tables in her flowered backyard and that was it. There was no sign on the front gate as the locals just knew her. Her homemade pasta was so different from everything I had tasted before that I understood in a gulp why the place was always busy.

"Her ravioli filled with spinach is the best," Carlos proclaimed. "Do you know she wakes up at five every day and goes to the central market? When she gets there, she picks the ingredients she thinks are the best and then she creates the sauces based on the ingredients. She has no recipes for anything."

On our way back home, Valentina couldn't have been happier. "Felipe, when we get married, I want us to be exactly like Carlos and Teresa." She held my arm tighter and got closer to me on the bus seat.

"Do they talk about having kids?" I asked.

"No, not that I remember."

"Don't you think it's strange? They are married, they just talk about traveling, places to go, different food all over the world, but never about real life?"

"Why do you think traveling and work and all of these interesting things are not real life?"

"They don't seem real for me. A married couple who

doesn't have children seems unreal. I think they are just too different. Carlos, for example, have you seen how he dresses?"

"You never thought about seeing the world? Or going to college?"

"I might have thought about that, but it's something I will probably do when I am older, when I have enough money for—"

She interrupted me and took her arm from mine, straightened her back, and looked at me in the eye. "Sometimes you are too, too, too…simple for me!"

I raised my voice and the few souls who were on the bus looked at our direction. "What are you talking about? Do you want me to go to the Bienal and start licking Picasso's painting? Or to start wearing those stupid turtleneck sweaters to impress people who didn't go to *college?* Am I not good enough for you now that you have smart friends?"

Valentina was embarrassed and didn't say anything. She crossed her arms over her stomach and kept her head low. She was crying silently, but it didn't move me. I was furious. I ignored her and looked through the window until we got close to our stop. I pulled the cord, got up, and she followed me. We walked side by side but didn't speak for the rest of the time.

"I sometimes think about going to college, to have a career, to have a purpose," she said, when we were approaching her house.

"Getting married and raising your own children are not a purpose for you?"

"It's not about that. It's about seeing what the world is about."

"All right, you want to go to college, be smart and sophisticated, but you forgot you need money to go to college. Education is not that cheap around here and. Even if you get into a public school, you have to spend money with books. You can't work full time, et cetera, so it's not that easy for people like us."

"You speak for yourself."

She said that and turned her back to me. I felt blood coming up to my forehead. I couldn't think straight any more.

All I wanted was to scream and shake her until she came to her senses. Who did she think she was? "Come back here!"

I think my voice was so loud and so upset she stopped right there, but she didn't turn back to look at me.

"No, Valentina, I never thought about going to college. I never thought it was for me. You know why? Because when I was seven, my father died and left my mother with all of us with a meager salary, gambling debts, and no savings. We had to come to São Paulo to escape shame and starvation. I had to pretend I had an injured foot once at school because one of my shoes was gone and we had no money to get another pair. I was too embarrassed to go to school barefoot, so I put a false bandage with old rags and went to school like that for days. Yes, Valentina, for me it's all about surviving, it's about making money, putting food on the table, raising kids to be decent people, honest people, which in this fucking corrupt country, is not a small thing! But if I am not smart enough for you, you are free to go and look for an *almofadinha,* a stupid dandy!"

"You don't understand anything!" she screamed and looked into my eyes. Tears were coming down her face in torrents. "I don't want us to be different from what we are. I just wanted us to see beyond this stupid squared place where the virtues of a woman are set between her legs, and men just think about buying bigger houses and procreating. Is that what you want?"

"I don't see anything wrong with buying a house and 'procreating.' But maybe you would like to open your legs more often, as your 'virtue' is probably at college."

As I finished the sentence I knew I had gone too far. She didn't say anything, not a word. She walked toward the front door, opened it, and slammed it on my face. I stood there, alone in her quiet street, in the darkness for about a minute.

Then I walked home as I felt my blood going back to normal temperature.

# Chapter 18

*São Paulo, August 1954*:

A ugust 24, 1954, Tuesday, an unsuspicious day for a president's suicide. Getúlio Vargas shot himself in the quiet of the night, leaving the whole country in disbelief. He had indeed come back to power "in people's arms," as he predicted. In 1951, after Dutra's presidency, he ran again for president and had the largest number of votes in Brazilian History until that day.

During that memorable August, everybody's attention was tuned into the president's scandal and the imminence of his resignation. It seemed that, finally, Getúlio's Era was coming to a close. The last few weeks had been a turnaround in the country's politics—the murder of Carlos Lacerda's security guard, with a shot that was meant for him, the opposition key man. One of Getúlio's allies confessed to the crime, leaving the president in a complicated situation. The military leaders were willing to take the power—it took them one more decade, but they ended up doing it. There was a lot of pressure for the president to resign and deliver everything in a tray to his enemies.

"I will leave the presidential palace when I'm dead," he had declared the day before to all the newspapers.

Mother was so consumed with Getúlio's fall, and tired

of joining every single street march in his favor, that she decided to go on superior court appeal. God. She was in a church vigil since the previous Saturday, praying for the "Father of the Poor," praying "for the nation's destiny" in her own dramatic, *radionovela*-style words. She came home with a couple of *getulistas* ladies from the neighborhood just to eat and sleep. I always thought Mother had to get into politics herself.

The day before his suicide, she was inflamed, preaching in the kitchen with large gestures, the bobby rollers almost falling from her hair while she waited for the milk to boil in the stove. "How can we turn our back on the man who allowed women to vote in this country? Do you have any idea of what voting means? Yes, our mission as wives and mothers comes first, but that's why we needed to have the same rights. We count, we raise the children, and we squeeze our husband's salary until the end of the month. We know better."

Getúlio Vargas shot himself in the heart during the night at the Catete Palace. News exploded in the early morning as a neutron bomb. People took over the streets. Mother and the *getulistas* transferred the vigil from the church to our kitchen where everybody was sitting under his photograph on the wall. Our old demolition table became an improvised sanctuary with dozens of candles people brought all day long. It was a sudden national holiday, and we got stuck at home with the radio news on. Shops were closed in fear of riots. The opposition was suddenly quiet and *getulistas* exploded in anger and revolt. People were gathering in the streets, and not even the usual winter drizzle of São Paulo kept the masses from being outdoors trying to come to terms with such an emotional end to the Vargas Era.

Getúlio, in his last trick, "left life to enter history." These were the words he wrote on his suicide letter. Not even the best *radionovela* writer could create such a dramatic ending to the crisis. His death had the desired effect. He was now a national hero.

Dozens of people came to our house during the day. We became a sort of a branch of his funeral in the neighborhood. As nobody went to work, I ended up in charge of the countless cups of *cafezinho* and water to the visitors who talked politics non-stop, discussing funeral processions and whether the vice-president Café Filho was a good choice or not.

It was about five in the afternoon when I saw Dona Marieta at the door. A cold wave went all the way through my spine as I saw there was somebody behind her that looked like Valentina. Since that night, when we had the big fight in front of her house, we had never been the same. We tried to mend it, but she was too upset about what I said, and I was too embarrassed to explain myself. More than embarrassed, I was mortified. I thought she was too good for me, I didn't deserve her. We had other discussions, but we decided to have a break during the Winter Festivities in June. She was still talking about going to college, and I couldn't put marriage and higher education in the same package. I thought it was an excuse for her to leave me. Those last few weeks were the worst of my life.

There was a permanent hole in my stomach and sadness in everything else.

Yes, it was Valentina at the front door. Her hair was a little longer. She wore a navy blue plain dress and a white cardigan over her shoulders. She looked more beautiful than ever, as there was light all over her. She entered the living room and met my eyes. I was carrying a tray of little coffee cups:

"Is this your night job?" she asked, looking at the large tray.

I smiled to mask the noise of my heartbeat. "Well, one has to survive. How are you?

"A little in shock, aren't you?"

"Yes, same here.

"How is your mother? She must be devastated. She has always been a great fan of the man."

"There's some drama going on but she will get over it." I couldn't let her go, I had to find a way to keep talking to her. "How is work at Light?"

"Good, all good. How is the paper factory?"

"Same old. I am actually thinking of studying accountancy in the evenings to have more chances at the office. Not college, just technical, but it will help."

"Oh, that's a great idea. I am happy for you."

She smiled and lowered her head. She avoided my eyes.

"Your smile is beautiful. I miss it."

"I miss you too."

She looked at me and her eyes were teary. I felt tears coming too. I put the tray away and took her hands in mine. We remained there, a moment frozen in the living room, no words until I heard my name.

"Felipe, coffee is getting cold on the table!"

Mother was aware of everything even on a day of mourning. I looked at the tray and at Valentina. I didn't want to let her hands go.

"Go, Felipe, we will talk later."

That's all I needed to hear. I grabbed the tray and passed it around. Valentina went to the kitchen and started helping Mother to unpack the food people brought in—fish cakes, sandwiches, *croquetes de carne, empadinhas…*

Every person who crossed the front door had something in hand. There was no space for plates anymore on the kitchen table, and we started bringing bowls and small trays to the living room or placing them on the stove. I didn't stop working while Mother commiserated with everyone, got hundreds of hugs and condolences. In a certain way, she was a widow all over again. In the meantime, my eyes followed Valentina to make sure she wouldn't leave without talking to me. I was anxious until things calmed down in the small hours, and we finally had a break.

Most of the neighbors had already left when Valentina and I sat together on the front door steps. My muscles were sore but I didn't feel tired. All I wanted was to be close to her, smell her flower perfume again, and notice the details of her body—the golden hair on her forearm was as light as fluff, her hands were pale, and her nails were short and painted red. I wanted to touch her so badly. While we were chatting, I looked at the curve of her breasts under the dress, going down so smoothly and squeezing into her small waist, as she was tightly embraced by her own skin. We stopped talking for a moment and I took her hand again. She didn't say anything.

"I'm sorry, Valentina. I never wanted to hurt you."

"I'm sorry too."

"I still love you."

"I love you too."

I looked into her eyes. I could see the dark sea into her pupils. My gaze went to her mouth and I approached her lips, taking all the air from her breath. When my lips touched hers, the whole world trembled and then disappeared, soft and dry. I moistened them with my mouth, taking her slowly with my kiss, my passion, and my longing for her.

# CHAPTER 19

Gilda and Lana were the most beautiful women in our family in different ways. Lana had a movie star quality. She knew about fashion and wanted to become rich and famous like her idol Rita Hayworth. She transformed her undesirable carrot color hair into something exotic, daring a very short, cropped cut, to Mother's dismay and shame.

"It's *vagabunda's* hair!" she proclaimed when Lana came from the hairdresser.

My pretty sister was not afraid of wearing black clothes to highlight her own skin color and freckles. Finally, she knew how to attract men and had always a boyfriend at arms' reach.

"This one soon is going to be a *perdida!*"

Mother never thought Lana could get married, as her reputation could have been already stained in her eyes, but she ended up finding a good prince who would take her far away.

Gilda, instead, was a natural beauty with dark brown hair, long sensuous eyelashes, olive skin, and curves. She never wore make up, her hair was always tied in a simple ponytail, she was shy and insecure, always dressed in plain shirts and black pants. Gilda married Ernesto at eighteen. He was our neighbor, and we knew she liked

him for at least three years before he made the first move
and invited her to have ice cream at the Polar Patisserie.
They went to the movies sometimes, and I was normally
their designated chaperone. They mostly sat for long afternoons in our old brown couch while Mother's vigilant
eyes were on their hands and gestures. I always thought
he proposed to Gilda not because he was in love with her,
but because he couldn't stand our boring living room anymore, and it was probably too late for a break up. At that
time, if you were dating *at home* you had to marry or you
would ruin the girl's reputation forever. Some angry fa-
thers even committed murders to save their daughter's
honor from men who just wanted to play with the girl's
feelings or worse, with their breasts.

"Once they are out of this house, it's their husband's
business. I wash my hands. I have nothing to do with
them anymore. They can do whatever they want," Mother
used to say.

It was a relief for her when Gilda married Ernesto. His
parents were from the Madeira Island.

"They are *gente de bem*," Mother used to say. Good
people.

It meant they had a better financial situation than ours,
not a difficult achievement. We had to scrape the bottom
of our purses at the end of the month, trying to find precious forgotten coins to take the tram downtown or to buy
bread for the afternoon *café com leite*. As many Portuguese people living in Brazil at the time, Ernesto's family
had a bakery shop at *Carandiru*. Their business was not
the richest but they had just one son to feed. Ernesto
could even have turned into a much better catch if he
wasn't so lazy and spoiled by his mother, who served him
breakfast in bed until the day he married my sister.

After the wedding, his parents, all of a sudden, tried to
make him a responsible man and gave him a small bar, a

*boteco,* so he could start his own business career. Differently from most of the people we knew, Ernest had finished High School without thinking about leaving school
to work and help out with the family expenses as all of us
and our neighbors had to do.

Gilda was radiant on the day Ernesto took her to see
the little townhouse he had rented to settle down after the
wedding. It was not very far from us, in a quiet private
road with a funny name: Sanitary Lane.

We all burst into laughter when we heard it. Decio
even made up a song about it. Gilda was not happy. She
didn't have the greatest sense of humor.

Her fairy tale lasted until their only daughter Anita
was born two years after the wedding. By that time, Ernesto had already started to drink the whole stock of his
own business. When Anita was barely walking, the *boteco* went bankrupt, he came back home completely
drunk every day, and he owed money to a lot of people.
One Saturday afternoon I stopped by Sanitary Lane to see
my niece, and Gilda didn't want to open the door.

"Gilda, come on, it's me."

"I am busy, come back tomorrow."

"You can be busy, I just want to see Anita. I can
babysit if you want."

"No. Go away."

I didn't, I sensed there was something wrong and sat
at her doorstep. "I will stay here until you open the door."

"Please, don't stay here until Ernesto comes."

"I will stay here. I don't care. It's better if you open
the door now."

Sanitary Lane was everything but sanitary: I could
smell sewage and there were stray dogs roaming around
and drinking from the muddy puddles, barking loudly.
They were all dirty, skinny and desolate.

I sat there at my sister's doorstep for ten minutes before she decided there was no way to get rid of me.

I heard the turn of the doorknob. She opened the door, just enough space for me to get into her living room. The first thing I noticed was the wooden floor, immaculately polished.

Exactly like Mother had taught all her girls. "Even when the house is not perfectly clean, shiny floors make a great impression, everything seems dignified."

I turned my face to say hi and give her a kiss on the cheeks when I saw it.

"Gilda, what happened?"

She looked at me and started to sob. It seemed she hadn't slept for a week. I just held her and didn't say anything for a while. Then Anita started to cry upstairs.

"I will get her," I said.

Gilda closed the front door and stayed there, like a scarecrow. When I came down the stairs with the baby, I could see it better, a big dark swollen circle around her left eye.

"He hit you, didn't he?"

"He was too drunk. He was not himself."

I felt a rush of blood coming up to my brain. "And is this your excuse?"

"It happened just once, it won't happen anymore. Please don't get upset."

"We will go home right now."

"No. I can't. He is my husband. Do you think Mother will accept me?"

"Gilda, he hit you!"

"If I leave, he will probably go there, and hit Mother too."

"Don't be stupid. Do you think anybody would touch her?"

I regretted it as soon as I said the last syllable.

"I am stupid. If I were like Mother, he wouldn't have

touched me. But I am a fool, I am nothing like her."

"Why, Gilda, why did he do it?"

She didn't say anything and walked toward the sofa, so small it looked like a toy from a dollhouse. We sat down. Anita was very quiet. She could feel the tension in the room. The sofa was as uncomfortable as a park bench.

"He came back home one day from the bar. He always comes a bit altered. It's too much drink available all day. I think it's actually a good thing he's leaving the business."

"You mean the business is leaving him, right?"

"Anita had a cold and I told him we had to go to the doctor. I was waiting for him to take me, I was scared of going on my own with the baby. It was too cold and it was getting dark. He got furious, he got so angry! He started to scream, to say that I didn't have a clue about taking care of a child, and if Anita got worse, he would kill me. He said I should have gone to the doctor long before on my own, that I was a stupid woman, incapable of doing anything. I started crying. I didn't know what to say, I was so embarrassed."

"And how did he hit you?"

"He got more and more upset because I was crying. He told me to stop it but I couldn't. It was out of control. So he slapped me and said that it was for me to stop whining. He left and came back just the next morning. He went to bed and fell asleep without talking to me. Then he woke up around one o'clock in the afternoon, went downstairs to the kitchen, and asked me in a completely normal tone if there was any food left for him."

"And you never said anything about it?"

"What I was supposed to say? I'm scared."

She just looked down at Anita, who was quietly playing on the rug. I didn't know what to say as well. Gilda was afraid of everything. She made me promise I was never going to tell Mother about her fight with Ernesto. I didn't have a good feeling about it but I said yes.

I went to see her more often in the following weeks. Money was very short as I worked as an office boy at a paper factory, but eighty per cent of my salary went to Mother's hands. She said I had to contribute a larger amount because I was too young to have money in my pockets. It could be dangerous, and it could lead to bad temptations. So, I walked home a couple of days and used the tram money to buy Gilda some coconut candy, her favorite since we were kids, just to cheer her up.

Later, she reassured me that fight was an incident. It wouldn't happen again. I thought everything was okay. Maybe that was part of married life. What did I know about it? I started to visit her less often. I had other things in my mind on that spring.

# CHAPTER 20

The car was gray, but I don't remember if it was a Gordini or a *DKV*. All I can recall is the strawberry and honey taste of Valentina's mouth, my hands moving up and down her back, my arms glued to the plastic seat as they were melting in one piece. Her brother had given us his new car for the evening, and instead of going to the movies, we went to see the famous Sunset Square, where couples parked cars and had a little privacy for romance. The square was on the top of a steep hill, with bushes and flowers and a spectacular view of the sunset on the west side of the city.

We were always sneaking out to kiss and make out after the movies, in her house when her parents got distracted, in the darkness of bars and parties. We never had any chance to be alone for such a long time and the car trip was a revelation. Valentina, who has always been shy and worried about the possibility of being caught, finally let go. For the first time, I realized she was not the teenage girl I fell in love with anymore, but a real woman with curves and desires.

We spent a couple of hours on Sunset Square. We talked, we kissed and I unbuttoned her blouse, touching secrets under her clothes. It took me a while to get back to reality. It was late when we decided to go home. We told her brother we had gone for pizza afterward. Nobody said anything but I could sense he knew what was going on. At that point, I was so much part of that family and our wedding seemed to be so certain that any evidence might be ignored, unless it was as visible as a baby bump.

Valentina and I didn't talk about it afterward. I wanted more but I didn't know how to ask. Our moments alone became more advanced, and she was comfortable with that. By the end of November, she started talking about doing something special on December thirty-first. I never understood why people get so excited about New Year's Eve. It goes all over the country and it's like a big preview of the upcoming Carnival in February.

"It is the beginning of summer season, that's when the thermometer starts to rise, when the spring rains end, and we are ready for partying," Lana used to say when we were younger.

She always loved to celebrate January first. All her dreams were out of the shelves one more time, blessed by traditional saints and *orixás*. After getting married, she and my Italian brother-in-law, Pietro, always went to the beach to see the arrival of the New Year, even if the trip lasted just one day as nobody could afford the hotel room. She carefully chose white clothes—"for peace and good energy"—and pink or yellow underwear—"for love and money respectively"—all brand new.

I still think it's a nonsense festivity. People now face massive traffic jams to go to coastal towns days earlier, or even in the afternoon of December thirty-first. Then they go to the beach when night falls to watch the celebrations of Afro-Brazilian religions: the offers to *orixás*, the boats overflowing with flowers sent away to the waves in order to please the beautiful *Iemanjá,* the goddess of the waters, her image with the blue mantle everywhere to be seen. There is live music, dance, lots of alcohol, and finally, at midnight, the fireworks fill the sky with the magic of new dreams. The crowds cheer, hug friends and strangers in peace unison for five minutes and then, let's sing and dance again until the sun comes up. A lot of people will go for a swim—and also for a pee—in the ocean at midnight. They say it's to "purify your soul." Bollocks.

I never found it very attractive as I don't like big crowds, but Valentina's argument convinced me right away.

"We should go all the way—I mean, sleep together for the first time. Let's do it on New Year's day, to start 1955 with a big change," she suggested.

"Yes, honey, great idea!"

"I planned everything, let's go to Santos with Teresa and Carlos, you remember them from the Paribar, don't you? Then we will all stay in a hotel right in front of the ocean. You and I can stay in the same room! My friends are very liberal, they don't mind."

"It sounds good, but what are you going to say at home?"

I also thought about another problem, even bigger than her parents—money. Where would I find money for this extravaganza? Hotel in front of the ocean sounded really great, but I wouldn't let her pay for it. My end-of-the-year bonus, the thirteenth salary, was already reserved to help Mother change the tiles in our bathroom. It was leaking again all over the place. I also needed a suit, because I was seriously thinking of looking for a different job this year. I could borrow money, but from whom? On the other hand, how could I say no? I had to admit I was flattered but a bit in shock when she came up with the idea. I ended up making the worst decision. I tried to borrow money from my brother Decio, who always had the dirtiest mind and told me I was a complete idiot.

"She has done it with somebody else, maybe with more than one guy. It's obvious. Now she wants to 'legitimate' it with you. Then you are even more obliged to marry her. You will be cleaning her stains and won't even get the honor of being the first. You are a fool, Felipe, a damn fool! And you are even paying for that? For crying out loud!"

Would my older brother be right? I couldn't believe Valentina was capable of such a scam. She was a bit too liberal, that was true, especially with her set of artistic friends and late nights at cool bars downtown, but she always took me with her. Maybe not...

*What if she's lying to me? Maybe she goes out with her friends, she even sleeps with some of them—maybe with two at the same time, all together?—and then she brings me to some parties just to keep everything normal. I am the good boyfriend who's going to marry her. She will have her moment before becoming a respectable housewife and mother. Now, when I think properly, she seemed so at ease when we went to the Sunset Square...*

I always thought it was because she loved me and felt comfortable with me. I couldn't picture her as dishonest, but truth was she had been changing a lot in these last few years. She was far away from that shy girl with braided hair walking every morning to her Catholic private school. I missed that girl who held my hand on the kitchen floor while drinking a chocolate milk shake. That girl had become a woman.

All of my friends thought more or less like my brother. They said that women wanting to marry didn't behave like her. They shouldn't be interested in sex, they should be even afraid of it. There was something wrong with Valentina.

On November fifteenth, Republic Holiday, she had lunch at my house. Mother cooked roasted chicken with potatoes and sweet peppers. I was walking her back home at evening time when she came up with the college conversation again. "Felipe, I am seriously thinking about going to college to study law."

"Well, how are you going to pay for it?"

"I can always try the public University. If I don't get in I can work during the day and do an evening course."

"Too much work. I prefer to learn a job just by doing it."

"People say you never get too far nowadays if you don't have a college degree. Times are changing, Felipe."

"This is not for us. And I don't have time for all of this intellectual stuff."

I said it and immediately regretted it. I touched a sensitive key and I didn't want to hurt her feelings again. But I thought she couldn't be serious. Why did she need to go to college? She already had a decent job. What about our plans to get married? We didn't speak for the rest of the way, until we said goodbye in front of her house, I kissed her lips briefly and left. We knew that was dangerous territory.

Even if it was the beginning of summertime, a chilly wind was blowing. By this time of the year, I usually missed the mild São Paulo winters of July and August, when humidity goes away and a deep fog covers the city in early morning, engulfing everything in a peaceful cloud for some hours, until the sunlight and the noise of cars and buses dissipates it all.

As I walked home, I was thinking about the fog and the mysterious atmosphere it brought to such a suffering city when I saw the bus going downtown, its yellow headlights emerging from the end of the street. I was passing by the bus stop and jumped in on an impulse.

Fifteen minutes later, I was at Victoria Street, the red light district, *zona das putas*. Decio had taken me there a few times, explaining how we should act with the ladies, full of himself. We normally walked around side by side, had a couple of beers at the bar at a *boteco* on the corner, and just watched the women getting busy. They wore lots of makeup—red *rouge* on the cheeks, dark eyeliners, lipstick. Their dresses were black or red, short and tight. They also wore black stockings. Many of them lifted their skirts when the cars passed by. It attracted a lot of men. Cars stopped by with happy men inside. They came mostly in small groups. They talked to the ladies for a few seconds without leaving the car or turning the ignition off. Sometimes the girls ended up in the passenger seat. But the vast majority were pedestrians like us. Good old times when we could walk this city everywhere and any time, day or night. The only problems were drunk men asking for cigarettes or money. Pickpockets were the worst that could happen.

I liked the idea of being alone that night. Without my older brother, I felt as a butterfly getting out of its cocoon. I sat at the same *boteco* from the last time with Decio, and I was not through the first bottle of beer when a girl with enormous dark eyes approached the table. Her mascara was melting with sweat under her eyes and it gave her a look of melancholy and a statement of poverty.

"May I sit here for a second?" she asked, already pulling out the chair.

"Sure," I said. I was a little uneasy as this was my first time here alone and Decio always, obviously, did all the talking.

"I'm Virginia, nice to meet you." She extended a very cold hand with short bitten nails toward me.

I was surprised as I imagined all *putas* had long and dangerous red nails. I touched her hand with a certain reluctance, and she sensed it. She sat on the chair in front of me taking all the space with her. Her hair was thick and black as a crow's wing. It was done in a bun with curls falling all over her face. It looked like a big nest.

"Do you want to drink anything?" I asked.

"I would love a beer too."

I ordered a second one. I knew this was part of the rules. You always pay them one or two drinks before we get into negotiations. We did small talk for about ten minutes. She asked my name, what I did for a living, what kind of girl I was attracted to—I said blondes and she ignored it. She drank her whole bottle of beer in two minutes and leaned over the table:

"I have a room. My price is six réis for half an hour. If I like you, you can stay a few more minutes and try a second time if you want."

I guessed she said that to everyone, expecting a tip. "Never give them tips," Decio would say. "They will follow you like vultures over rotten meat next time you come here."

I said yes and we left together. I didn't feel secure to start a negotiation or to look for somebody else.

We walked two blocks in silence. We turned right and there was her apartment building, a three store ancient *prédio*. It smelled like dogs as soon as you opened the door. I hated dogs.

She led me through one flight of narrow stairs, and stopped at number three, and unlocked a dark green door with chipped paint all over. There were so many cracks I initially thought they were some kind of pattern. Would it be her own apartment? I was afraid to ask. I felt a bit scared as I imagined she would take me to an hourly rated hotel, as there were many around that area.

It was a very small studio with a double bed in the center, which took almost all the room. There was a kitchen sink in one corner and a little wooden cabinet

over it. On the other side there was a door. I presumed it
was the bathroom. The apartment was cleaner than what I
expected.

"Please put the money on the bedside table first," she
ordered. Her voice was suddenly harsh.

I obeyed and didn't say anything, even if I really
wanted to tell her I was not dishonest.

After she counted the money and put it in her bag, she
took my hand. I realized my fingers were colder than
hers.

"First time?" She had a businesslike-trying-to-be-nice
tone.

"Not really."

"So you know the way."

She let go of my hands and started to unzip her skirt.
She took her clothes off piece by piece without looking at
me in the eye, and I was suddenly petrified. I sat on the
bed. After she took off her panties, she placed them on
the chair with the other items. She then looked at me.

"What do you want?"

"Surprise me."

She came closer. Her breasts were much smaller than
what the structured bra suggested. Her legs were muscu-
lar, pale white, and as well shaped as the legs of a runner.
Before she sat on my lap and started to kiss my ears, I
realized she had kept her high heels on. She kissed me
everywhere. I mean everywhere—where I had never been
kissed before. She was very precise, but also sweet, and
we were finished in a few minutes, before I could enjoy
the moment as I should.

It all probably lasted less than fifteen minutes and, afterward, all I wanted was to leave the place. Sex was not
different from other times, not even when I had a fling
with a showgirl for a couple of weeks, and we used to go
to her apartment every time I could afford going to *Salo-*

*mé* cabaret. That night, when I left the dark-haired woman's building and the fresh breeze hit my face, I had a rock in my stomach instead of the sense of relief I was supposed to feel.

I walked to the bus stop and lighted a cigarette. I had just started to smoke thanks to Valentina, who thought you had to do it if you were in clubs and intellectual bars. Every cool person in the city smoked. When I was a kid, I used to admire Clark Gable, always with a cigarette dangling from the corner of his lips. I thought women liked it, but as a teenager I was too afraid of trying a cigarette on my own. Mother used to smoke the pipe with her friends or when her sisters visited us. I can still close my eyes and smell the sweet smoke that came out of her mouth as she exhaled it. She loved it, and I guess she associated the pipe with festive moments, dear visitors, and good times. On the other hand, I was sure Mother would get mad at me if she found out that I was smoking cigarettes to look cool. We all smoked, except for Gilda, and we all hid the evidence from Mother.

The night bus appeared on the corner. I threw the cigarette butt on the sidewalk and jumped in. There were two other men sitting inside the car, one of them fast asleep. As I looked at the dim streetlights outside and watched the few pedestrians go by, I tried to guess what was that heavy feeling I felt. Maybe the *puta* was sick and I got some sort of bug from her. *Impossible, no bug acts that fast.* Then I remembered Valentina. I imagined what would happen if she saw me having sex with that woman, if she could watch everything. *Well, I'm sure she wouldn't care, as she knew every man did it.* Women, I knew, were supposed to just close their eyes to these facts of life. Men needed it, women didn't. Would I go to the *zona* again after doing it with my girlfriend? Maybe, who knows?

Why was I thinking about it now? My brother's words came back to my mind:

'*You are a fool, a stupid fool, Felipe.*'

Would it be true? My brother and I were very different. I liked music and radio, I went to the movies every week. He couldn't care less about all of that. He said I had conversations of an *efeminado,* a gay man. He was already on the military service, proud of his uniform. He saw life in black and white: right versus wrong, girlfriend or *puta,* man or woman, family and *putarias.*

The bus went all the way down Santos Dumont Avenue. It went fast at that time of the day with no traffic. We were now on Zona Norte, the northern part of São Paulo where we lived. After passing the Luz train station, the streetlights were placed more apart, and some of them didn't work. Cobbled streets gave place to dirt side roads. Houses were smaller, looking improvised, temporary, always with something to be done: front walls needing a coat of paint, roofs with missing tiles, doors and windows of different patterns. There was still some charm, a few backyard herb gardens, chicken coops, flowerpots.

I got off the bus and started the walk up Coroa Street. I still felt a rock in my stomach when I thought about Valentina and the path we were both taking. I thought about the girl I'd fucked half an hour ago, and I just pictured Valentina instead of her, taking her clothes off in that sad bedroom, lying on those faded sheets with anybody: old, young, sick, big, small, dirty, clean, all sorts of men.

# CHAPTER 21

*São Paulo, 1954, New Year's Eve*:

December thirty-first was a perfect summer day with a cloudless blue sky, soft breeze, and no humidity. Everybody was talking about a new samba called "Teresa da Praia," from Tom Jobim. We didn't know much about Bossa Nova at the time, but this song was in the beginning of the musical revolution João Gilberto would ignite a few years later. The magic of Rio's beaches, sweet life, and the bohemian smoothness of Jobim's piano were already present. The song was a dialogue between two friends, talking about a girl named Teresa they met at the beach. This was the soundtrack of our trip to Santos, a coastal town close to São Paulo, where my first night with Valentina would finally happen.

*"Ela é minha Teresa da praia, Se ela é tua, é minha também.* (She is my Teresa from the beach, if she's yours, she's also mine.)

I was nervous. I bought new underwear, checked all my clothes, and made mental calculations every time I bought an extra cup of coffee or a pack of cigarettes. I borrowed from two different friends to pay for the hotel and also for dinner and drinks. Two hundred and fifty *réis* in total, almost half of what I got in a month, but I was happy to see Valentina so lively on that journey down the mountains, squeezing my hand on the back seat of Carlos and Teresa's blue Volkswagen. We left São Paulo at the end of the afternoon, with enough time to get to Santos, check in the hotel, have dinner at a fishermen's shack and then drinks, before going to the beach to meet other friends and wait for midnight.

I felt excited and uncomfortable at the same time. When Valentina was with Carlos and Teresa, or with her new friends from work, she was different. She never excluded me from the conversations, but sometimes I couldn't follow anything: European painting, Existentialism, Clarice Lispector's new book, *Cold War*, the whole night was about it. I was realizing there was much more in the world than *radionovelas,* popular music, and the plastic table cover in our Coroa Street kitchen. Valentina had a glow when she mentioned the books she was reading or the movies she wanted to watch. She was more interested in everything else than the world we actually lived in.

At eleven o'clock, we decided to walk from the hotel bar to the beach. *Caipirinhas* were flowing and everyone was laughing and embracing. To be honest, I couldn't wait for the party to be over on the sand so I could go to the bedroom with Valentina, and we would have our night. It seemed awkward to me the way we planned such a romantic moment with all these friends around that meant nothing in my world, but what bothered me the most was that I realized over dinner that they meant a lot to her.

"Felipe, have you seen Lucia's new scarf? Somebody brought it from Paris. Imagine that?"

"Yeah, it's beautiful, lovely."

I was so bored. Valentina kept talking on and on about

fashion, about new magazines, she apparently tried to keep up with everything these people liked.

The feeling of rough sand in my toes made me forget the boredom for a few seconds. Walking barefoot on the beach meant that the world was being held, that my steps would always be safe as far as the sand was beneath. The sensation was even stronger at night, when it was dark and I couldn't see the sand. People were talking and singing everywhere. There were thousands standing on the beach. Valentina's loud slightly drunk voice mixed with Teresa's laugh, Carlos and his cousin Marcelo were silent, observing the afro ceremonies that always take place before midnight. Several small boats were loaded with white lilies and roses surrounding the image of *Iemanjá*, the goddess of the waters, a beautiful woman enveloped in a blue robe, with her arms stretched, the robe falling over her hands as a waterfall. It was almost midnight when the boats were pushed into the vastness of the sea, small little candles flickering on their sides as their reflection in the dark water disappeared together with the year of 1954.

Suddenly everyone started counting down. *"Cinco, quatro, três, dois, um, Feliz Ano Novo!"* Happy New Year! Valentina and I were holding hands. At midnight we kissed and her mouth tasted of *cachaça* and beer. As I was holding her, she started unzipping my pants and tried to reach my penis.

"Let's go to the hotel," I said.

"Why? No one is looking, it's dark, everybody is busy partying. Let me touch you."

She whispered in a way I've never heard her before. She had never tried to touch my penis, even when we had intimate moments, she always waited for me to start something new.

"Felipe, I want you, let me feel it."

I let go. It was overwhelming, even if I didn't like to do it on the beach, in the middle of all the party, but nobody seemed to bother at all. Her friends were busy watching the fireworks and kissing."

She moved her hands fast under my pants. I was starting to forget about everything else when I saw Carlos and Teresa walking in our direction, drinking from a bottle of *spumanti.* Valentina recoiled and turned to face them, standing in front of me as a shield.

*"Feliz Ano Novo,"* Carlos said while handing me the opened bottle.

I drank from it and passed to Valentina, making sure my shirt was not tucked into my pants but hanging over my waist. She grabbed the bottle and threw all the remaining drink over her head, laughing and licking her lips the way *vedettes* did at the Teatro de Revista when they sang sexy songs. I was embarrassed, but I didn't know the party was just starting.

"Come, Felipe, let's dance!"

I thought it was better to come with her and persuade her to go back to the hotel. I was mortified, but I realized her friends didn't care.

"Don't you think Valentina is much more fun when she drinks?" Carlos asked.

I smiled a fake smile.

Music was louder now. A few bands were playing Carnival marches in different parts of the beach and people started dancing, running and diving in the water. We were all dancing together as a group and changing the pairs as we moved around. I had a few *caipirinhas* and felt more bored than drunk. I danced with Teresa and then with Cristina, Carlos's cousin's girlfriend. I looked to the side and saw Carlos's hands on Valentina's waist. He was caressing her in a very strange way, almost touching her bottom. They were moving together like just

one body. His wife didn't seem to care as she was talking
to Marcelo farther away. I realized she knew what was
going on. I pushed Cristina away and walked toward Carlos and Valentina. Without saying a word, I pulled her
from his embrace and started dragging her toward the hotel. She complained and started crying. I didn't say a
word as I knew she was drunk, and I was too angry to
speak.

All I could feel was the heat of boiling blood in my
face. We got into our room and I left her on the bed. She
was now crying loudly. I went out again, closed the door
behind me, and headed for the street, leaving her alone. I
don't remember how many miles I walked around that
unknown coastal town. I suddenly missed São Paulo and
its vastness that I knew well, the chaos that in some way I
could control, knowing the moods and ways of its streets.
Here I was lost and felt out of place. All I wanted was to
go back home. I wanted to feel myself again.

I passed by some *putas* in a dark street. They were
standing against the wall, with skirts so short they didn't
even need them. One of them was a beautiful *mulata*. Her
skin was the color of caramel. Her afro hair was long and
made her skinny frame look even more fragile. She was
smoking a cigarette and her hands were big, almost the
size of mine. I was not interested but couldn't resist looking back when I passed by. She was tall and more attractive as she endured less suffering than the others. She
threw the cigarette away and walked in my direction. I
stopped.

"If you want it here, it's just ten réis. In the room, it's
thirty."

"I don't think I want it today. I—"

"Come on, it's New Year's Day, I could make you
happy for the rest of 1955. Why don't you give it a try?"

Suddenly, the hotel room, the money, the trip in the

small car with the annoying couple, everything came back to my mind as a movie with an unhappy ending.

"Let's have it here."

"Are you sure? You don't want—"

"No, here, right now."

"Okay, money first and then we have to go to the corner where we won't be seen."

I handed her ten réis and followed her long legs to a dark corner where the wall had an angle, forming a perfect cubicle for our minutes of love. She unzipped my pants with precision and touched my penis the same way Valentina had done hours before. I closed my eyes and tried not to associate the two women, but I couldn't help it. When it was finished, I thought about going to the room and staying with the *puta* for the rest of the night. Instead, I gave her a tip and gained the streets again.

I entered the hotel when the day was bright and the sun was already watching over the last disheveled partygoers on the beach. There were people walking around with sandals in their hands, there was confetti and serpentine everywhere in the street and a lonely cleaner trying to tame the mess with a huge yellow broom. As I crossed the hotel reception, I prayed not to face Carlos, Teresa, Marcelo, or Cristina. I just wanted to deal with Valentina and go back to São Paulo.

She was half asleep in the room and, as soon as I came in she started crying again. I couldn't deal with that and I said we should pack our bags and go back.

"But what about our first night together? You ruined everything."

"I ruined everything? You got drunk with your snobbish friends, you embarrassed me, acted like a whore, and then I ruined everything?"

"You don't understand anything, Felipe, you are such a small mind."

"I am a small mind who loves you. So, if you think it's still worth it, come back to São Paulo on the bus with me now and leave these people here."

"You know I can't do that."

"Why not?"

"They are my friends, we came together, we go back together. You are acting stupid."

"Well, maybe I should keep acting stupid but alone. We are not good for each other anymore, Valentina, you are not the person I think you should be."

"What is this all about? Are you upset because I got drunk? Because I wanted to touch you? I thought you would love it, that it would please you."

"You don't need to act like a whore to please me."

The fight didn't end well. I grabbed my bag, paid for the hotel, and left her to come back with her friends. On the bus I kept thinking about what Decio and my friends told me about her. The magic was gone. We broke up the following week.

# CHAPTER 22

*São Paulo, 1959*:

In those last months of a revolutionary decade, it was clear to everybody that we were the "country of the future." Juscelino Kubitscheck was the Bossa Nova president. We were building Brasilia, the new capital, from scratch in the middle of nowhere, in the central plains of Brazil, far away from the coast. We had car industries coming to invest millions, producing and selling four-wheel dreams to people who could afford them. There was Bossa Nova, Tom Jobim, João Gilberto, and Carlos Lyra. Bars in São Paulo imitated the glamor of the Rio southern zone, with smoky restaurants and clubs, where the finest new wave of musicians sang love and smoothness to the rest of the world. We were finally on the map.

For the first time, there would be just Mother and I for mass and supper on Christmas Eve. I had no plans of leaving the house, and getting married was now a distant thought. Even Rá was working her shift at the hospital, and she would come just for New Year's Day.

I worked at the paper factory until five o'clock on December twenty-fourth. There was always a little bonus on that day, and I used it to buy two bottles or red Portuguese wine, imported chestnuts, and a *panettone* filled with candied fruit. Mother was already at home, marinating two whole chickens, washing the rice to be fried later, and improvising a salad. On the previous day, she prepared our favorite Christmas dessert, coconut flan with prune sauce.

While the chickens where in the oven, we listened to the radio. Angela Maria, the Radio Queen of 1954, was singing "Lábios de Mel." Then we left for church and came back just after midnight, enjoying the warm starry night on our walk back, greeting friends and neighbors. Our old street was bright as the stars above, and people kept windows and doors opened to get the summer breeze inside, some showing the glow of the Christmas trees if they could afford them. We just had a wooden crib that we mounted on the coffee table every year since I was a kid.

"This is Christmas and we are as poor as Jesus," Mother pointed out every time we talked about buying a tree.

We got home and ate our supper very slowly, talking about friends, dead and living relatives, the new president and his plan to take Brazil from the ground in five years.

"As if we could change a whole wrong country like this," Mother said, with one quick clap of her hands.

We drank all the wine and sat at the kitchen table until the roasted chickens were just bones, dessert plate was empty, and the first morning *Bem-Te-Vi* birds were singing outside.

On Christmas day, Mr. Russo came in the afternoon. Mother was just waking up, complaining about the unusual taste of red wine in her mouth. She was wearing the new pink apron Lana gave her. She asked me to answer the door when she saw who was downstairs from her bedroom.

I opened the door and there he was, standing at our small front gate: a short man, thin as a leaf, holding a bunch of white roses in his right hand. I noticed the thick blue veins popping up on the top of his hand. They almost blended with the stems. He was also holding a grocery bag overflowing with fresh lettuce.

The smell of grass and farm soil was stronger than the smell of roses.

We were not expecting anyone.

"Good afternoon, how are you?" I said. "I'm Felipe." I didn't give him a handshake as he had both hands full.

"Hello, I am Mr. Russo, from the grocery store. I don't think you remember me. You used to go there with your mother when you were a little boy. I realize now it's been a long time ago."

"Of course, of course. I remember that, Mr. Russo. Do you want to see my mother?"

He now seemed to hesitate as he tried to find the right words. "Ye...ye...yesss. I came to bring her these flowers and say Merry Christmas, but I actually wanted to have a...a...a little word with yourself, if you are not too busy at the moment. I can always come back later, maybe this is not a good day."

Now multiple drops of sweat were coming down his forehead. His gray hair was greasy with Brylcreem, carefully combed and parted on the side.

"Sure. Please, come in and have some coffee."

I opened the gate, and he walked after me through the narrow passage that would end at the door. I remembered we didn't tidy up the living room in the morning, and Mother would be mad that I told the visitor to come in. But what was I supposed to do?

"Thank you," he said as he walked into the house.

At that point, I realized he was wearing a dark gray suit and tie. The humidity of late December was already difficult to bear with shorts, let alone walking up the hill on Coroa Street in that outfit.

He gave me the bag of lettuce. "They came from the farm just yesterday, I hope they are still fresh," he said.

"Thanks. I will put them in the kitchen." I was feeling a little awkward, as I never had any conversation with him at the grocery store he had owned since before I was born. I thought I would love a glass of water if I were in his shoes. "Do you want some water?"

"Oh, yes, please," he said. He was a little over polite and it got on my nerves.

"Please sit down, I will get it in the kitchen." I went inside, wondering where my mother was. I had a feeling she went back to bed on purpose so I would have to get rid of the man on my own.

I picked up a glass and poured the water from the clay *moringa* we had. It always kept the water fresh.

When I came back, he was there, petrified, sitting on the corner of our sofa, with the bunch of flowers in his hand. He drank all the water at once and looked at me, still holding the glass.

"Felipe, I came here because, well…because I want to ask for your Mother's hand. I want to marry her.

I tried to keep my cool. "I didn't know you two were dating."

"No, no! We are not! God forbid, I have respect and admiration for her. I really want to marry her and be her companion in our old age."

"Well, I think this is up to my mother to decide. If she wants to marry you, I will respect her decision."

He seemed surprised with my response, but said nothing. We were silent for a while in the living room. I took the glass back to the kitchen and told him he should ask her directly.

"May I talk to her now?"

"Sure." I was standing there, trying to think fast how to break the news to Mother upstairs. I decided to disappear for a while. "I will get her, she will be down here soon."

I went upstairs. She was just out of the shower, combing her wet short hair.

"Mother, he wants to talk just to you, you better come downstairs soon."

"Oh, Jesus, not even on Your Holy birthday I have peace..." She was complaining and she didn't even know what was waiting for her down there.

I was afraid of telling the truth beforehand. I thought it was better to go and have a beer at the *boteco* on the corner and leave them alone. I went downstairs, said goodbye to Mr. Russo, who was still like a statue on the sofa, and left the house. As I walked, I thought about my mother's hard life. She was getting older and still worked long hours. She still made her corn fried bread to sell, eventually, and did haircuts in the backyard on Saturdays and Sundays. Her legs were swollen at night, and she complained about pain in her knees and hips, but there was something lively and strong about her that never changed or got old. Her laugh was loud and sincere and her face had minimum wrinkles.

She dyed her hair religiously with cheap color tablets she dissolved in hot water before applying the mixture to her gray head. Mother was in her late fifties and, even if we didn't have to go to the end of the street market every Friday to grab leftovers from the vendors or even ask them to give us a bone for soup, our situation was comfortable, but not ideal.

Lana was gone to the south part of the city with her Italian husband. Maria was still in Taubaté with three children. Rá lived at the hospital, since she was now a helper at the pediatric ward. She came back home every other weekend and gave us a small part of her minimum wage, which was not much.

Decio was in the military, and he was dating Elvira, a quiet small girl with curly hair, her skin the color of a mouse. He never talked about her at home and rarely brought her for Sunday lunch. Mother and I thought they would get married. We didn't like or dislike her. She was insipid. He didn't seem very much in love to me, but I always thought my brother would choose a wife in a more clinical way.

When we asked about her, he would reply, "She cooks the best fried rice I've ever had."

"Well, food is important," Mother replied, her face buried in a huge bowl of *café com leite.*

I came back home after one hour, wondering if Mother and I would still cook our Christmas day lunch together as we had planned. I found her sitting at the old kitchen table, smoking her pipe, and listening to the radio. The radio was now permanently sitting on the top of the long table as if the sound machine and the wood had become one inseparable piece, the most important in our house as we were almost all the time around them.

"Where is Mr. Russo?"

"Gone."

"So, how was your conversation with him"?

"Good."

"What did he say?"

"Well, you know what he said."

"And what was your answer?"

She looked at me and rolled her eyes.

"So, Mom…"

"They can't take a woman like me easily."

"I agree. Do you like him? Did you have anything, a fling?"

"Hey, Felipe, respect! Of course not! Fling? I am your mother, I don't go around having flings!"

"Well, he comes here on Christmas Day with a bunch of flowers in his hand and asks you to marry him. I assumed—"

"You don't assume anything. Respect, please!

"Sorry."

"I have been going to his grocery store for years, and he has always been a gentleman. We've got to know each other over this time and, knowing our difficulties, he always put an extra bunch of bananas or an extra pound of tomatoes in my bag. He talks to me a lot. I imagine he is very lonely, and I am always up to a good chat. He needs company."

"Do you think you will ever remarry?"

"Remarry for what? I won't have children and, at this point, I don't need anybody to take care of me. I've done it all by myself."

She finished with the pipe and threw the ashes in the stove. Then turned the radio off. She sat again at the same chair, her favorite.

"Aren't you afraid of being alone, of getting old and having nobody to take care of you?"

"By this time, I am used to not having the company of men, and I learned how to cope. Once a man enters your life, he expects you to cook, clean, and take care of him. In a man's mind, this is what he calls taking care of me. No, I don't need that."

"Come on, not all men are the same."

"And what do *you* know about that? That's all I need now, an old rag dragging his sleepers over the house and asking me to cook him soup. No, Felipe, I don't think I will ever remarry."

I wondered what was my own idea of a marriage, but decided not to give too much thought about it.

"Mom, I think it's time to start cooking our lasagna. We have to make the sauce."

"Yes, good idea."

She got up and came in my direction. She held my head and pulled it down gently, kissing me on both cheeks. Mother was not very affectionate. That was an exceptional gesture. I took it as a Christmas present.

"Merry Christmas, my son."

"Merry Christmas, Mom."

# CHAPTER 23

*São Paulo, April 21, 1960*:

Celebrations and parades lasted for days. Brazil had a new capital, built from scratch in the middle of nowhere. The curvy lines of Niemeyer's architecture were set to reach the future. Presidents and diplomats from all over came to set their foot in the central plains for the first time and see the new city, shaped as an airplane, and the Palácio da Alvorada, the Sunrise Palace. The parties in Brasília were endless. President Juscelino Kubitscheck was in all the magazine covers and newspapers. He had made it and fulfilled his promise of building a new capital in four years. Meanwhile, in São Paulo, all we could see was rain that fell in waves for days.

The neighborhood gathering Mother had organized, with tables outside and a potluck that should end with chocolate cake with the word *Brasília* written with vanilla icing, had to be canceled because the street became part of the Tietê river. The riverbank's curves, that followed the line of our street, disappeared by midday, giving way to a pool of water that got deeper by the minute. At three o'clock in the afternoon, dozens of people had to leave their houses, carrying bags, dogs, and radios on their shoulders. The water rose fast and, one more time, we were lucky just to be in the highest part of the road with four large steps leading to our front door. The flooding reached the middle of the third step by the end of the day. To be on the safe side, Mother, Gilda, and I had already placed our old armchairs and the *cristaleira* on the top of the kitchen table and had taken our precious radio *Pekan* upstairs. We still had a few leaks in the house, but nothing that a bucket in the living room to catch the drops wouldn't fix.

Gilda had been living with us for months now. It was not difficult to convince Mother to take her back after Ernesto left for Brasilia to work on the construction site after losing his business and all the other temporary jobs he had found. He had left in the beginning of 1959 and never sent her a penny. Not that we expected it. She couldn't even pay the rent so we had to pay off her debts with Mother's thin savings and bring her back home with Anita.

"They are parading the *candangos* all around Brasília in open cars, Anita. Your father is there," Gilda said.

*Candangos* were workers from all over the country who came in torrents to get jobs in the Brasília construction site. There were hundreds of them in open cars, brought to a parade around the new capital. Gilda was glued to the radio as if she almost could see him on one of those trucks.

By the end of the day, many neighborhoods in São Paulo were flooded. In our street, a man found a small canoe, not sure from where, and was charging ten *réis* to take any dry belongings to other parts of town. It took a few days to see the water disappear, clean the putrid mud from the roads and houses, and start over again. We were not the brand new Brasília, after all.

# Chapter 24

*São Paulo, 2009*:

T he driver was going too fast, but I was enjoying crossing the city without traffic, as it didn't happen very often. The car went down Anhangabaú tunnel in such speed it felt we were diving. After the tunnel lights we emerged again to see the old decadent buildings close to Luz Station, the *treme-treme,* shake-shake. It seemed they were going to fall any minute. Motorcycles zoomed by, crisscrossing the traffic like supersonic snakes. I looked at Mariana. She was quiet, looking through the window. When we stopped at a traffic light in front of the old *presidio* arch, which is now the entrance of a theater, she got agitated.

"It's okay, Mariana, the traffic light will be green in a minute. There's nothing to be afraid of."

I was sitting in the front with Wilson, Emilia and Mariana were in the back.

Going out was still a torture for my niece. She couldn't drive anymore and, even with us, she thought we would be attacked any minute. The pills she was taking for panic disorder were starting to help her, but progress was slow. She was skinnier than ever and had eyes of somebody who never sleeps. She just felt safe at home.

It was the day before Carnival, and we were heading to a small farm outside of São Paulo with some friends and Maria's children. A quiet holiday: no parades, no samba or masked balls. It was so hot that you would sweat just by looking at the melting asphalt. Streets were feverish with expectation for the wild partying.

While I was looking at the boys selling candy on the traffic light, I remembered going to the *corso* on São João Avenue with Mother and my siblings the year after we arrived in the city. There were clowns, women dressed as ballerinas, odalisques, lots of confetti and serpentine covering everything. I loved to run after the colorful serpentines as they were landing on the ground. I chased them and, luckily, there could be still half of the roll intact, so I could throw it again into the air.

The driver made a turn close to one of the bridges, and there it was, the samba school practice, the rehearsal for the big parade that happens on the first day of Carnival. Now we were going to be stuck in traffic for a while until all the floaters and people in customs were gone. The drums were loud and the closer they got to us the sound took over everything, the whole street seemed to vibrate with its power. It's always the same in this country. Every time the *batucada* passes, people stop, sing, and dance, as if nothing else exists in the world. Some cars in front of ours opened their windows and people started to wave. There was no point complaining, as there was nowhere to go.

"It's going to take a while," said the driver. "It has just started, and the rain is coming."

I opened the window and looked up to the sky. Heavy clouds were forming in different shades of gray. Soon thunder was roaring far away, and I could hear the first one through the *bum bum bum* of the drums. Nature was inviting herself to the party. It was going to be an epic storm, just seen in places where tropical and temperate climates cross paths.

"The air is so heavy you can almost hold it. I can feel these people's heat," I said to the driver.

The wind started to blow from all directions, sweeping the landscape before the thick rain started. Colored feathers from customs were flying. I got dust in my eyes from the air conditioning. There was a strange music in the air, and it was not part of the samba, it was a warning of danger.

Mariana was lying on the back seat with her head on Emilia's knees. "I am scared, *Tia,* I am so scared!" She covered her ears and closed her eyes tightly. "I want to get out of this car, please! The noise, I can't stand the noise!"

"Soon, my dear, soon. It's just Carnival, it's just a party, people are dancing, nothing bad happens here," Emilia said while striking Mariana's dark hair.

I looked back and noticed Emilia's forehead getting sweaty. She was almost as pale as Mariana. *She is nervous*, I said to myself. I tried to look into her eyes but she didn't look at me.

"Bad things happen everywhere, *Tia.* A fight can break out, somebody might be shot. There will be a lost bullet, dead people..." Mariana was pale as a sheet of paper. She complained about sweaty hands and being short of breath.

Thunder was getting louder and the first thick drops hit the glass on the front panel of the car. After a few seconds, the torrent came down at once, taking over the streets and blurring our view from inside the car. The noise of the falling hail on the top of the car was louder than the drums. As people started to run in many directions, some hit our black Mercedes. Others, just for fun, pressed their faces against the glass and looked at us with wide eyes. Young boys dressed with white tunics hit the front of the car with the palms of their hands, as it was a drum. Everything was shaking, and the driver looked at me with a question mark on his face. What could we do?

Mariana started to scream so loudly I feared the windows would break.

"They will take me, they will take me."

She wanted to open the door and grabbed the handle. Emilia tried to hold her arm but Mariana was stronger.

"Felipe, help here!"

I turned my back as much as I could but couldn't even reach her. Muscles were no longer obedient. Wilson took over.

"Excuse me, Dona Emilia, I can get her."

He held her arms with a strong grip from the front seat, stretching his arms as much as he could. In her desperation, my niece just wanted to run away. She couldn't reason at all, but breaking the barrier between the mob and us was not a good idea. In her loss of control, Mariana was throwing herself at the situation she wanted to avoid.

"You have to do something," I told the driver. My own voice was shaky.

"Please, please Mariana." Emilia was now screaming as well and almost crying.

Who was more out of control? Emilia was holding Mariana's hand right on the door lock and Wilson pulled her arms back. She was fighting both in despair.

I started wondering what would happen if I had a heart attack right now.

Wilson didn't loose his grip. People outside looked at us through the car windows as if we were a museum exhibit. After a long ten minutes of rain, the samba school and the crowd behind were almost gone, and Mariana started to calm down. Wilson let her arms go. Street life resumed as if nothing had happened. In a few minutes, we were on the highway, and Mariana fell asleep in Emilia's lap, tears still on her cheeks. I noticed my shirt. It was completely wet as if I had been outside myself parading with the samba school.

Once we were at the farm, I was happy to see family and friends together but I felt exhausted. The property was on a small town called Mairinque. We had bought it many years ago, when I started to make extra money. We needed an escape from São Paulo. I liked it but I had to confess that, after twenty-four hours in deep silence and surrounded by green, I missed the hub-hub of the city. I missed even the combined smell of pollution and humidity.

After dinner with neighbors from a condo nearby, I left for bed while they were still talking about the news with Emilia. As I lay down and looked up the ceiling, I remembered the leaks on the roof we had in our house on Coroa Street, the sound of water drops falling in the buckets all night. I closed my eyes and remembered the famous Tom Jobim song.

*"São as águas de março fechando o verão*
*É a promessa de vida no teu coração"*

These are the waters of March closing up the summer
It's the promise of life in your heart

# CHAPTER 25

*São Paulo, 1965*:

M r. Petronio Fisher was nothing like I imagined. I always thought such a powerful man would be as imposing as his job as general manager of Alvorada Radio Station, with one of the biggest audiences in the country. Instead, when I first stepped into his office, I saw this diminutive man with wild curly hair that seemed larger than himself, its proportions similar to a lion's mane in relation to the animal's body. Then I understood his nickname, *leão*. Lion. Not because he was the king of radio, as I assumed before, but just because of his messy hair.

I was nervous to meet him. I applied for a job at the accountancy department many times before they started to consider me for an assistant position. All I knew how to do was stupid office work and, if that was the only door to a job at a radio station, it was the way to go. I used to go to the Alvorada Studio at least once a month. First they didn't even let me pass the doorman downstairs, but on a sunny Wednesday in October, I managed to sneak into the elevator among some of Angela Maria's fans. She was being interviewed and performing live that day, and it was chaos at the door with more than five hundred fans screaming at the main entrance. I stretched my lunchtime at the paper factory and joined the crowd at Riachuelo Street to see her. Six fans were picked from the crowd to go upstairs with her, take autographs, and watch her sing. As there were just a few men among all the fans I presumed this was the reason they chose me to follow the big star.

Everyone knew Angela Maria was very small, but I never thought she could be so tiny. I stood close to her in the elevator, and she looked like a teenager beside my five feet, ten inches. Her dress was belted at the waist, brown with orange small flowers. Being so close to her, I could observe every detail. I had never been face to face with a celebrity, but I was really in shock when I looked at her foot and realized she was that small, even wearing high heel peep toes. She was very polite, answered all the questions people asked her, and gave us autographs. I didn't have a chance to talk or ask any question. It was just a slow elevator ride, but I got Angela's autograph on my handkerchief. I framed it afterward and it's still on the wall in my office as a talisman.

Then I had to think fast. I couldn't waste the opportunity to find out the right person to ask about a job. After charming a receptionist, I was sent to the Accountancy Department, where I begged for an opportunity. A fat woman with spectacles shaped as cat's eyes got out of her eternal boredom and gave me a phone number.

"We don't have any availability now but you can call Mrs. Fini occasionally and we will see. Something might come up."

I thanked her so effusively she started to step back.

Months later, I stepped into *Leão's* office for an interview. The place was as disappointing as its occupier. The studios were actually less glamorous then one could hardly imagine. Rooms were small. There were boxes piled in corridors and walls all covered with dark wooden panels. Mousetraps waited for victims in a few corners. When you listen to the radio—those velvety voices coming out of the box, songs, jingles—you can never picture all that magic coming from this single floor of an old fashioned commercial building.

"Come in, Mr. Navarra, have a seat."

*Leão* was signing a few papers on his desk, and he barely lifted his chin to look at me. He just pointed to the seat with the pen he was holding. He finished with the papers and asked for another minute to answer a phone call. I paid attention to every word but couldn't figure out what he was talking about. He hung up the phone and finally looked at me. His eyes were dark and small, too close to each other.

"You seem to have a decent job at the paper factory. Here we pay less for the same type of work. Why do you want to change?"

"That's my dream. I always wanted to work at this radio station, since I was a kid."

"A lot of people have this curiosity about radio, about what lies behind the waves, but it's a job like any other job. You are not going to work at the studio, meeting the artists every day. This is an office job, you will be on the B side of the record.

"I know. It doesn't matter. This is the place I want to work, I really would like to have an opportunity."

"You should at least consider going to college or do some courses once you are here. It could improve your opportunities and your salary a lot."

I thought about Valentina and the whole college issue for a second. Where would she be now?

He took a stack of papers from a pile on the left side of his desk and started to look at them, reaching for his pen. He kept talking, asking me about my work, but was not looking at me. I sensed the conversation was coming to a close.

I couldn't waste the chance. "Would you give me the job if I promise to go back to school and do some courses?"

"The hours here are long and the salary is not as good as the one you earn now."

"I am aware of that. It's fine with me."

"Listen, you are not a twenty-year-old anymore. Do you have a family?"

"Not yet, sir."

"Soon, you will probably have one and you might realize this dream of working on radio or TV won't feed your kids."

"I always wanted to work on the radio, please, give me this chance."

"People who want to work on the radio, normally want to stay on the glittery side: production, management, DJ. Your experience is in accountancy books—"

"I don't mind learning new things."

"So, you admit that what you really want to do is go to the other side. Once you are here, you will leave accountancy as soon as you can and become a producer. Is this your plan?"

I didn't know what to say. If I said yes maybe he wouldn't hire me. If I said no I would be lying. I knew I had the voice and the talent. Then I don't know what came into my mind at that moment of despair. I decided to pretend I was on air. "Ladies and Gentlemen, here is your Reporter Esso with the last entertainment news. Elis Regina, the new singing sensation, just won the Music Festival or Record TV last Sunday. She now has a contract with EMI Records."

I almost sang a piece of her famous song "Arrastão," but thought it would be too much. Instead, I kept going with different news, pretending I was a radio host.

Of course *Leão* was not impressed. "You are persis-
tent, my man. I think it might be your best quality. I will
let you stay but I am going to ask your boss to watch you
closely. You will start as a messenger and we will see
how it goes."

The salary and the position were even lower than what
I expected.

"Thank you, sir, I'll take it."

"Go talk to Mrs. Fini about the details and close the
door behind you."

# CHAPTER 26

*São Paulo, 1967*:

We were ready to watch the Miss Brasil beauty pageant when a march for "restoring freedom" took over our neighborhood. Mother had baked an elaborate vanilla cake to take to Ambrosia Bahia's house, the first in our street to own a TV set. Everyone was invited to watch the contest on that evening of July first. Marches and protests were popping everywhere during that time. Mother considered ditching the whole Miss Brasil event to join the crowd outside, but the neighbors didn't let her go. She never lost her taste for politics, even if her legs were not as strong to march in the streets as before.

New music, hippies, men with long hair, and rebellion exploded all over as it happened around the world. It was the boiling cauldron for the twists of 1968 that would resonate everywhere. In Brazil, we could feel the same wave but we could also feel a chilly wind, a shadow, a sheer dark cloak slowly unfolding its fabric and waiting for the right moment to cover the entire country, tying us all in a tight knot. In March of 1964, Brazil was shaken by a military coup. The generals took over the power and sent President João Goulart into exile in Uruguay. A lot of people celebrated the "bloodless" revolution and the return to order. Leftists were hunted everywhere, sent to jail or into exile, and many people were happy about it. They said we were free from the "Cuban Ghost" and we were not going to be communists in the model of the Castro's revolution.

"It's forbidden to forbid!" Caetano Veloso would soon yell this catchphrase from the stage of the Record Music Festival, a huge live TV contest for new composers.

It had the power of stopping the country on its finals, on Sunday, October twenty-first, like a World Soccer Cup. On the following day, Caetano was interviewed at *A Hora da Bora,* our most prestigious program at Alvorada. He had gotten fourth place with the song "Alegria Alegria" and thousands of fans crowded the street downstairs to see the man who would create the *Tropicália* cultural revolution a few years later. Police were called and I was one of the radio employees in charge of helping to control the mess. I felt very important and Caetano Veloso passed just a few inches from me. He even said, "Hi, how are you?"

I worked more than twelve hours a day and often did weekend shifts, but I was happy. My job was unglamorous but I didn't care. Later, I found out it was not about seeing Caetano Veloso, Roberto Carlos, Dick Farney, Carlos Lyra, and Emilinha Borba in person, but much more about seeing how everything worked and came to life on the waves. I also had made a good friend with a funny name, Boscobino, an assistant producer.

The radio station took three entire floors of an old corner building in the heart of old downtown São Paulo, overlooking the Chá Viaduct—a place where I came so often when I was a kid with Mother and later strolled around with Valentina when we were together. Many girls had crossed my path after we broke up, but nothing good enough to sparkle my heart. I'd heard she married a Varig commercial pilot and moved to Rio.

Back at the radio station, I worked on the first floor where all the boring departments were located—accountancy, correspondence, Human Resources—but as a messenger, I gained the streets a lot as I had done when I was a teenager. On the second floor, there were four studios. Three of them were not much bigger than a bathroom. Walls were dark with soundproof systems and normally one or two tables with microphones. The fourth studio was for live performances or for recording programs with lots of musicians. It was twice as big as Mother's kitchen with many microphones standing or hanging up from the ceiling, two cellos, piano, a set of drums that could be heard in Africa, stools and chairs. On the other side of the glass the sound control table with thousands of buttons and a constant smell of sweat. The few *radionovelas* that survived television were also recorded here, and we could always see two big carton boxes in the back of the room with equipment for special effects: maracas, coconut shells, cellophane, whistles, and a whole bunch of old stuff that could easily be perceived as garbage and taken to the bin on the curb downstairs. At home, we heard the sound of rain, thunder, closing doors, ships coming from far away, and all your imagination could create as you listened to the stories that came from that small box.

Finally, the third floor was almost inaccessible to mortals, as that's where the big shots worked. All the rooms had fluffy carpets, heavy furniture, and a special room for lunches and dinners with artists and agents. I was there a few times, bringing documents to be signed by *Leão* and other directors. I realized there were many more important men in the company, and *Leão* was the one who held less power, who used to deal with all the mess from

downstairs. The others didn't have to talk to employees
or go down to studios. If they had any interest in one artist, the artist and his manager would go upstairs and have
lunch with them. Normally, the managers and record
companies would fight for access to the third floor. Later,
I found out they controlled much more than money. They
decided who was going to be on magazine covers, what
march would be the next Carnival hit, what song would
open the next *radionovela a*nd become an instant success.
Everything people loved, they had loved it first.

On a Monday afternoon, I was sent to the third floor
dining room to bring back some papers to the legal department. There was a meeting going on for hours and
there were problems with an exclusive show broadcast
deal. Everybody downstairs said The VIPs were in the
meeting. They were charming brothers, Ronald and Marcio, a big hit at TV festivals, singing cute rock'n roll bal-
lads. All the girls made me promise I would describe
them in detail when I came back to our ordinary office on
the second floor. I met Boscobino at the elevator, and he
bet that I wasn't brave enough to chat with one of the
brothers. We were not allowed to ask for autographs at
work.

I was instructed to knock on the door and get into the
room quietly. When I entered, I felt tension. The president was talking to a tall man with long hair and a purple
long-sleeved shirt. Marcio and Ronald were standing in
the back of the room, whispering to each other and peering through the window. A maid had just served them
two small cups of *cafezinho.* Marcio was shorter than
Ronald. Both were wearing black pants with large belts,
shirts similar to their manager's. Ronald's hair was long
to his shoulders and curly. He looked older than he did on
TV.

"Here we go, my man. You can leave now, thank

you," the president said and handed me a few papers.

"Yes, sir. Excuse me."

I looked at The VIPs once more, but they didn't notice me.

I left and decided to go to the bathroom before taking the elevator. Bathrooms on the third floor were much nicer and always clean with soft toilet paper and imported soap available in a china bowl on the sink. I always went there, took one or two of the little soaps shaped as roses of different colors, and gave them to Mother. She started to collect them in a jar in our bathroom, but nobody was allowed to use them to wash their hands at home. They were just for decoration and fragrance.

As I prepared to leave the bathroom, I made sure I hadn't forgotten the signed papers I brought with me from the dining room. I opened the door and suddenly a force of nature, hair, and sandal fragrance took me over, pushed me into the bathroom again, and locked the door behind her.

"The wait was too boring until you came along, my dear. Your eyes are so dark, so big and deep. And I love your hair."

Her voice was very soft and almost childish. She had blonde hair almost to her waist. She stroked my dark curly hair with her big hands.

"Somebody might want to come to this bathroom."

"People that matter have another bathroom in the main room. Don't worry, it will take just a few minutes."

"What will take just a few minutes?"

"I will show you."

She took her tie-dyed multicolored blouse off. She wore no bra and I suddenly felt a reflex tickle underneath my pants when I saw her small pink nipples getting closer to me. She almost ripped my shirt off, and I heard the sound of a button falling on the tile floor. I had a last

moment of good sense and placed the documents carefully on the sink, making sure its border was dry. Then it all
happened really fast. We both came silently against the
wall. Afterward, I realized she was small and light as a
young ballerina as I kept her in my arms for a few
minutes and felt I was just holding a blanket around myself.

"Where do you come from?" I asked as she stood up
and reached for her blouse on the floor.

"I am one of The VIPs backing vocals. Nice to meet
you, my name is Elana."

"Nice to meet you, I'm Felipe."

Somebody knocked on the bathroom door, and I suddenly remembered the papers, the work, people were
waiting for me downstairs. A small torrent of panic went
through my blood, but I still had the good sensation of the
past ten minutes. I closed my eyes and tried to stay on
that feeling.

I suggested one of us should hide in the toilet com-
partments while the other left sooner but she gave it no
attention:

"Felipe, you are hot! I hope to see you again. It made
this boring waiting much more exciting."

She stood on the tip of her toes, and gave me a kiss on
the left cheek. Before I had time to say anything she
opened the door and left without even looking at the unknown man who gave us a puzzled look before going into
the bathroom without comment. I left and went down almost running by the stairs.

In the end of that afternoon, I left the studios earlier
with Boscobino. We were both happy to go to the movies
to see a rerun of *Terra em Transe*, one of Glauber Ro-
cha's films that were making a revolution in Brazilian
cinema as the Rossellini movies had made in Italy years
ago. I had been working so hard I barely had time to go to

a theater anymore. My closest friends were still people from the neighborhood, and they were all getting married and having children. I don't know if it was because we worked long hours in the same building or we were meant to be good buddies, but Boscobino Bandeira was becoming one of my best friends. We used to have a beer or two at a *boteco* on Monday evenings, the quietest day at the radio. We worked a different schedule because the weekends were the busiest time on radio stations, with special entertainment programs and artists performing live in the late afternoon *"Chá com as Estrelas*, Tea with the Stars,"* was the biggest hit at Alvorada, with Diego Antunes. He was the richest and most famous radio presenter at that time.

On Fridays and weekends, we pulled fourteen hours, running up and down with guests and celebrities in and out for live programs. I was still a messenger, but I'd accumulated coverage at the production and at the offices lately. I had to work more for a meager raise in my shameful salary. Boscobino was already an assistant producer, the job I wanted to learn. Apart from work, he was really good to me, but he was a little mysterious, to tell the truth. He was not the sociable type, tall, skinny with a huge nose. His official job was to provide the studios with whatever they needed during live interviews or performances. He spent most of his day bringing coffee and cigarettes to singers, technicians, and producers. Not ideal, but more glamorous than my job. We talked about work, girls, families, and the scary times we were living in the sixties.

"There is so much going on in the world, it's like an explosion of freedom in America and in Europe, and here I feel we are being squeezed, our mouths glued with tape, our brains sterilized."

Boscobino used to get inflamed when he talked about

politics, the dictatorship and the coup of 1964. I used to be so naïve and think the military generals were going to step out for real in a few months, maybe in a year, and give us some space.

Boscobino laughed and always proposed an ironic toast. "To my friend who still lives with his mom, believes in fairies and in the good intentions of our government. *Viva* Felipe!"

We used to laugh while ordering another cold Antarctica beer and talk about something else. He didn't talk much about his own family and his longtime girlfriend. I think her name was Julia. They lived somewhere in the countryside, a good seven-hour drive from São Paulo. He visited them often and I thought it said a lot about his good heart. He took the bus at least once a month on Sunday evenings to be back on Wednesday afternoon, straight to work.

I was still single with no girlfriend and living with Mother, who was now entering her seventies and was getting ill and tired. I didn't miss living on my own. I had all the freedom I wanted but still had some long Sunday lunches and talks with her. She was refining more and more her sharp sense of humor as her body became weaker. Her knees bothered her all the time, and she started to take medicine for high blood pressure, not without challenging the doctor's abilities.

"Let's go to the monastery again. The Friar's pills are enough to heal, doctors are full of shit."

"Mother, the pills probably don't even exist anymore, and doctors study all their lives to be able to give you a prescription. They deserve some respect."

"The pills are holy, they come from God. *He* deserves more respect than stupid doctors with their manners and all their talk, always looking down to you, as you are an idiot."

Her trouble with doctors had started to worry me. She was supposed to do some sort of exercises for her legs and to take more medicine. I used to give her the pills in the morning, but I always had a feeling she was throwing them in the sink. The future would prove me right.

When I was at home on weekends, I noticed her difficulty climbing the stairs and always thought about getting old myself. I kept thinking that the way you lived your life really came back to you. Mother was a tough woman who gave blood and tears to raise us free of drugs, crime, and all the misfortunes of poverty. She never remarried because she was afraid it would be bad for us. Now my siblings were all far away, taking care of their lives. Would Decio stop on a Sunday evening to see how tired she looked? Did he ask what he could do about it? They certainly contributed with money, so she didn't need to worry about the grocery shop or the doctor. Sometimes Gilda dumped her daughter in our house on weekends so she could go to a party or a walk in the park with her husband, now that they decided to give the thirtieth chance on their marriage, and he was just out of AA. Lana lived on the other side of town and was too busy spoiling her only son. Maria was three hours away in our old Taubaté. We saw her once a year, normally around Christmas time when she came to visit, dragging a bored Louis by the arm and bringing her three girls to say hello to Grandma. Then there was Rá, who came every other weekend to complain. I wondered at that time if Rá was just unhappy, damaged, or purely bad.

"I think I will finally get a chance to become a senior producer, or a real one," Boscobino told me a month later on another Monday at the bar, while he slowly filled up his glass with beer as he always did—the glass a bit inclined to avoid excess of foam that I instead loved to taste.

"How come?"

"Abelardo is leaving. They invited him to work on *TV Record.* People are flocking to take jobs on TV now. It pays better. It's growing fast. The radio age is at the end, my friend."

"I don't believe it."

"You should." Boscobino emptied his glass in one gulp and grabbed the bottle on the table again.

I was silent.

He started to fill another glass. "Did you hear about the new Globo TV in Rio? They have just started and people say it will be powerful. They are already investing millions in high quality *telenovelas.* Some actors from TV Tupi are packing their bags to Rio to start working on their programs, and two of the best writers from the radio were hired a few weeks ago. That's it, Felipe, we soon will have to start shopping for jobs on TV."

"But I never thought TV would become that big, radio is simpler. Poor people from neighborhoods like mine don't have money to buy TVs. They have to gather and watch it at somebody's house. Can you imagine having a little party for every *telenovela* episode?"

"If this country was not so fucked up people would get less attached to what's going to happen on the next t*elenovela* episode," he said.

"What do you mean?"

"I just think we had a great push in the fifties. There was so much music, new theater, new books, new blood. It seemed like the future had started. But now I see this fucking country going back to Middle Ages."

I shook my head. "Well, they say life is improving, there are more jobs."

"It's all fabricated, Felipe. How can we believe in anything we hear or read if the military censors are occupying TV stations, newsrooms, publishing houses. They are everywhere. Most people don't know what's really going on."

"So, do you know? How can you know?"

"Well, people talk. Journalists talk. I hear their conversations. They whisper, they try to be careful, but I sometimes hear them."

"So?"

"They talk about people that have been kidnapped and nobody hears about them anymore. The *political police* takes them to questioning in secret places, they torture them for information about communist organizations, *guerrilhas,* leftists in action."

"Do you believe it's all true?"

"Maybe. Anyway, we better talk about something else."

# CHAPTER 27

*São Paulo, July 20, 1969*:

I was not convinced about TV until the day I watched in disbelief as Neil Armstrong set foot on the moon, live, right in front of my eyes. Brazil was falling apart in that first semester of 1969, but on those days of a cold and humid July all people talked about was men on the moon. Even Mother got a TV set. We decided to make a joint effort and buy her a *Telefunken* for her seventieth birthday. The image came in different shades of gray. Just visible when we put a dark blanked over the living room window as a black out curtain during the day, but she couldn't be happier.

On that Sunday, she woke up early to prepare fresh *gnocchi* she had learned with Maria Pagliucca. She only cooked it on special occasions.

"Felipe, come and see. I polished the old kitchen table all by myself. It will be perfect for the *festa da lua*!

"*Festa da lua?* Moon party? That's how you call it now? I didn't know it was going to be so fancy."

"Well, people don't walk on the moon every day. These Americans are unbelievable, I have to say—"

"Mother, you shouldn't be polishing tables on your own, this is a heavy piece of furniture, you could dislocate your shoulder, you can feel pain in your back later, you—"

"Aah stop! You are so negative! Look at our table! It's part of history now, it will host the first *festa da lua* of Coroa Street and you worry about my back. My hands won't fall because I spent a few hours cleaning it."

The table was shiny but not sanded. Mother always said the marks on the top were the book of our family. The knife marks of *gnocchi* slicing—"*matar cobras*" or "kill snakes" as we said when we were kids—pencil marks from our homework, chipping here and there, round stains from cups, pans, and *bules*.

"You don't need to make history with the party then. The table is history already."

"True."

She turned her back to me, placed her hand on her lower back without noticing, and walked toward the oven to check the *bolo de fubà* she used to make in the afternoon. She let it bake slowly, the pan only covered with ember and cinder still remaining from lunch preparation. It took more than an hour for the cake to be ready, but it came out as fluffy as a cloud, and there was nothing better to pair with a cup of black strong coffee. The house had a sweet smell waiting for the event of the century and soon it would be full of neighbors and friends.

At Alvorada instead, everyone had to work on July twentieth to help the news desk. We were not that many, anyway. The streets were so quiet, I decided to walk to work, to stroll all the way downtown, watching the city around me. I stopped at a small bar close to Praça do Patriarca to have a *média e pão com manteiga*—coffee and hot milk in a little glass cup and a toasted roll, cut in half and with melted salty butter in both slices. That was our usual breakfast in São Paulo before espressos, croissants, and twenty-four-hour bakeries. Rolls were always fresh, small French baguettes baked three, sometimes four times a day. Butter was rich and sold in cans. Aviação was the best brand.

The roll had just landed on the bar. The smell of melted butter right in front of my nostrils filled my mouth with water. I'd adjusted the first half between my fingers for a bite when three men came in and the world stopped, paused for a horror movie.

They parked a blue VW in front of the bar. They were all dressed in dark suits without ties. I was horrified when I realized one of them had a gun in his hand and the other two had *cacetetes,* the police rubber sticks. People said they were good to beat people because they hurt but didn't leave marks on the skin.

"Police! Where are José Maria and Olavo?" asked the man with the gun. He stopped a few feet from where I was standing. He was looking at the owner, Miguel, a short Spanish man with a thick moustache and sweaty forehead who I saw behind that bar almost every day.

He raised both hands, as if by instinct, palms facing the policeman. "Who—who are you talking about? I don't know these people."

"Don't lie to us or you will have the same destiny." The man's face was as inflamed as Boscobino's cheeks when he talked about the military dictatorship. He showed Miguel the gun. "Are you going to help us or do you want to come with us to the precinct?"

"But—but I really don't know what you are talking about." Sweat was now dripping on his forehead.

I was still holding the buttered roll midway between the plate and my mouth. My heart was beating so fast I could hear it. Even I could tell the Spanish man was lying.

"Where are they?" The man with the gun was now yelling.

The others looked around the place. One of them jumped over the bar and started to look for something. He broke plates and cups on his way to the kitchen in the back and threw on the floor everything he could reach. Overwhelming clattering noise.

"I am going into that room." The man said it and pointed at a small blue door in the back of the bar. "And if I find somebody hiding there you are dead. I swear I blow up your brains right here! We have very reliable information that they are hiding here, in the back of your dirty bar!"

"Who are you?" Miguel managed to say, his eyes leaping out of the orbits. His hands were still in the air.

"Police, I told you. You know José Maria and Olavo are involved in subversive actions. And they know people who might be dangerous for national security. We need to take them for questioning. If you don't help us, you will go too! We are entering now."

I could see that Miguel was getting more and more agitated. Every day at the bar, he was nice but very quiet, not the chitchat type. Now he was shaking and stuttering while answering the policeman's questions. He looked at the ceiling and took a deep breath. "They just asked me to spend the night. They are friends of an old friend whom I owe a lot of favors. I never thought they had anything to do with leftists, with *resistência*. I am sure it's a mistake. You are probably looking for somebody else."

The three policemen didn't say a word. They kicked the back blue door and stormed inside. I should have left at that time but I was glued to my spot by the bar as a dummy in a shop. We heard noises of people going down the stairs. Things fell on the ground, clattering, echoes, and voices. Behind the bar Miguel had heavy tears in his eyes: "There was nothing I could do. They are old friends but I don't want to go to jail to die."

"But if you didn't do anything, they would let you go," I said.

"You people, you have no idea about what's going on in the dungeons of this city, in the basements of police stations. If they hunt you at home as they are doing now, you have a very small chance of coming back."

He spoke in a low voice now and started to cry nervously.

The policemen came upstairs, bringing the two men. I was surprised to realize how young they were, no more than twenty years old. One of them didn't say a word and I saw he was handcuffed. The other, who I understood was José Maria, screamed, cursed and fought. Before they got to the front door, the gunman hit his head with the revolver. I saw blood pouring from his skull and a cold chill went through my spine toward my legs. I thought I was going to faint.

"*Comunista de merda*," the policeman said and shoved him into the car.

I realized I was shaking as much as the Spanish man.

One of the policemen came back and held him by his collar from the other side of the bar to deliver the final message. "You better pack and go back to your dirty country, I am giving you a chance, *comunista de merda!* Otherwise, you won't be alive too long in this town. I will let you go this time but I don't want to see you anymore. If we cross paths again, you are done! I know your background, I know who you are. *Comunista!*"

He pushed Miguel, who fell on the floor. The policeman turned his back on us and left. Then I heard the car engine. They were gone.

"Please, get out, I need to close the bar for the day."

"But, Miguel, who are they? Who are these guys you were hiding here?"

"Ask no questions, it's safer. Go, Felipe, go. I am sorry about all of this."

"Will you be okay?"

"Yeah, yeah. *Tchau, tchau, vá embora.*"

He waved his hands sending me away. I left the bar without saying a word, in shock. After walking one block, I heard the sound of the rolling metal door of the bar being closed. I threw the rest of the cold bread and butter in the garbage and then I regretted not waiting to find a beggar as there were always people asking for money or food on the corners downtown. I thought about stories I'd heard about the military hunting leftists, communists, and conspirers. That was the *repression* people talked so much about, all these comments at the small mouth, whispered at the coffee break at work, all the anger Boscobino felt. I always thought it was an exaggeration as we never saw or heard it on the news. I actually never cared or paid too much attention to it.

I still had a few blocks to walk until I got to the radio station. During that walk, I finally understood a lot of what Boscobino talked about with so much passion. A chill ran down my spine as I recalled a conversation we had a few days earlier:

"These ghosts in suits, they are censors. They are everywhere now. Did you see? They come here, they never need to be announced for the important offices on the third floor. They don't even need a pass downstairs."

I'd heard they were everywhere, on TV and radio stations, on newsrooms all over. Some newspapers had been closed, and others would be for sure. But it all could be an exaggeration as well. How could we know?

"There are spics, spies all over. You can't trust anyone, Felipe. Anyone. They can pretend they are your friends and if you say something stupid against the military, even if it's a joke, they call the censors and they start to investigate your life. Even if you don't have a real connection to the Communist Party or with any leftist, they will find one and take you to torture. I think they enjoy killing people."

How did Boscobino know that much? Maybe I was stupid. Reality was unfolding in front of me, and I just didn't want to see it.

I reached the building and everything was more silent than on Good Friday. I took the elevator to the first floor and, as I entered the newsroom, not a single person noticed me. Everyone was mesmerized, speechless, standing up in front of the TV set placed on the top of a tall chest of drawers. The legs of the lunar module were slowly descending onto silver ground. The Apollo 11 had just landed on the moon.

# CHAPTER 28

*São Paulo, 2009*:

I browsed some photos from a pile on the coffee table. In the first one, I could see The Museum of Modern Art's red walls jumping out of the gray landscape. The building sits unusually over four pillars on its four corners. The space underneath, where the ground floor should be, forms a large vault. A contortionist used it as a stage. A few people were watching. A woman nearby looked very tired and disappointed, her arms folded over her chest like a comforting embrace. In the background, there were the museum gardens and the long road going north and passing under Paulista Avenue.

The second image was a motorcycle accident. Many of them happened here every day. Motorbikes are in huge numbers, as a trick to avoid traffic and move faster. The biker was lying on the ground with a bloody leg in the center of a circle of people. Some seemed to be yelling, most of them just stared, and a man was talking on a cell phone. We couldn't see the biker's face since he had his back turned to the camera. It was a bright sunny day and the light sparkled on everything.

The third photo showed the Consolação subway station's long escalators. They started on street level, separated from the noise and smoke just by an enormous glass case. Then they went down a long path to reach the underground.

"What the hell is interesting about the escalators going down to Consolação subway station?" I asked myself.

The photo showed just the line of faces on the escalator—two black men talking side by side and one incredibly fat woman, who probably took all the space around one step. She was holding tight to a colorful plastic shopping bag. A girl of around eighteen held books and a folder. She was right behind the black men and seemed to be paying attention to their conversation. Finally, on the top of the escalator was a man in a dark suit with shaved head and colorful tie. He seemed to be looking nowhere. On the very top of the image I could see a part of street sign with the name of the station in white and green.

The intercom rang from the main gate downstairs. Rita yelled from the kitchen:

"Seu Felipe, it's Dominic, can he come up?"

"Of course."

Mariana came from the bedroom, her hair wet from the shower. "So, Uncle Fe, what do you think of my photos?"

"They are good, very good. Still a little cliché, but it's a good start."

"Listen, this is not a contest and I am not becoming a professional. It's just an exercise. You should try to be less grumpy."

"Well, I always tell the truth, remember? By the way, Dominic is coming up."

"Ah, good…"

She seemed a little embarrassed. She sat on the sofa in front of the one I was sitting on.

"Are you back together?"

"I think so. Well, we are just getting closer again I

should say, I can't manage a relationship right now."

The bell rang as she finished the sentence. Rita came rushing to open the door. She was all agitated when she knew Dominic was coming, I bet she had a crush on Mariana's boyfriend. He was the usual type women fell for— six feet tall, light brown wavy hair, ocean blue eyes with a touch of melancholy, a swimming instructor, American from New York. A show-stopping, heads-turner kind of gringo, even in a diverse city like São Paulo. Had I been like that when I was twenty-five? I can't even remember myself at that age. Would I leave my girlfriend if she started to have panic attacks and was unable to go anywhere without creating a fuss? Who knows? Well, he did, at least for a while. It just added to her confusion to be dumped by the handsome guy. Now he was back, ringing my doorbell. At least he was polite and made an effort to speak decent Portuguese.

"*Bom dia, Seu* Felipe, *tudo bem?*" He touched my shoulder with one hand and extended the other. I made a move to get up, but he kindly pressed my shoulder. "No please, remain seated." His hand felt like a pillow and his voice was always warm.

I bet girls fell for the accent too.

He kissed Mariana briefly on the lips. They sat side by side on the couch in front of me.

"So, how was your first day as a photographer?" he asked.

"Well, a bit scary in the beginning but I could walk up and down Avenida Paulista without fainting."

"It's a smart exercise. Your therapist had a good idea," he said and looked at me, trying as to include the old uncle in their conversation before I felt uncomfortable.

"But it was scary," she said. "At the same time I always get fascinated by it, there's so much of São Paulo in these images." Her face got serious. "Months ago a friend was robbed on a traffic light at Paulista at lunch time. He was stuck in traffic and some boys came to the window with a knife. They took his watch and money. Nobody did anything."

"You have to start avoiding these stories…"

"Well, I shouldn't be going on and on about it again. It's not interesting to talk about it."

"You can talk about it, but just if it helps you, it's a great idea from your therapist, taking photos from the city every day as a healing method. I am proud of you, I really am."

The bastard. He was proud now, but when Mariana had nightmares every day and couldn't go out without freaking out he left her, couldn't "deal" with her suffering…

I pretended I was reading the paper and not paying attention. I thought about going to the kitchen to give them some privacy but my curiosity won.

Dominic was still talking. "…I like this city, I really do. It's ugly in the beginning, there's no easy attraction. It's like being adopted by an angry stepmother. But, as time goes by, you find out she has a big heart beyond the anger."

I emerged from the wall of newspaper: "Dominic, *meu filho,* it's nice to hear something positive about this place. But sometimes I think we are never going to solve the real problems, I love this place but I am getting tired."

"What's the worst problem for you, Seu Felipe?"

"Well, traffic is horrible."

"But they are extending the subway."

"Well, to understand better why we got to this point you have to understand our class system."

"What class has to do with subway?"

"Everything! Upper middle class from fancy areas like this one are not interested in having a wonderful subway.

They can afford bulletproof cars. Why would they allow people from the suburbs to reach beautiful Ibirapuera Park in thirty minutes? A lot of people in this town want segregation, walls, and boundaries.

Rita came from the kitchen, her hands dug in the pocket of her apron as if she was embarrassed of showing them. "Lunch is on the table."

"Thanks, Rita," Mariana said.

Suddenly she was the usual cheerful person. She looked at me while she held Dominic's hand and pulled him gently to the dining room.

# CHAPTER 29

*São Paulo, 1972*:

In those first months of 1972, Boscobino Bandeira took three months of unpaid leave. I sensed there was a problem with his family, but when I asked about it, he never gave many details.

"I have to see some relatives in the countryside. My father is dying, and there's a dispute over his small farm." That was all he said.

I thought that he might come back married to Julia or she might even be pregnant and he had to go there and fix the situation. I wished him luck.

Boscobino became strangely quiet those days, more than usual. We even stopped going out for drinks, and it made me sad. I had other friends, and the more time I spent at work the more it became a second and more diverse home for me. But with Boscobino I could talk about anything, and he even started coming to our house on Sundays to enjoy Mother's roasted chicken.

I also participated at the Radio Alvorada staff monthly reunion*s* at Bar Brahma, a classy place on the corner or São João and Ipiranga Avenues, all marble floors, mahogany tables and heavy doors. This part of town would be later theme of a very famous song that would become a classic, "Sampa."

On a rainy day in March, when our hot summers start to become breezy falls, the newsroom received a telex about a shooting somewhere in the south of the city, around the Interlagos racing car track. Apparently, more *terroristas* were involved in some action and the police caught them. Two reporters were sent to check it.

Late that night, I was on my shift answering the phone and checking telex messages, when most of the staff was gone. Lucio Vaz, one of the reporters, called:

"Felipe, are the censors still there? "

"No, everyone is gone now. I am here with the cleaning crew, the news writer, and the night DJ."

"You will need to call the director and tell him what's going on here."

"What's up?"

"Did you hear about the two terrorists in the Volkswagen that were involved in a shooting with the police this afternoon?"

"Yes. Last update said they were stopped by traffic agents and got very nervous. Then police found documents in the glove compartment leading to a *guerrilha* cell. The information I have here says the passengers had a gun under the front seat and started shooting at the policemen. There are no names until this moment. Do you have anything else? Should I put you in contact with the writer in the newsroom?"

"No. The story is more complicated."

"I don't get it."

"One of the two terrorists who died in the car was Boscobino."

"Was *who*?"

"Boscobino was a terrorist. *Our* Boscobino."

"*What*?"

"You heard me. I'm sorry, Felipe."

"No, it's not possible, he is at a farm with his family."

"Well, that's what he said. I was at the morgue waiting for identification before calling you. They just confirmed his identity. He lied, Felipe, he lied all the time. He was involved with the ALN."

"ALN?" I asked.

"Aliança Libertadora Nacional, one of the leftist guerrilla groups involved in clandestine actions, trying to fight the military by kidnapping important figures in exchange for amnesty of political prisoners, using violence and guerrilha tactics."

I shook my head, stunned. "No, no, it's not possible. There must be a mistake. Let me try to contact his family. There must be a phone number—"

"We already called them, Felipe. It's hard to believe, but he hasn't been there in the last two years. He was probably in *guerrilha* training in the jungle or even in another country. We are trying to find out something about it now. We have to inform the general director because I am sure there will be questioning. The police will try to find out if somebody else at the radio station knew about it. God knows what they can do to us to find out. They can even close Radio Alvorada indefinitely if they think we are trouble."

"But do you think somebody here knew anything?"

"Well, if there's a suspect, it will fall on you. You guys were close, weren't you?"

I thought I was going to lose my breath. My throat became dry. "Oh my God, he never mentioned anything to

me about it! He didn't even like talking politics. He said
he went to see his family every two weeks, every time he
had time off. I always thought he was on the bus to the
countryside. Now you say he hasn't been with his family
for two years..."

Confusion and fear were then mixed with disappointment. Boscobino, my friend, was dead. The one who
spent Sundays eating lunch with us, the one who even
met my nephews from Taubaté. I didn't know where the
biggest shock was: from finding out he was a liar, that I
actually never knew who he was, or because he put us all
in jeopardy. The scene at Miguel's bar suddenly came to
my mind. I felt a chill that quickly froze my stomach.

It took me a few minutes to come back to reality and
make the call to the director's home. He said he was coming as soon as possible and rudely hung up. That's when I
remembered I had the keys to Boscobino's drawers and
locker. He had given me those keys months earlier. I
couldn't even remember why. I lost them and never gave
them back to him. During his "time off," I finally found
them on the back of a drawer at home and I was planning
to give them to him as soon as he returned to work. I had
to act quickly, before everyone arrived.

I was about to discover something that would change
my life.

I knew I had just half an hour to do it. I got Boscobino's keys from my locker and checked if the few souls
that were roaming the corridors were busy enough not to
pay attention to me. Of course, nobody cared about where
I was. I first sat on his desk and put the key in. It opened
three paper drawers at once, all of them on the left side of
the desk. Inside the top drawer, I found old train tickets,
pencils, erasers, and rulers, and a few receipts from a
nearby *lanchonete*.

In the second drawer, there were just drafts of scripts

for programs he was working on. The third one just had dust.

I quickly moved to his locker on the corridor. The second key on the set easily opened it. In a small shelf on the right side there was a small bottle of deodorant, a razor, and a tube of shaving cream. Two small towels were carefully folded on the bottom. I found very peculiar that the interior walls were all covered with sheets of magazine pages, mostly from soccer and car racing publications with photos and news. I knew he was a sports fan, but never thought he would go through the hassle of covering his locker with photos cut from magazines. It looked like a schoolboy's room. I saw a photo of Emerson Fittipaldi, the car racer, and my hands reached for the page to read a subtitle on the photo. That's when my fingers noticed it: there was something lumpy behind the wall cover. I tore a small piece of paper and, Oh Jesus!, there was a large envelope hidden between the paper and the back of the locker. A rush of blood went through my head. What should I do now? Without too much thought, I ripped the paper completely away, as if it was never there, and got the documents. I quickly closed the locker and took the envelope with me, hiding it in the briefcase I carried to work every day.

I went to the newsroom where the editor-in-chief had just arrived, certainly after the director made a few calls to half of the staff. He was on the phone, and I just made a sign saying I was going to eat something down at the bar and would be back soon. I disappeared in the elevator with my briefcase and took a taxi home where I hid the envelope under my mattress and went straight back to work, again by taxi. It cost a total of twenty-two cruzeiros, a fortune for my thin pockets. Currency in Brazil had changed a couple of times over the twentieth century. Cruzeiros were the currency from 1970 to 1986.

Turmoil was the best word to describe the following hours: people were in and out from the third floor. A group of police officers arrived with angry faces opening drawers, cabinets, spreading papers, clips, and fear around the offices. They talked to some people and watched everybody's movements. All documents were confiscated. Boscobino's real identity and death was a bomb and Radio Alvorada was making an effort to dismantle it before it went public. Nobody wanted that type of attention to a high-audience broadcasting station. I am sure they had to negotiate with the political police to avoid closure. I left work when a glorious sunrise could be seen through the concrete of buildings. I jumped into an empty bus going *contrafluxo* on the opposite side of heavy morning traffic. I slept on the bus. I was so tired I ended up at the final stop all the way down to Jardim São Paulo, a quiet new neighborhood in the outskirts of Santana. I had to take the same bus going back for about twenty minutes until I reached my stop. Even if I was a wreck, the sight of the city waking up, the first workers walking or taking the bus to face one more day, was refreshing. The mornings in São Paulo always smelled of soap and wet hair and people looked clean. I loved to close my eyes and hear the sounds—the streets getting noisier, the movement of cars and people increasing by the minute. It made me forget about Boscobino for a few moments.

At home, I checked all the documents in the envelope: there were a few sheets of paper with typed addresses, phone numbers, contacts from different countries, names of people I'd never heard of, people Boscobino never mentioned in any of our conversations. I still didn't believe he was involved in a *guerrilha*. In the back of my mind, I thought something would suddenly come up and this incredible mistake would become just a legendary story. We would go for beers on the following week and laugh about it all.

I went to his funeral on that same day after work, and just Lucio Vaz from the radio came as well. All the others didn't want to be seen as friends of the *terrorista* and get in further trouble during those heavy and uncertain times, when being at the wrong place with the wrong people could cost you one or two fingers under torture in prison. But I couldn't bear the idea of not going, I felt guilty, especially after finding the envelope with all those names and not knowing what to do with it. I decided to keep it under my mattress and not talk about it with anyone.

A week went by until the censors and the police decided to talk to me after questioning other employees. They had been around all week, smelling the evidence of more potential terrorists or accomplices. There were three of them, and they called me in right after I came back from my lunch break. They asked me to follow them to one of the third floor offices. They didn't waste any time, but came straight to the point:

"You and Boscobino Bandeira were very close, right? What did you know about his involvement with the ANL?"

"Nothing."

"It would be better if you tell us. Your friend is dead. You won't help him being quiet. We need to find other terrorists. Do you understand this is a matter of national security?"

"Yes, sir, I understand. It was a shock for me as well to find out about it when he died, the way he died. He never mentioned anything about ANL to me. He told me he used to see his family every two weeks, and I found out recently he hasn't been with them for two years. I was caught by surprise as much as everyone else."

He raised his voice and banged the table. "We cannot

believe it. You, who were out with him and who invited him to your house many times, didn't know what he did in his spare time? You better start telling us."

I was now afraid they might take me to the police station. All the secret comments people made about torture started to come to my mind.

There was another policeman who was firm, but still polite, somehow elegant. He took the lead and asked me other questions, repeating the same questions over and over, to see if I would contradict myself. They wanted to seem smooth and smart as detectives in old American movies, but their cheap, wrinkled suits and nauseating Continental cigarettes denounced their real origins. The man who talked directly to me was the shortest and his hair was dark and greasy.

"Don't try to lie to us, it will be worse. You will have to go to the precinct with us."

"But I am telling the truth, I can swear."

I could feel the sweat dripping from the sides of my fore head.

"We will give you a day to think about it. We will be watching you. We know where you live, and where your family is. So, don't try anything funny."

How I could find myself in this situation? And what should I do about the envelope? If they found out I had it, if they realized somebody had opened Boscobino's locker, things would get complicated. Could they get into my house and investigate? My stomach churned.

I left the room without saying a word, I couldn't think. I didn't sleep that night and, the next day, I still didn't know what to do by the time they called me. But before that happened, I was summoned to the director's office. I thought it was something related to work and, for a moment, I forgot my personal drama. When I got into his all-beige/brown room with heavy burgundy curtains covering large windows, I saw he had a serious look.

"Sit down, my man, please."

He had never spoken to me in that tone. I obeyed.

"The police and the censors want to make a deal."

"Why? Sir, I swear, I didn't know anything about Boscobino's connection to terrorists. He used to vent out against the military every now and then, but that was all. It never crossed my mind—"

"Felipe, if you know anything, any little detail, tell them. If you have anything that belonged to Boscobino, please give it to them. I have an offer for you, but this has to stay between us forever, otherwise, it will cost you this job and any other job on radio in this city."

"Yes, sir."

"If you have any information and if you are willing to give it to them, I can make your dream come true—" He paused but didn't look at me directly. "I can give you the night time program. You could finally become a DJ. If you make it work with the numbers and the audience, well, that's your chance. But you need to help us and give them some information."

My mouth was dry. "But, what if I don't have anything to give?"

"Then we pretend this conversation never happen and all stays as it has always been."

"Sir, I know they have reasons to believe I knew about his private life. But, if you allow me to ask, why are you giving me something so big in exchange for information that might not be that important?"

"The police and the censors are so furious about the Boscobino story, they are talking about intervention, arrest, questioning, closing this radio station for good. They need to know the connections to our dead friend. We discussed it, and they can negotiate. If I give them anything you might have, they wouldn't take any of us into custody, they wouldn't interfere in our programs, and they even considered letting the censors go. We obviously have to behave and not broadcast words that are offensive to the regime, but that's not the end of the world nowadays. Felipe, please, think. I give you the rest of this day off so you can pause about it and try to remember any information Boscobino might have slipped out while he was with you.

"Is your promise for real, I mean, turning me into a presenter?"

"Yes, I give you my word and a contract of two years on the job. Here it is."

He showed me three pages typed with all the details of my new job running a night live music program.

"Take it with you and read carefully. You will have more than enough time to prove your talent on air. Today I will talk to the policemen, I am sure they can give you one more day to decide. You will be saving Radio Alvorada from serious trouble, Felipe, even from extinction."

"I will be back tomorrow, sir."

"Think, Felipe, please think. Don't disappoint me!"

"No, sir."

"You may go now. See you tomorrow here in my office, same time."

"Yes Sir, excuse me."

I left the room, got my briefcase and didn't speak to anyone. I went downstairs, stepped out of the building and, when I reached the street it was as if my neck had been relieved from a metal collar. I decided to walk home. It was a warm sunny day, almost as warm as January or February, but the breeze was different with hints of autumn.

The city didn't have the usual smell of hot asphalt as in the summer, and I didn't feel sweat dripping over my face and my back when I reached the second block.

On the way, I stopped at the same bar at Patriarca, the place where I witnessed the arrest a few weeks earlier. There was no sign of Miguel behind the bar. I ordered a black coffee and it came immediately from a percolator as big as a beer keg. The server was fast and didn't talk. He placed the small glass half filled with coffee, which was already sweetened in most bars at that time, with generous amounts of sugar added still on the percolator. After presenting the glass with the coffee, the server quickly gave me a small coffee spoon and the sugar bowl.

"Just in case you want to add sweetness to your life," he said with a smile.

I drank the coffee quickly. It was at the right temperature and as sweet as *balas de côco*, coconut party candies. I looked at my watch: eleven-fifteen, time for coffee break at the radio. Everyone was probably congregated in the narrow corridor on the way to the restrooms, smoking, talking, and pouring extra sweet coffee from the recently filled thermos in small cups. The *continuas,* our mix of janitors and cooks, brewed fresh coffee three times a day: at eleven-fifteen, two-thirty, and four-thirty. They brought three thermos with hot coffee, one with hot milk, the sugar bowl, and coffee cups with saucers and spoons. They were all placed on trays along a narrow table that stood along the wall at one side of the corridor. When they brought the fresh coffee, it was like recess time at school. Everyone left their desks, bringing cigarette packs and lighters, hanging up the phones. It was our gossip and friendship time. What were they talking about in a day like today?

I put the money on the bar and, before leaving, I decided to ask, "Where is Miguel, he used to be always here at this time, didn't he?"

"He left for Spain more than a year ago. He said he might never come back. He sold the bar."

"Pity. He is a nice guy."

Yeah, we all miss him."

There were long seconds of silence. We both knew the reason and it was better not to talk about it.

"Okay, well, see you soon, *até logo, obrigado.* "

*"De nada, tchau. "*

I kept walking and feeling a heavy shadow over my head. When I got home, there was nobody there. Mother was involved with a lot of church work at that time, and she was always among priests and nuns. I was relieved to be on my own. I went to my room and pulled the envelope again from under the mattress. I looked at every line, trying to find a connection between any of those names, phone numbers, notes and addresses. It was like reading in another language. I noticed coffee stains in some of the pages. Would it be coffee from the thermos in the corridor? When did he spill coffee on those pages? Maybe it hasn't been Boscobino, but somebody from that list on his own coffee break or maybe the man who died in the car shooting with him. I would never find out.

I lay down on my bed and closed my eyes until I fell asleep. I slept for the whole afternoon. I got up, had dinner with Mother. We talked about different things, from soap operas to soccer. When she asked why I was back from work so early, I said I was feeling a bit under the weather. She was usually very smart for lies but this time she didn't pick up anything. Maybe she didn't want to. I went to bed early that night, slept until five-thirty in the morning, and got ready to go to work.

# CHAPTER 30

*São Paulo, 2009*:

The bus door opened in front of me, and my knees felt like jelly. Dominic pushed me in, and I hyperventilated. I couldn't breathe. I was holding his arm so hard he had to pull my hand out."

Sunday lunch. As it happened every other week, we were at Rubayat, my favorite barbecue place. Emilia, Mariana, and now, for the first time, Dominic, totally marveled with the abundance of delicious meat and the colorful parade of side dishes: fried rice, grilled vegetables, endless types of *saladas*, *farofa,* sauces, perfect French fries. Mariana was telling us that he took her to a bus trip to Praça da Sé, scary even for me with the waves of people in the streets pushing you along as in a chain, street vendors yelling, buses and cars all over. To make it more of a challenge, he took her by bus, which I thought was a little too much. I didn't say anything, it was almost a miracle to keep my mouth shut.:

"I looked at every person who got into that bus," Mariana continued, "and I studied their behavior. I was just predicting the moment when somebody would show a gun, yell and say '*This is a robbery!*' Or '*We are taking this bus!*'

"But it didn't happen, nothing like that happened," said Dominic.

I saw Mariana's eyes get somber. She sighed. "I still have to get over a lot of other things before I take a bus on my own again. It might never happen here."

"You should talk about it more often, it might help."

"I can't, I just can't—"

She was getting more upset. Emilia intervened:

"Why don't you show us the Praça da Sé photos? We want to see them!"

Dominic held Mariana's hand in a gesture that was sympathetic and comforting at the same time. She looked for the photos in her bag. They were black and white and more suggestive than the shots from Avenida Paulista. She passed them to Emilia who handled them to me.

There were about a dozen photos of women: young girls wearing colorful miniskirts and talking in front of a kebab restaurant; an old lady, carrying two shopping bags, trying to cross a busy road; a mother, wearing a yellow cap, holding the hands of two little girls; a couple sitting on the cathedral steps, kissing passionately; another couple apparently having a fight, with angry looks at each other and caught in the middle of a sour discussion. There was a sequence of shots of the couple fighting: on the first shot he held her violently by both arms, the photo suggested he was shaking her. Then she pushed him but he didn't let her go. The last shot was a blurred close up of her face in tears, still trying to get away from his grip. She was pretty, in her twenties, long straight hair, sexy dark eyes, full lips. She seemed trapped in beauty and violence at the same time.

I looked at the sequence for a long time. I looked at Mariana. She was quiet, holding Dominic's hand, and eating her fried rice. Table conversation changed to world news, teasing each other, and food, our all-time favorite subject. My questions about the photos dissolved into the happy lightness of family gathering, and I realized it was not the moment to ask her anything.

# Chapter 31

I thought about it, I really did. I thought about all the people who were going to be arrested, some of them would probably be beaten to death, or suffer electric shocks, maybe have fingernails pulled out, fingers cut off if I gave them Boscobino's address list. I knew the dictatorship police was not joking when they hunted militants from ANL, MR8, and other anti-regime movements. I didn't know them. I didn't even know they existed, and that's why I gave the envelope to the director in the morning. I told him I found it accidentally in his locker when I decided to recover a borrowed shirt there after I learned about his death. I told them Boscobino had given me the keys before his supposed vacation, just in case I needed to open his locker. I gave them the envelope and the keys all together.

"Thank you, Felipe. We will always be grateful. Let's sign your contract right now. Welcome to our presenters' team!"

The director showed me a copy of the same three sheets of paper I had read at home many times. They were the terms of my contract for the next two years.

I signed it, we shook hands, I said "thank you," and

left without any other word. Two weeks later, I had my debut as a radio speaker. The program was called *Entrando na Madrugada, Entering the Night,* and featured old musical hits, marchs, *samba-canções,* boleros that I knew so well from my young age. I presented the songs and read letters from listeners who asked for them to be played in the program explaining in the letters why that song was important in their lives. I was anxious before the first program started but once the red light was on with the words "On Air," I felt I was in Mother's living room chatting with the neighbors.

Mother, by the way, organized a Pantagruelian meal at home with all our friends and relatives to listen to my first radio live program. Even if most people had TVs at the time and radio evening programs were not the richest slice of audience compared to TV Globo and TV Tupi *telenovelas,* that got all the attention.

"Good evening São Paulo. This is Felipe Navarra, I will be with you for the next two hours. Fasten your seat belts. This is a time machine on its way to the past. Take a ride with Radio Alvorada and listen to the best of the twenites, thirties, forties, fifties, and sixties. The first song today is 'Boogie Woogie na Favela.'"

> *"...A nova dança que faz parte*
> *Da política da boa vizinhança..."*

# Chapter 32

*São Paulo, 1974*:

Hi, I am Felipe Navarra. I am reporting for a special program for Radio Alvorada. It's about the migrant workers from the North—"

"Oh, yeah, they told me you were coming."

"Are you the social worker here?"

"Yes. Nice to meet you, my name is Emilia."

She shook my hand and I looked straight into her round dark eyes. They were peaceful and sad.

"Nice to meet you," I repeated.

Her hand was warm and soft as a cotton ball.

She then took me on a tour around the place where she said she worked twelve hours a day, sometimes on weekends.

"People call this place the reception, like in a hotel," she said.

It was a warehouse besides the *rodoviária,* the bus station. The first stop for workers from the North of Brazil and from *paulista* countryside after a long bus ride from places I'd never heard about: Caruaru, Assis, Dourados, São Félix—small villages scattered in the huge Brazlian plains, stricken by poverty, bad luck, or lack of rain.

"They come here hoping to find a place to sleep on

their first days, most of them don't know a soul in this city. We also try to find them jobs, but this is getting more difficult. The prosperity fountain of Sul Maravilha, the wonderful south, is drying." She said it while opening a heavy sliding door. "Here is the waiting room."

It was an old basketball court. The floors were covered with a crust of dirt. There were no seats and just two windows. At least fifty people were sitting on the ground and I couldn't say which of them looked more miserable. There were no suitcases. All their belongings came on *trouxas* or shopping bags. Men were skinny and a few women were heavily pregnant. Children ran around as if they were in their backyards. Everything had the same color of dust.

"Here we try to help them as much as we can," she continued. "We try to place them in pensions. We send them to farms or factories in the outskirts of the city. But in the last few years, so many people are coming, there is no space anymore."

"And what happen to the families who find no job?"

"They end up in slums or in abandoned houses that shelter many families at once, you know, the *cortiços*. But even if conditions here are so miserable, we can never talk them into going back, it's never an alternative."

I thought about the cold evening so many years before when we saw São Paulo for the first time at Luz Station. I could relate to that—going back is the last thing you might want when you uproot your existence toward new sceneries. Nothing can be the same back there, ever.

"Is there a way of stopping them from coming unless they have a job previously arranged?"

"Where do you think you are? Of course not, we can't do that!" She raised her voice: "These people don't need passport or visas to come here. We are all in the same country. You can't build a wall…"

I looked at those families sitting on the floor, and I felt embarrassed. I realized I had never traveled to any other place in Brazil except Rio and within the state of São Paulo. I had no idea about the rest. I just knew we had thousands of kilometers of beaches and so much land we could even be a continent.

"Have you traveled a lot in Brazil?" I asked her, more out of personal curiosity than of professional duty.

"I traveled a little, mostly for work. I spent six months on Indian reservations in Mato Grosso and a year in villages at the *caatinga* in the Northeast."

I was impressed. She was not particularly beautiful but her aura of goodness pleased me. After my visit, she took me to a *lanchonete* close by and we had a few cups of black coffee, sitting on old wobbly benches around a small table. I almost forgot it was a professional visit. I asked about her age. I asked if she was married. I asked if she was happy with her career. I asked what was her favorite food.

She answered all the questions with careful words. She knew I was crossing the line, but she seemed not to care. She rarely smiled. Emilia's hair was the color of honey, she had very thin lips but they were drawn carefully to decorate her pale face. She was short, not more than five feet, one inch, and I noticed a disproportionally large bottom under her pants and colorful tunic.

"I listen to your night program sometimes. I didn't know you did reporting news too."

"Well, I am not officially a reporter. The audience has been very good, so we are starting to produce a different program in the afternoon slot. They are trying to teach me how to do it. It's more of a test."

"Good for you. Evening time is quickly dying for radio, right? The whole world is glued to *telenovelas*."

I wanted to stay in that bar as much as I could. We

talked for three hours. It got dark and I offered to escort
her home. We took the bus to Perdizes, where she lived
with her aging mother, and I thought about kissing her in
front of her house that night. I didn't, but I came back
many times before we got married a year later. I felt it
was about time for me. I never felt this crazy rush all over
my body when I saw her, but being with her made me
feel safe. We rented an old two-bedroom apartment in the
same street of that hilly neighborhood where her mother
lived.

Our wedding was simple, the way she wanted: just a
religious ceremony at a chapel, followed by cake and
champagne for family and close friends. Emilia was pure,
simple, and altruistic, and I loved her for that. I admired
her. Time didn't stop when she was with me, I was not
breathless every time I kissed her, but it just felt right.

# Chapter 33

São Paulo, 1981

In October, Emilia and I finally got to terms with the fact we would never have children. She had had several miscarriages since the year we got married and she was now taking Valium at the end of every loss. She was paler, thinner, and she was not even working anymore. Her purple veins could be seen through the skin and her eyes were always lost. I started to fear for her. Another failed pregnancy would have been a serious risk.

We had barely talked about adoption when Mother died of a stroke the week before Christmas. Her funeral was the first ceremony attended by the whole family since my wedding. The wake was in Araçá Cemetery, where she was going to be buried later. It was a hot and humid summer day, the sun was impious outside and the heat indoors increased the warm and sweet smell of flowers, like cheap perfume on a sweaty *puta's* skin. Burning candles surrounded the coffin and everyone was praying and patting their foreheads with Kleenex.

I was sure this was the reason people didn't do long funeral ceremonies in this country: die and you were buried on the next day, before you started decomposing in front of your family.

"Felipe, my dear, you look good! But, damn, it's so hot!"

Lana kissed me on both cheeks. Her eyeliner was slightly melting under her eyes, her eternal dark circles even darker. Behind her was her son Pietro, a tall man with the same red curly hair as our father. He was shy and didn't exchange a word with me. I was almost relieved by that. Her husband was outside smoking a cigarette:

"I would love to come visit you and see Emilia," Lana said. "It's been at least a year. We don't see each other."

"I know, living on the other side of town now means a two-hour trip."

"Traffic has been awful!"

"Well, thank God, I never wanted to drive!"

"Now I ride the subway almost all the time. I love it."

"By the way, sorry about the miscarriages, Emilia must be exhausted."

"Yes, she is."

"Are you trying again soon?"

"No."

Her face changed with the realization she said something wrong. We were silent.

I looked at her and at her tall and grown up son. I always thought he was a nerdy and a quiet kid. Many times I imagined myself having a completely different child, but at that moment I was envious of Lana. She tried to change the subject.

"I am happy for you, brother. You deserve money and success. When I listen to your program on the radio, when I see your name on newspapers, sometimes it's hard to believe the famous radio presenter and interviewer is the same boy who sold live frogs to the Italian restaurants to get a few coins and buy condensed milk." She said it with a laugh and held my hand while we were sitting side by side on those terribly uncomfortable chairs outside the wake room.

"It's good to hear that from you. Sometimes there's so much around...I wish I could see you more often."

"Me too." I could see a tear rolling down her left cheek.

A loud crow voice came from the back:

"Where is the coffee? How we can have a wake without any coffee? I didn't have my breakfast today."

Lana turned back to talk to her. Rá was standing up but she was almost the same height as me when I was sitting down. She was wearing a twenty-year-old black dress with long sleeves and beige thick tights, even in that heat, but she didn't seem to be uncomfortable. I thought maybe Rá was not human at all. Lana took action. She knew I was not in the mood for anything.

"Why don't we go down the road to the bakery and we can have a *media e pão com manteiga* together?"

"Are you going to buy me breakfast, Lana?"

"Yes."

"Good."

They left and I didn't move from my chair. I thought of Mother again, and I couldn't think about eating. I still could hear her laugh and her voice across the kitchen table. How passionate she was about Getúlio Vargas, and how fiercely she protected all of us from danger, drugs, gangsters. I remembered the sound of the egg beater against the bowl when she was making *bolo de fubá*. I would never taste her cakes again. How long would I be able to remember? More than sad of losing her, I felt a sudden terror of forgetting.

When I started to make more money, we thought about buying her an apartment close to ours. She never wanted to leave Coroa Street. Mother spent her last years between meals and visits to her grandchildren, hanging

out with old neighbors, and spending more and more time
at church. She became even more religious in the end.

"I have to give it a big push, I don't have a lot of time
left," she used to say.

She still cooked her famous *feijão preto com toucinho*,
black beans with bacon. She got better with time and the
dish was now so famous she had to cook twice the
amount she was going to serve at home just to give a few
bowls to some friends or neighbors. A generous amount
always went to the priests and nuns.

Decio came to sit beside me, on the same chair left by
Lana. "Mother had a hard life but she aged well in her
own way. She was happy, wasn't she?"

"I think she was happier than any of us."

"You are saying you are not happy, little brother?
With all the money, with the famous people you interview every day? Come on! It would only be better if you
were on TV. Imagine that—there would be a hundred
photographers outside this funeral room now."

"Why in heavens did Mother protect you so much?" I
blurted out and immediately regretted it.

"Oh, now here it comes...the jealous little brother...same old blah, blah, blah. Felipe, get over it!"

"You know what? It's Mother's funeral for God's
sake. Let's not fight again. I'm sorry."

"Apology accepted."

"How is your job going? How is Elvira?"

"Job is always the same shit. At the army, once you
get older, they give you a desk and some papers to sign.
If you are lucky you have a secretary good enough to
fuck. Not my case. I have to find amusements in other
places."

"You never feel guilty about sleeping around that often?"

"Not at all. If you have a penis in good condition, you

have to use it as much as you can. And my wife doesn't
have a clue. She doesn't have a clue about many things.
She can't even sign her name properly.

"She might be smarter than what you think."

"If she's smart, she pretends she doesn't see anything.
Most women do that. That's how we survive marriage.
Soft on eyes, softer on your heart."

"You never think about your two kids?"

"They have nothing to do with my private life outside
of the house. I provide them with all they need. I am a
good father and a good husband. I still fuck my wife every Sunday during our afternoon naps!"

"Priceless details."

He laughed and patted me on the back. Decio would
never change.

"Felipe, we shouldn't be talking about fucking at
Mother's funeral."

"Tell me about it."

"As we are here, tell me just one more thing: don't
you ever, ever jump over the fence? Come on. With all
those *gostosas* around you every day."

"People at radio are pretty just in people's imagination. It's actually very unglamorous."

"Stop playing saint, come on. One dirty detail, come
on!"

"Decio, my marriage is not like yours." I got up and
decided to walk away before the conversation got sour.

"No, it's not. You have money, little brother. And
money makes the difference. If a gossip magazine pic-
tures you in bed with three women who are not your wife,
you will be called eccentric. If it happens to me, I am a
disgrace."

"That's what it's all about, right, Decio? Jealousy and
money."

"Do you think I am jealous of a *bunda mole* like you?"

"Yes, you are. You have always been."

"I am a real man, I have a real, steady job. I am not in *entertainment.*" He changed his voice when he said that, like in a comedy sketch. "One day you are not that cool anymore and you are out. Enjoy while it lasts, Felipe."

He left before I could do it. I felt a hot flush taking over my face. I wanted to smack him as I did so many times when we were young, but Mother wouldn't be happy watching us.

She was buried at the end of the afternoon when the sun was going down, but the temperature was still unbearable, everyone was sweating buckets around the tomb. Four men lowered her coffin carefully and the priest Nonato, from Coroa Street, waved the aspergillum with holy water, a magical instrument to sanctify her soul as she flew on her way to heaven. I looked around and saw all my family: Maria, Louis, and their three grown up children, their in-laws and grandchildren, all nicely dressed, showing a good lifestyle but still tired from the car trip from Taubaté. Lana with the red-haired-silent son and her husband, the tallest of all. Gilda and Ernesto were side by side in one of their countless on-off moments. Anita, now a young lady who resembled Gilda years before, was on the other side of the coffin holding Rá's hand. Her strange and ugly husband was watching everything from the back. Rá cried out loud. At one point it seemed fake, exaggerated. Decio, with his wife and sons were on the opposite side, as if he had to prove he was something different or special. They didn't shed one tear during the whole thing. Our uncles from Taubaté were too old and sick to attend the funeral, but some cousins came. Behind the family, I could see the entire neighborhood, all the people who became family to us over the years: Maria Pagliucca, still with her hair pulled in a bun, but her hair was now white as a cloud. Her eyes were red with tears she couldn't contain. All her sons, daughters, and grandchildren were there and more than fifty people I knew from Coroa Street surrounded us at the cemetery.

# CHAPTER 34

*São Paulo, January 25, 1984:*

D iretas!" they yelled from the tribune.
"*Já!*" one million people responded, voices echoing a few miles around.
"We want to vote for a president *now!*" he said again.
"*Now!*" the crowd yelled, applauding.

São Paulo's 430th anniversary was celebrated on this warm Sunday evening in style. One million people occupied Praça da Sé, the central point of the city, to demand elections for president. That was the *Diretas Já* Movement, finally signaling the official end of a moribund dictatorship and marking the top of my career on radio. Many personalities from TV, sports, arts, and music were invited to the tribune. I was among them, and my face was in all the newspapers on the next day, side by side with Caetano Veloso, Gilberto Gil, Pelé, *telenovelas* stars and TV news anchors. I was finally famous beyond my voice. I was a voice with a face. For months, people recognized me on the street and asked for autographs. My contract advance for the next year was way beyond expectations, and I even did a few commercials for cough drops on TV. With the money I got from the ad, we bought our apartment in the Garden District, top floor, doorman, pool, all the amenities, and security that people dream about in São Paulo. I reached my fiftieth birthday and everything seemed so perfect, so predictable. I started wondering what could go wrong. I could smell something going wrong as I always did when life showed us no mercy.

Instead, we got two presents: the elections bid was approved and Brazil finally could vote for president on November 15, 1984. Side by side with democracy, my niece Mariana was born on the same day, when we also celebrate the birth of our Republic.

I didn't remember being that happy. Emilia and I felt a connection with that little girl from day one, and I got so inspired that at Christmas I decided to reunite the whole family: the pieces of us scattered around, leading different existences that seemed to be never interconnected. Our new big apartment was ready to become an entertainment theater and we invited everybody for Christmas Eve supper.

I hadn't seen my younger sister for almost a year. Gilda and Ernesto, who had been living in a little room in the back of his mother's house for the previous ten years, were the first to arrive. Gilda marveled at our apartment, with a kitchen that was a crossover from TV ads and science fiction, all metal and marble. Marble was also in all the bathrooms, from floor to ceiling. This is the shit that impresses people so much and make them think you are the happiest guy in the universe.

Emilia—who has always been a down-to-earth woman, never denying her old social services past—spent the whole Christmas supper trying to play it down to make Gilda and her husband feel more comfortable. Ernesto sat at the tip of our bottle green silk chairs, as if the precious fabric couldn't be maculated by people like him.

"Are you comfortable, Ernesto? Do you want another

dose of scotch?" Emilia asked, and I immediately gave her the wide-eyed look as if saying "Don't offer alcohol to him so fast, you know where this is going to end by the time we start to sing 'Jingle Bells.'"

She was so concerned in doing her best, she pretended she didn't see my signal. I am sure Ernesto did and he said "no thank you, not now." He would never refuse whiskey otherwise. He was holding the Waterford crystal glass with both hands.

"These glasses are so heavy, they must cost a month of my salary," he said.

Gilda turned her face to him for a split a second and frowned without saying a word. I tried to change subject:

"I can't wait to see Mariana, I haven't seen her for a week."

Ernesto played with the whiskey glass as it was a little piano and he could hear a song while patting its border, alternating an imaginary rhythm with his fingers.

"I just saw her on the day she was born."

Even if it was Ernesto, I was a bit surprised and just blurted out: "But you are her grandpa, you didn't visit Anita after she left the hospital?"

"No."

Gilda stretched her back from the tip of the sofa where she was sitting beside him and, as usual, tried to fix the unfixable. "We live very far away and we have to take three buses to get to her house, it's the opposite side of the city."

Ernesto replied as only he could do. "And you forgot to say we don't have the extra money to make all these bus trips back and forth. Our daughter is better off without us, anyway."

The ring of the doorbell saved us for a while.

Emilia rushed to answer:

"Oh my God! Do you have a spare room in this place where I can move in?"

The loud voice was unmistakable. I felt a stone in my stomach as if I had just eaten a whole pig. I took a deep breath and thought, *Just deal with it.*

"Welcome, Rá!"

"Wow, very impressive!"

She stopped at the foyer like another exotic piece of decoration, not even bothering about my wife, who was standing there, waiting for her to come in and say "Hello, Merry Christmas."

Rá looked all over, to the crystal drop lampshade, the heavy cream curtains, the Persian rugs. She wanted to steal it all, engulfing all my fortune just with her narrow eyes of gluttony. "My little brother, my little brother!"

She now forced a higher tone, trying to emulate a child's talk. That always drove me crazy. She came toward me for a hug. She was such a *mão de vaca,* tight fist, she couldn't even get some decent clothes for Christmas Eve. She was wearing the same old brown knee high socks, sandals, a pencil skirt from circa 1940 and—cherry on the cake—the ancient red sweater missing two buttons. Good old Rá.

"How are you, Rá?"

I tried to hug her as briefly as possible. I was afraid of her smell, but she actually had a clean soap scent. She hugged and kissed Gilda and shook Ernesto's hand. Afterward, she collapsed in an armchair with all her weight. I looked at Emila, who was bringing a tray from the kitchen, and we thought the chair legs would break with the impact.

"Aaaah! This is very comfortable. You could buy one extra chair and ship it to my house."

"I can give you this one as my Christmas present."

As the only single person among all the siblings, we

all agreed that Rá should stay in Mother's house at Coroa
Street. She was now retired, with a minimum pension, but
she would surprise us in the near future buying a much
bigger house on the Santana hills, the same area where
Valentina used to live decades ago. Rá had a side business of lending money at high interest, and she saved a
fortune during her years at the hospital. She bought the
house, totally restored, in cash and it took us a while to
realize it really happened the way it did.

"Rá, do you want something to drink? A glass of wine,
beer…?"

"Just a tiny little drop of wine. I can't drink it because
of my liver problems." She turned to Gilda and started to
talk with no pause. "Two months ago I started feeling
nausea every morning. I went to the doctor and now I
have something on my liver, I don't remember the name
of the thing…it's….it's…."

Rá loved to talk about diseases. She liked to have people's attention and being sick was a good strategy. There
was always something wrong with her: this year was the
liver, last year her legs were swollen, the previous summer she had athlete's foot, and so on. Medicines were
also a hot topic: she used to try every single cream, pill,
or syrup people recommended. Years ago we went to the
bank to open an account, and she started to talk to a
woman on the line about her arthritis. The woman
bragged about a miraculous root that she could find at the
street market at Sé Square.

"Rá, for God's sake, are you crazy? Sé is the busiest
place in São Paulo, there are muggings everywhere! So
many people cross the square every minute, they just
push you along, you don't even need to walk. You can't
go there alone! How can you believe in any crap people
talk you into?"

"The woman drank the foracea root tea and her arthritis disappeared. Why somebody would lie about that?"

I ended up going with her, of course. We were shoved into the subway one Wednesday afternoon and were spit out of it at Sé station, together with thousands. I had refused to go for days before that, but then I realized she was going anyway and I thought I would feel a bit guilty if something happened to her on the trip. Secretly, I wanted her to suffer but I didn't want anything to do with it.

It didn't take long for her to find the vendor and the damn root. At least it cost one *real* for a package, quite cheap. Back in her house she made tea with it and drank a gallon in a few hours, just to find out the taste was horrible and the potion made her vomit for the next two days. No improvement on the arthritis, but not even this experience cured her from accepting any recommendation to run to the nearest pharmacy or stall.

As Emilia came back to the living room with a half glass of white Portuguese wine the bell rang again. I felt a certain relief when I saw Lana at the door with her tall husband, so tall his back was a little curved, like a giant hunchback of Notre Dame. We have always called him goose's neck, since the day she brought Giuseppe home for the first time, but he was as gentle as his height and their son was similar. It was as if they agreed to leave all the conversation in the family on Lana's account, and she didn't complain. Their son Pietro was celebrating his twentieth birthday the day after Christmas. He had Lana's carrotcolored curly hair, freckles, and a strange beer belly. Maria, my older sister was right behind them in the elevator. Her children were all married with kids, living in different parts of the country, so she came arm in arm just with Louis. Maria's hair was shiny silver, and she had the same haircut Mother used to carry, squared by ears' length. She looked like our Walkyria in her last

decades: large shoulders, full and wine colored lips, dark
brown eyes contrasting with her gray hair. The only thing
Maria could never match was Mother's easy laugh. She
was heavy and serious, it was hard to pull a smile out of
her.

"Felipe, I never knew working on radio could make a
person rich," said Louis, who looked 130 years old. "I
always thought just TV people made money."

"Merry Christmas, Louis, Merry Christmas, Maria," I
said, ignoring his comment while coming in their direction after hugging Lana.

Louis shook my hand in a professional manner. "Merry Christmas, Felipe. And thank you for inviting us. This
will be a beautiful party."

We talked about politics for two minutes and Louis
started again with the TV conversation. "But you really
never thought about moving up to TV?"

"Truth is, dear Louis, poor old radio reaches more
people in this country than TV. We just don't have the
same appeal. I love radio since I was a kid, I own it everything I am, I don't want to work on TV."

"Maybe because you are getting old for it," he said,
patting my shoulders and laughing, making sure I was
getting it as a joke. The stupid pharmacist. What did he
know?

The apartment now looked much smaller with almost
all the family in the living room. I looked at the Christmas tree and felt sad.

It was becoming fashionable to have paper or plastic
trees, sometimes their branches and leaves were red,
white, or blue, not even green anymore. It all came in a
single box: the unassembled tree, the glass ornaments that
often matched colors with it, and a string of lights. No
more smell of pine in the living room, no more making
ornaments with yarn leftovers as we did a long time ago.

"Emilia, this is the most beautiful tree I've ever seen. I love the white branches like snow," Rá said.

"Well, it's eighty degrees outside, snow is far away from here," I said.

Rá sighed. "They say this summer will be one of the hottest in history. Oh my God, I know my blood pressure will go down and I can even faint in the street. I think I need a new fan…"

I stopped listening. Gilda was close and she tried to pay attention. She was always nice to Rá, unlike me. Louis was standing by the window and I approached him.

"Well, after the *Diretas Já* your name is everywhere and your program has high audience, he said. "Now all you need is a contract on TV and your moment will last longer, imagine that!"

I thought *But how does a seventy-year-old pharmacist from Taubaté knows what's best for my career?* But I didn't say anything. I put my arm on Louis shoulders and invited him to see the Christmas lights through the window.

For one blessed moment, we were silent, just looking at all the apartment buildings around my own: balconies had strings of lights hanging on, many shaped like stars in different colors. In a white Mediterranean building, somebody put a long ladder made of rope outside the window, and a smiling Santa was placed on the third step, his bag of gifts almost as big as himself waving at the wind's mercy. There was something in the air at Christmas Eve that I could never grasp. I always felt genuine happiness. For one moment, even with my brother-in-law by my side, I felt that peace again and I remembered my last Christmases with Mother: the mass, the wine, the simplicity of our chicken and rice.

When we turned back to face the living room again, there was no simplicity anymore, even if Emilia tried hard to hide the opulence: our china was expensive, the table was enormous, the turkey, just out of the oven, seemed the cover of a fancy culinary magazine. We didn't buy the new stuff we were getting introduced to recently: caviar and blinis, fois gras, blue cheese, wine from France and Italy and not just the old Portuguese *vinho verde*. Everybody was amazed by the amount of nuts we had on the table, an old tradition imported from Europe, but still expensive: roasted chestnuts, walnuts and hazelnuts. Brazil nuts and cashews, much more common in our shores, but not cheap, were also starting to become part of Christmas menus.

As we sat at the table, Lana asked about Decio and his family.

"They didn't come and they didn't call. To tell you the truth, I had even forgotten about him. Maybe he decided to spend Christmas with some new woman and poor Elvira is still sitting on the sofa waiting for him to come back home and drive here"

"Felipe!"

Emilia stopped pouring wine, half way onto Lana's glass, and just gave me the look. "I can't believe you said that in front of everybody."

"Well, we all know Decio."

"Come on, it's Christmas," said Lana. Emilia finished pouring her wine and she muttered a "Thank you."

As Emilia moved to Ernesto's place holding the bottle and serving, Rita was coming from the kitchen with the turkey, rice, *farofa,* and salad in a cart. The phone rang.

"Please Rita, answer the phone, I can serve the food," Emilia said.

Gilda and Lana stood up at the same time and reached for the cart, passing the dishes to the center of the long table. Rita came back in seconds.

"*Seu* Felipe, it's your brother, he wants to talk to you."

I didn't say anything but got up, a bit annoyed. It had to be Decio, right before the Christmas toast. What would be the excuse?

I still could hear Lana telling Rá not to make noises while she was eating when I brought the phone close to my ear:

"Hi, Decio, what's up? When are you coming?"

"Sorry, brother, I will be late but I am on my way. Paulo and Jonas are not coming, just Elvira and I.

"Anything wrong?"

"Jonas was arrested. Don't tell anyone please. I will tell you all about it later."

"Just tell me why."

"Drug possession. They caught him selling drugs at a bar entrance, two blocks from our house."

"Oh, boy."

"Yeah, I know. But it doesn't surprise me. I will tell you about it later."

"But where is he? I know it's Christmas but—"

"He's out. I paid the fine and he's free for the moment. I won't let him spoil our party, so I will be there soon. He will go home, stay on his own, and think of what he has done."

"Decio, don't you think you should go home with him and talk, did you know he was into drugs?"

"I always suspected, but he is twenty years old, it's hard to have a conversation with him."

I thought it was hard to have a conversation with Decio too, but in a rush of Christmas spirit, I decided to keep my mouth shut.

"What about Paulo?" Jonas was Decio's younger son just a year younger than Paulo.

"He is surfing with friends."

"At Christmas Eve?"

"Well, he said he wanted a fun Christmas this year.

Elvira was not super happy, but again, they are adults now."

"If you say so…"

"See you in half hour, sorry we are late."

"No worry, come whenever you can. If you decide not to come, we will understand."

"Hey, little brother, did you invite me just for the protocol or you really want me to come?"

"Yes, I really want you to come," I lied.

"So, I shall. But I don't want the others to know about this now, it's not the right moment. Can I trust you?"

"My lips are sealed. But what should I tell them when they ask me why you are late?"

"Tell them, I don't know…that my car had a problem, and I was trying to fix it."

"Lame…you could have called from a public phone."

"They know me, I wouldn't care about calling."

"True."

"Thank you."

"See you soon."

"See ya."

I went back to the table and did as we said. Rá, of course, had a comment:

"That's why I never cared about having a car. Driving in this city is mad and, when you need it the most, the car just breaks and leaves you hanging there on the road. You can even be mugged, city is getting so unsafe now—"

Louis interrupted. "Come on, woman, you never had a car because you could never learn how to drive, you are afraid even of leaving the house on your own."

"And you would never open your purse and buy a car, you are too cheap," said Lana blinking at Rá in a joking tone, trying to lighten up the conversation.

We all laughed and Rá turned to face me. I was sitting at the head of the table.

"Well, now that I have a rich brother, he could buy me a car with a driver."

Everybody laughed again and suddenly there was a void of seconds while they all waited for my response, of course the rich brother should be the one setting the tone.

I sipped my wine and placed the goblet on the table so softly it seemed it was flowing over the cloth. "You guys think I am swimming in golden coins. I still work a lot, and I still have to do it. I work on weekends and late nights, and I rarely take vacation. I am not sitting on a fortune as you may imagine. This is all very beautiful and it seems another planet if we think of where we came from, but it's not that much if we compare to other people in this neighborhood, and I couldn't retire tomorrow if I wanted to."

"Well, you are rich for people like Gilda and I. We were not as lucky as you were, Felipe." That was Ernesto with the extra alcohol kicking in his blood.

"I was a bit lucky, but I worked hard."

Our tone of voice was getting higher.

"Come on, Felipe, your career started when the military were sitting their asses in that studio and your producer friend died. Suddenly you went from being a nobody to a presenter with your own time slot. There must have been so many professionals with college degrees and credentials to fill in for that job, but why did you get it? What did you give them? Information? Maybe you knew your friend's real identity and blew it up to the *milicos.*"

"Well, if it happened as you say, I wouldn't still be on the same radio station if I hadn't worked for it, right?"

Emilia intervened, always polite. "Ernesto, this is not fair. We are trying to reconnect, to share our blessings with you all, because you are Felipe's family, and we should try to get closer, at least for Christmas sake. I know he really liked Boscobino, they were good friends, but he never, never mentioned to Felipe he was a terrorist, never! You can't say something like that." She looked at me and her eyes were all disappointment.

I tried to follow her:

"You even use the word they used at the time: terrorist. We all know the leftist militants were just fighting with the weapons they had during those crazy years. They were not terrorists as you should know by now."

Emila got up and decided to go no further. "I will get more rice in the kitchen.'

Everyone was silent. Even if we hadn't been together for many years, we always could expect some *arranca rabo*. There was not even the thick cloud of awkwardness that normally follows an exchange of that nature.

Ernesto just grabbed the wine, sitting in a nice bottle basket at the center of the table, and filled his glass so fast it almost spilled on the white embroidered cloth. He kept going. "I don't want to be rude, even if I am rude by nature, but that's what a lot of people might think, right? And sometimes we all think it's unfair the way things turned out. They always say on TV that we should extend Christmas for the whole year, the *spirit* of sharing should last 365 days. So, have you been helping us during these last few years? Did you remember to ask Gilda if she had money for the bus before saying 'how could you not go to visit your granddaughter?' Well, we thought we were not welcome there in the first place. Anita is ashamed of me for being a drunk bastard and ashamed of her mother because she owns just a few outfits, and they all look so shabby. She's embarrassed because my wife—your sister—works as a janitor, and I have no steady job, and I don't care about that, Felipe, I don' t care!"

Gilda had her head down and her lips were trembling, tears would start rolling at any moment. I felt sad for my sister. I felt something heavy sinking at the bottom of my heart and I was ashamed. I wanted to disappear, but life had taught me to stick it out, face the music, and dance, don't show regret or emotion. I could barely notice Lana and Maria muttering *"Calma, calma, Ernesto"*

"Excuse me, Seu Felipe. Seu Decio is downstairs already." That was Rita saving me from having to say something.

I felt a rush of blood up my throat but took a deep breath. Maybe for the first time in my life, I didn't react as I always did: yelling, bumping my fist on the table, sending Ernesto out, and humiliating him for what he had said while sitting on my table and drinking my good wine and eating my fucking turkey. No, I didn't do any of this and I was even surprised at myself. I took a deep breath and I don't know why this attitude came to me. "Excuse me, I will meet Decio at the door."

"I can go," Emilia said.

*"I'll go."*

I left the table in silence, leaving their faces buried in my blue china, all we could hear was the clink of the silverware.

I opened the door and waited for the elevator to bring Decio and Elvira. I suddenly had a flash: "What would Mother say?"

Well, if she was alive, the whole discussion at the table would have never taken place, she would have shushed everyone at the first sign of a disagreement.

The elevator arrived silently at our top floor. There was no other apartment and the door practically opened inside our living room. Decio was wearing his tenant uniform, holding the cap in his hand. I imagined he needed to make an impression at the precinct earlier. Elvira had a navy dress, crisp and just right on her tiny frame. She looked young and was always very pleasant, even if too shy when Decio was around. I couldn't imagine what life would be with my brother for so many years.

"Hi, how is everything?"

"All under control," Decio said. He was serious when he shook my hand and there was no sign of his usual debauchery.

I kissed Elvira on the cheeks.

She looked into my eyes and just said "Thank you."

"Of course."

I guided them straight to the dining room, their formal shoes leaving soft marks on our intricate woven rugs. Emilia did a nice job decorating this apartment. It could easily have become such a *nouveau riche* statement with price tags hanging from each piece. Instead, it looked solid and elegant.

We all sat down for desert and I was relieved to see that our table conversation got back to socially acceptable standards: food, recipes, TV personalities, what was going to happen in the end of the *telenovela*.

Christmas Eve meals always ended after midnight, when we saw fireworks by the window and opened the presents. Emilia remembered to buy a present for each one.

Nobody ever mentioned the episode about Decio's son until the end of the following February, when he was murdered in front of his house with two shots in the head. Apparently, he owed some money to drug dealers in the area. Needless to say the dealers were never caught.

We all went to the funeral and that was the last time all the siblings were reunited. Later that year, Gilda died of a heart attack and, till this day, I believe she died of deep sadness. We never laid eyes on Ernesto after her funeral. He moved away and nobody cared about asking for an address, not even his daughter Anita. It was important for me to pay for the entire funeral, I wanted to offer her this last comfort, as I failed to rescue Gilda during the last half of her life. We were so close as children, I was always protecting her until I moved on with my life, and she stayed in the same place. Even went backward when we look back at the small house on Sanitary Lane, where she cried during the day and kept up with Ernesto at night. Instead of accumulating possessions as I did, they kept losing them, dropping their belongings along the road as they got older, as if they were carrying a heavy *trouxa* with a loose knot. First the bar went bankrupt, then they lost their house and had to move to an apartment close to Luz Station, an area that had become more and more dangerous, very different from the glamorous park we encountered when we saw São Paulo for the first time. Finally, after Anita got married, they went to live in the back of his mother's house, in a tiny studio built to shelter maids and garden workers. His parents could have helped them financially but I guess they lost hope long ago of seeing their son doing something better. Giving him money would just keep him drinking.

After 1985, death was sitting at our front steps for a while, taking one by one as in a procession.

# Chapter 35

*São Paulo, Winter of 1992*:

Politics turned my life upside down in a way I could never predict. I was crossing the age border after fifty-five, where nothing happens that often. When your job is stable and you are just supposed to navigate in predictable waters toward the inevitable bone-cracking and penis-shrinking sadness of being too old. But the world around me couldn't be more exciting.

For weeks, the city was a sea of yellow and green as the *caras pintadas* took over the streets, demanding the impeachment of president Collor de Mello, who was accused of a mountain of corruption schemes. First students and later millions of people repeated their newly acquired democracy rights and went out to scream, sing, and protest, painting their faces with yellow and green stripes, the main colors of the Brazilian flag.

President Collor tried one last trick. On August fourteenth, he went on national network asking everyone to go out the following Sunday, wearing the national colors in support of his presidency. On Sunday, August sixteenth, millions took to the streets again, walking and beeping horns in *carreatas,* but wearing black instead. I was posted on Avenida Paulista broadcasting live all day.

Even if I got pretty good at transmitting the energy and atmosphere of a particular event throughout radio waves—that was my strongest talent—nothing prepared me for what I felt on that sunny and breezy afternoon.

Paulista is probably the most famous symbol of São Paulo. That was where the New Year's marathon ended and where people celebrated soccer championships and political victories. The avenue was first traced on the top of a hill in the end of the nineteenth century. Coffee barons built their incredible mansions there, and later the first industrialists did the same. Banks, shops, theaters, and a famous modern art museum came later. Finally, people took over. On that bright Sunday, they really occupied every single squared foot, and traffic was completely jammed over three miles while all the people beeped the horns as loud as they could. Cars and buses had large black cloths on the top or at the windows. Thousands were walking around, singing or blowing whistles. There was not one person who was not wearing black, and most had also the yellow and green stripes painted on both cheeks.

"Impeachment now!" a group of young ladies screamed from a convertible waving black sheets as flags.

"Yes, Collor out, Collor out!" a group from the sidewalk yelled back.

They had matching T-shirts saying *United against corruption*. They were waving national flags and had black towels around their necks that fell over the shoulders like Superman's cape.

I was walking around holding a microphone all day, talking to all sorts of Paulistanos, and I didn't see a fight. It was all about hope and justice. Finally, we were doing something against our longtime ingrained corruption. Of course, we had to do it in a carnival fashion, with music,

beer, and noise. At five o'clock, my broadcast was supposed to give room to another anchor, but I was not tired,
quite the opposite. I was not live on radio anymore, so I
decided to grab a beer and join a small band party on the
corner with Campinas Lane.

*"Eta eta eta, Collor é picareta."*

That was the chorus of the band's recently composed
song to dismiss Collor for good. More and more people
were gathering at the corner. I had a couple of beers and
didn't even notice it got dark. As the sun went down, political speech gave place to a more lustful atmosphere.
Women were getting closer and dancing was getting dangerous.

"Oh my God! Is that Felipe Navarra, the famous radi-
oman? I can't believe it!"

She said it loudly and I didn't need to turn my head to
guess who that voice belonged to, but I did and we didn't
say a word for a few seconds. We needed to adjust to reality as one adjusts the eyes when the lights are suddenly
turned off.

Valentina hadn't changed a lot. Time had been gentle
to her: the same small figure, a slight, almost imperceptible bulge of belly under her black turtleneck sweater. Her
hair was short now, she reminded me of Audrey Hepburn
when she wore boyish haircuts. Some tiny wrinkles
played hide and seek around her eyes, which still had the
same shine.

She bit her lower lip and finally broke our silence.
"Oh my God! So many years. You haven't changed that
much!"

"Oh, yes I did! *You* haven't changed. Even your hair is
the same color. Mine is gray—"

"Well, thanks to L'Oreal," she said with a big laugh and hugged me really tight.

I gave myself to her embrace and felt at home, as if we have never parted. "I didn't know you were living here. Hadn't you moved to Rio years ago?"

"Yes, that's when I got married. It's more than twenty-five years ago."

"And how is your husband? Does he still fly? He was a commercial pilot, wasn't he?

"We are not together anymore. I got divorced four years ago, after my youngest son started college. But yes, he is still flying and traveling all the time."

I felt something funny in my stomach, as if I had eaten a chocolate with a mysterious filling and the filling just opened up inside my mouth.

"Are you still living in Rio?"

"No, I moved back here after my divorce was final. I live two blocks away, on Lorena Lane."

"Oh my... I live on Franca...I'm right beside you."

"How funny is that!"

She gave me a big smile, and her teeth were still perfect and white. Time accentuated the deepness of her sight. She had a smarter aura. I was envious. I started to mentally check on myself to see if I looked older than my actual age, if my hair was too gray, if my tummy was too big.

But she interrupted my thoughts. "I sometimes listen to your program on the radio. I am proud I met you in the old times. You've made it! Exactly as you wanted!"

"Well, nothing is exactly as we predict or as we want. My prime is way past now, a lot of new and noisier voices are on air, and in many cases radio became just a trampoline for jobs on TV "

"Not exactly. There are lots of radio listeners and fans everywhere."

"Well, we are treated as the poor cousin on the hidden side of the table now."

"The world has changed, and I bet you have changed too."

I nodded. "Change is good, we are still alive."

"Yeah."

We were standing on the corner. Young people passed by, dressed in black, faded yellow and green stripes painted on their faces. The political act had evolved to a festival with people playing drums here and there, cars passing by beeping horns, small gatherings for drinking and laughing. The bright streetlights made everyone look more tired and paler.

"Do you want to have a drink or some coffee?" She pointed to *Campinas* Lane, down the hill from Paulista.

"Sure, it's a good idea. Too noisy here."

She smiled.

We went down the road while talking, as we had never stopped seeing each other. She had become a lawyer, and she worked a lot, while her husband traveled often. At a certain point they were together just because of the children. Once the kids grew up there was no more connection. She had an affair that didn't work out, but she realized it was time to stop faking the marriage.

"My divorce was clean and painless. I know it's a difficult thing to believe, but we were both ready to separate."

"I am sorry about it, but I am glad you both didn't suffer too much. It must be hard."

"Are you married for a long time?"

"Eighteen years with the same woman."

"Congratulations! How many kids?

"No kids."

She got caught in her own silence and there were those inevitable few seconds of not knowing what to say. It always happened when I told people I didn't have children.

"It's okay." I smiled. "Nobody knows exactly what to say."

There was a familiar comfort between us. I felt I didn't need to be social or polite. I just had to go straight to the point as we would understand each other.

"Why?"

"We tried but she couldn't get pregnant. We thought about adopting a baby but my grandniece's mom died when she was a toddler. Her father was not the best parent in the world and we adopted her."

"That's great. I think destiny put the right child in front of you at the right time."

I didn't remember anybody who had said that to me before. Normally people would preach about the legal implications of adopting a child *informally* or they would say "how great," but implying and not being able to disguise the "poor you, ended up raising somebody else's child as a consolation prize."

She moved fast and was skinnier than I could remember. Her frame was gamine and I realized how young she looked, even if she was as old as me. We turned the corner on Lorena and passed a few bars with tables outside. They were all crowded with people in lines, waiting to sit down. The neighborhood was busy in the aftermath of the *passeatas*. I thought about inviting her to come to my house and have something to eat, but I found it weird. What would Emilia say when she opened the door and saw me with my first love of thirty-five years ago? Valentina read my thoughts.

"Why don't we go to my apartment? It's right on next block. I have some wine and we can order food. You must be hungry. Is your wife waiting for you at home? You can tell her to come over, I would love to meet her. Do you think it would look strange?"

"Yes, a bit strange as we haven't seen each other in such a long time. Maybe next time we invite her and you both can meet."

"It's nice to catch up. What a wonderful chance encounter!"

"Yes, it's great to see you again. I think our meeting really deserves a toast. Wine is not a bad idea."

I felt a simple, no frills kind of happiness. We could actually be friends after all these years.

"Here, it's me," she said as she pointed to a terraced new building, all tinted brown glass and stone, with a majestic entrance and doorman. I let a big laugh out:

"So amazing, we are neighbors again! How can we live so close to each other and I never bumped into you in the street?"

"Well, I work long hours. I work for a big office downtown, close to the Central Justice Court. I leave early and don't come back before nine o'clock every day. On weekends I go to see my sons in Rio or I just sleep."

"I don't walk around very often either," I said, and I realized how little time I had to enjoy the colorful life there was around on that beautiful and expensive neighborhood. I didn't see friends often, Emilia was the one organizing dinners, birthday celebrations, reunions. I thought about calling and telling her I was going to come home later, but Valentina interrupted my plan while we were getting into the roomy elevator with mirrors on all sides.

"Are you happy with your life, Felipe? Is radio everything you dreamed of?"

"Pretty much. Careers have their top moment, the pinnacle, and I think mine is just turning the curve down the hill now. There was a moment, maybe ten years ago, when a lot started to happen. I was getting more money, I was popular, my opinion was heard with reverence at every producers meeting. Now they don't even call me for some meetings anymore. I have my time slot, I am free to do a lot on my own, even to be a reporter at a *passeata* day…"

She smiled. "Yes, I listened to your program sometimes. I saw you on TV at the *Diretas Já* campaign. I was very proud of having known you."

She searched for the keys inside a huge handbag that looked like Santa's bag. She opened the door. Her place was neat, too neat to be real. There were two chocolate brown sofas facing each other with a fake farm coffee table in the center. There was nothing on the coffee table, not a vase or a fancy book. A small fireplace was set on the wall in one of the corners: a luxury and a status symbol in the new apartment buildings in a city where we have probably six cold days in a year. The opposite wall was covered with books and photos. Glass doors gave way to a balcony with lots of flowerpots facing other balconies with different flowerpots.

Valentina's plants looked so perfect they might be artificial or they were not tended. When they dried from thirst, they were simply replaced. I was curious to look at the photos on the shelves, but I thought it was better not to do it.

"Do you have photos of your kids?" Maybe I sounded pitiful now.

She didn't seem to notice or care. "Take a look at the shelves. There's one recent Christmas photo of myself with three very tall young guys. Daniel is twenty-seven now, Antonio and Alex are younger. They are great, but they don't call me very often. That's my only complaint about my sons, especially about Alex, the youngest. He felt betrayed when we divorced right after he got into college. He said we were just waiting to get rid of them and get on with our lives."

She came from the kitchen with two tall expensive wine glasses, holding them upside down by the stem as they do in TV commercials. In her right hand she had a bottle of red Bordeaux, a costly type of wine at that time.

"Do you see your ex a lot?"

"No, he travels all the time and he remarried a year ago. Since we don't have custody problems or financial deals anymore, and we don't live in the same city, we can even pretend we were never married."

"Are you happier being divorced?"

"Yes, much happier." Silence again. Something unusual and unknown about her reached me.

She gave me the bottle and an old fashioned cork opener. I decided not to let go the conversation:

"Would you remarry?"

"I don't know."

I beat myself for getting into that awkward silence again. The *plop* of the cork filled the emptiness.

"This wine looks good."

"I will get some nuts. I think that's all I have. Should we order pizza?"

I was starving and thought it could be safer to eat.

"Why not? But before you order can I use the phone?"

Cell phones were not very common in São Paulo in 1992. I dialed home and went outside to the balcony. She disappeared in the kitchen looking for a pizza place menu,

"Emilia?"

"Hi, where are you?"

"Listen, I met some old friends from radio covering the *passeata,* and I am having dinner with them here nearby. I will get home a bit later, just don't' count on me for dinner."

"Okay, have fun."

"Bye, see you soon."

"See you soon, love you."

Emilia was not the type to keep asking "Who is with you? What are their names? Do I know them?" She was always easy going, but if I did something wrong she would probably catch me red handed on the curve. She wouldn't say anything, but she would do her little investigation in casual conversations, dropping a question here and there. She would then put all the pieces together as in a detective novel. She had always been an avid detective novel reader, but I never had given her any reason to mistrust me, and I wouldn't.

I hung up and went into the living room again. Valentina called the pizza place and I could hear her voice inside. "Yes, a large Margherita pie and a green salad. How long? Okay, thanks."

Her voice hadn't changed. I closed my eyes and I could hear her talking years ago. I saw the two of us sitting on her mother's old kitchen floor, drinking chocolate milk, and holding hands for the first time. I realized I had long forgotten that mysterious heart lifting sensation of loving and kissing somebody with passion.

"You have good taste. Your apartment is nice," I said to start a conversation.

"And since when you know about decoration?"

"Since never!" I said with a laugh. "Okay, you win. Where's the wine? I am certainly better at opening bottles."

We sat on the brown sofa and poured more wine. We talked in an attempt to fast forward all the years we had been apart. Pizza came and we decided to eat the juicy slices sitting on the carpet, looking at the lights outside through the glass door. After pizza, we opened a second bottle of Bordeaux. I had a sensation of being back home, back at Mother's house on Coroa Street, to a young Felipe I had long left in the back of a closet. Feelings that I thought I couldn't feel anymore were suddenly running in my arteries. I almost could listen to my blood moving through my veins. I looked at her feet when she sat down on the ground. Her small toenails painted an almost imperceptible pale pink. My eyes ran up to her black pants, I could guess the shape of her legs underneath them.

"I think I should be going, it's getting late."

"Of course. I'm sorry, Felipe, we lost track of time. I hope we can continue catching up, especially now that we are neighbors again, like in the old days."

"Yes, old times…" I didn't know what else to say. "It would be a shame to lose touch. We won't let that happen."

"No, we won't. Let me get your phone number and we can have lunch next week."

I was glad she asked. I wrote my number in a small notebook she handed to me and left it on the empty coffee table. I wrote down her number on another page and ripped it from the notebook, tucking it into my pocket.

We said goodbye with a hug. I avoided her eyes when I left. I walked the few blocks that separate our apartments. My legs were light as feathers, but my thoughts were confused.

I tried to focus on the street: bars, tables on sidewalks, the colorful happiness of Ritz restaurant, the old corner of rua Augusta, a lonely electric bus going down the road. When I got home, Emilia was dozing off on the couch watching an old Audrey Hepburn movie, *Two for the Road.* I had watched it years earlier. Audrey and Albert Finney play a couple in crisis, who decide to go on a car a trip together.

Before I woke her up, I thought Emilia and I should do a road trip before we were both too old. I promised myself to talk about it in the morning as she would never pay attention half asleep.

I turned the TV off and woke her up with a gentle kiss. We went to our bedroom and made love before she went back to her dreams.

# CHAPTER 36

I never took that road trip with Emilia, but I had lunch with Valentina a few times over the following months. We used to take a break from work and go to old-fashioned restaurants downtown, at Centro Velho, near the Justice Court and the law school. Those were long lunches where we talked without noticing the clock. After paying the check, we were always late, running in opposite directions to get a cab and go back to life.

One hot Friday in January, when the city was empty and everyone was at the beach, we were going to the same area after lunch and shared a cab. There was no traffic and the car was speeding down south Nove de Julho Avenue. When we entered the tunnel our legs touched by chance in the back seat. For one second, I didn't want that brief contact to end. I looked at her and I knew she had the same thought. I kissed her on the lips quickly and softly, without a thought, as a way of catching the moment and not letting it go. As our lips parted, the car exited the tunnel and sunlight filled our eyes. We didn't say anything for the rest of the trip and said goodbye as if nothing different had happened.

I couldn't sleep the next few nights. I felt guilty and ashamed, thinking about Emilia, about my family, and what a jerk I had been. Another part of me was mortified knowing she probably wouldn't take me to lunch anymore or accept my invitations. The worse part was thinking how I wanted more. I wanted that kiss to last. I wanted it to happen again.

# Chapter 37

*São Paulo, March 1993*:

Carnival was over and the country resumed its normal rhythm in March. The torrential rains of the summer afternoons gave place to continuous showers that could last a week, bringing cooler breezes and calmer tempers. I took a family vacation in February and made an effort not to call Valentina. I believe she did the same. Weeks had passed after our kiss inside the cab, and the idea of having crossed the border was killing me. I expected her to call me as if nothing had happened, showing that she was not upset, but she didn't. Sometimes I caught myself talking to the bathroom mirror, imagining I was talking to her. I should call and apologize. I didn't want to lose her again because of a silly fall into the past. I used to walk from the radio station at Paulista to my apartment, a few blocks away.

One afternoon. I left earlier and made a detour to pass in front of her building. I knew she was not at home at the time, but I just sat at the café on the other side of the road. After an hour, I decided to call her and end the torture as I was being so stupid. I decided to leave a message, cell phones were not everywhere at the time and answering machines were still in high demand.

It rang once, twice, three times. I was rehearsing the message I was going to leave in my head when she picked up:

"Hello."

"Humm, ah…hello. Valentina?"

"Who's that?"

"It's Felipe."

It took her a few seconds to talk. "Hey, hi, how are you?"

"I wanted to talk to you, it's been a while—"

"Yeah, I know. Where have you been?"

"Same place, nothing changed. You?"

"I'm good."

"Can I see you sometime? Just for a minute, I won't take time, I promise. I feel so bad—"

"Why did it take you so long to call me?"

"Because I feel so bad about what happened…you know…in the cab, that day where—"

"Yes, I know. I felt bad too."

"I expected you to call because it would show you were not upset, that we could get over it, but as you didn't contact me, I assumed…"

"You assumed what?"

"I assumed you were really mad at me and wanted distance. I offended you, I am sorry. I like your friendship, I miss our lunches and want it to be back to what it was."

"Back to what?"

"To what it was before."

"Before when?"

"Well…before I kissed you in the cab."

"Don't feel bad. Let's not talk about this on the phone. Do you want to come over? I am working from home today."

"Well…yes, of course! And…what time?"

"How long would you take to get here?"

"Is one minute too short notice?"

"It's fine."

She hung up and my heart accelerated. I almost forgot to pay for my *cappuccino* before I left the bar.

# CHAPTER 38

*São Paulo, 2009*:

On a rainy Monday morning, we received the call. The police ordered us to go to the precinct and recognize the guys who robbed the bus and took Mariana with them. I answered the phone and, after I hung up, I had to sit down for a minute until I could articulate a word to Emilia. "They got the guys."

She was knitting a red sweater and just lifted her eyes. She didn't stop moving the needles. "What guys?"

"The guys who robbed the bus."

She stopped and placed both hands and the red piece on her lap. "Oh my God! After all these months? That's a miracle...How did they find them? Were you talking to the police chief?"

"Yes, but he didn't give many details over the phone. They were looking for a gang who falsified credit cards and there was a connection with drug dealers. The boys were stealing credit cards, kidnapping people, and taking money from ATM machines. One of them kidnapped a policeman who managed to make a call. The bastard gave the names of the others later. They traced back lots of other activities and finally they got to the bus assault."

"How are we going to tell to Mariana?"

"This is what I worry about. It's not going to be easy for her to see them again and I have a feeling she will try to avoid it. "

"But she has to go. It will give her some sort of closure."

"Well, this will be my strongest argument, Emilia."

Mariana came late that night. We waited for her in the TV room, watching *telenovelas* we were not following just for lack of anything better to do. When she got into the room to say hello I went straight to the point:

"Do you have a minute? I need to talk to you."

"Sure, Uncle Fe, what's up?"

She collapsed on the fluffy sofa, grabbed a cushion to hold as we'd hold a pet, and looked at me with no idea about what was coming.

I felt my throat dry before I started to talk. I told her everything, carefully but at once. We were expected in the precinct as soon as possible to recognize the kidnappers. It could be difficult but there was no other choice.

She took a deep breath and looked nowhere. She placed the cushion on the side and crossed her arms tight around her stomach. "It has to be tomorrow?"

"The earlier the better."

We went on the following day. She was silent all the time. It was not very much herself but I thought it was not time to talk too much. In the end, I thought it would be more difficult to deal with her emotions.

The precinct smelled like a combination of urine and humidity. It was a dark and damp small building, not very far from our street but on the rough side of the neighborhood. Emilia decided not to come. There were just the two of us. It all happened very fast, and it was like in a movie. They led us to a room with a huge window. We could see people on the other side but they couldn't see us. Four men came and stood in front of the glass. There were numbers on the wall above their heads. Mariana's first reaction was to get up. I held her hand tight. It was cold and sweaty. She was moving toward the door and I pulled her back. I knew three of them were our guys. We both recognized them, and Mariana asked if she could leave. She started crying in the car, but said she didn't want to talk about it.

"I think you will have to talk at a certain point. You will never get over that incident if you don't talk about what happened to you after they pulled you out of the bus."

"I don't remember. I just don't remember. There's a blank, just a big white spot on my mind from the moment I was pulled out of the bus until the moment I saw myself running on this unknown street, ringing someone's bell, and asking to make a call."

She cried more and I held her in the back seat. When we got home, I delivered her to Emilia's care, gave an excuse, and told the driver to go back to the precinct. I wanted to know what was going to happen afterward. I knew that in many cases the criminals were recognized, charged, but ended up on the street again shortly. There was always a reason: sometimes the law was too flexible, sometimes they were minors, sometimes they simply escaped from jail with the help of a drug traffic chief.

"May I talk to the *delegado* for a minute?"

The man on the counter was trained not to be nice. He didn't even look at me:

"And why do you need to speak to him? He's very busy, and it has to be important—"

"I know. I came this morning to recognize three defendants from a bus hijack, my name is Felipe Navarra and—"

He lifted his head. "Wait a second. Are you Mr. Navarra from the radio?"

"Yes, it's me, but as I was saying—"

"Oh my God! I am a great fan! I miss you on the radio! What an honor!"

And that's how I was sent to the *delegado's* office, quite embarrassed because I clearly cut ahead of some people in the line waiting line to see him. But the receptionist—who introduced himself as Mario Lopes—made such a fuss and even asked me to sign autographs for his whole family.

I probably signed twelve pieces of paper dedicated to different people. The effort was worth every word because, fifteen minutes later, I was sitting in front of Dr. Soares, a very small man in his sixties, wearing a wrinkled gray suit matching his gray hair impeccably parted on the side and combed with gel. He looked fragile but had an impressive way of staring that made you so scared you could shit your pants.

"Nice to meet you, Mr. Navarra, it's an honor to have you here in my precinct."

He looked right into my eyes and shook my hand. My first thought was to turn on my heels and leave.

"How can I help you?"

I tried to get over the chills his glance gave me and explained about the incident, the thieves, and our experience recognizing them in the morning. I told him briefly what Mariana was going through, and I wanted to know what was going to happen with them next.

"I am sorry to hear she is struggling, but I have to admit, this is becoming a common situation here, Mr. Navarra. I mean, people with panic disorders caused by traumatizing experiences. From my side, I can assure you I will do my best to keep them in jail. Two of them are already veterans and have been here before for other crimes. This time it is different, but to make sure they are not released by other powers, your niece should come and give more details of what happened during the kidnapping. It's already considered a severe crime, but we should know if they were cruel to her, if they raped her— sorry to say that in such candid way—it can help with the prosecution, even if we don't have a way to collect evidence anymore. A long time has passed."

A shiver ran through my spine. I asked about the third guy. The *delegado* changed to a confidential tone.

I had a feeling he wouldn't dedicate so much time to my case if I were not a radio personality, somebody relatively famous he could say he knew.

"This one is a shame. He is much older than the others and he comes from a very humble, but good background; a *normal* functional family as we say. No trouble in his family history. His father was an *operário,* a factory worker who barely knew how to read. As far as we could find out, he was honest but good at getting into trouble. In the worst years of dictatorship, around sixty-nine, seventy, he still distributed flyers, calling on workers to strike, complaining about minimum wage and stuff like that. He was not afraid of the *polícia política.* He could have become a *Lula,* Mr. Navarra, he was a very active labor leader, even if he had clear ties with Communism!"

"And why he didn't?"

"He tricked the police a lot during those years, but in 1975 he was caught. He was so good at escaping, and the police were after him for such a long time, that people who worked on the case said it was a miracle they got him. He was one of the best at hiding and plotting the resistance. A lot of militants helped him. He was a kind of hero among the leftists.

"And how did they get him?"

"Well, apparently—and this was found recently, after the dictatorship files where opened and so many people went after these pieces of history—a big list of names had come up a few years before, around 1972. This list was found after terrorists were killed in that famous car shooting, in the south side of the city, do you remember? His name was on the list."

I felt my hands sweating but I tried to keep an impersonal curiosity about the case. "A list? How amazing, it seems something from a mystery movie."

"Yes, I know, unbelievable how the police got something like that."

"But how did the police get it?"

"Oh, Mr. Navarra, this is a very well-kept secret. Nobody knows, apart from the directly involved, and they are probably all dead now. Everybody believes it was the work of a spy embedded in the resistance. As far as I know, this was the only way the police could lay eyes on such complete evidence kept by professionals who were protected in many levels. Names of people, the way they operated, and the address and contact of some *aparelhos,* their hiding places. A lot of militants were arrested and tortured because of that list. This guy's father was one of them. We believe he died in jail. The files say he hung himself, but photos released after the end of the dictatorship attest he was probably killed in torture sections. There's so much still coming out from those years Mr. Navarra—"

"Yeah, don't tell me. But what's the connection? The father was a militant during dictatorship and the son becomes a dangerous criminal? As far as we all agree now, they were just fighting for freedom, no? And you said the background is good."

"Well, yes, apart from his political beliefs, the father was a good worker and family man, but he was taken from home in front of his children and was never seen alive again. We know the wife just lost it after she realized he was not coming home. Our man was a toddler at

the time, who grew up seeing his mother become an al-
coholic who never recovered. It becomes a sad story and
falls into the common outlaw background: one grows up
in the streets, one learns how to survive and gets connect-
ed to wrong people who use children to get what they
want, giving them drugs, presents, money. You know,
Mr. Navarra, these kids have no perspective. They know
they will be miserable forever. Somehow getting into
crime or drugs is their opportunity to do something with
their lives. Once I heard a fourteen-year-old saying he
didn't care if he would die young. He said he had no interest in living a long life. Going to school or being honest was for idiots."

"Just out of curiosity, if you don't mind, what was the
name of his father? I mean, the suspect's father."

"Sebastião Mendes Caldas. It even sounds like an aris-
tocratic name, don't you think?"

"And the son?"

"Sebastião Junior, same as the father. But everybody
in the crime world knows him as Tião Galinha."

"What will happen to him and the others?" I demand-
ed. "I want to make sure they get punished for what they
did to my niece and to all the people in that bus."

"Well, they will go to court. We are waiting for the
procedures. I can't tell you when it will happen. They
might get something between five and thirty years."

"It's really slow don't you think, *delegado*?"

"Mr. Navarra, that's the way it is. If I were you, I
would consider myself lucky if I saw these men in jail for
at least five years."

The phone rang and he answered it briefly. He stood
up and faced me again with those terrible eyes. "I have an
appointment now, Mr. Navarra, I'm afraid I will have to
let you go."

"Of course, of course, I am sorry. It was very generous

of you letting me in here in the first place. I really appreciate it."

"It was my pleasure to meet you in person. I was a fan
of your program!"

"Thank you so much, thank you for your time, Dr.
Soares. If I can be helpful on this matter, please let me
know."

I made a mental note to contact somebody at the radio
and ask to send him a T-shirt, a cap, and a bottle of something.

"It was my pleasure to spend time with such a celebrity, Mr. Navarra."

"I am a former celebrity. I am retired now."

"You will always be Mr. *Diretas Já*, one of the sym-
bols of our fight for elections and democracy, how can
we forget that?"

"Thank you, you are very kind."

I left the building and saw Wilson waiting on the corner inside my black Mercedes.

*I have to tell him to always go to the garage. This car
will end up hijack*ed, I thought. *I wish I were healthy and
younger just to walk a few blocks on my own and clear
my mind.* I had a bitter taste in my mouth as I had swal-
lowed a whole bag of *jilós*. Would it be possible that the
list he talked about was Boscobino's list? The one I let go
in exchange for my big break? Did I truly have no clue of
what I was doing at the time or I was just burying my
head in the sand? How crazy it is to think that we start
dozens of different bolts from one whole engine when we
make one single decision and, at the time, the only thing
that matters to us is only our own little bolt. It couldn't be
possible. It had to be another list, a coincidence.

A few days passed by, and I gave Mariana her own
time. I told her to open up at least at therapy. I don't
know if she followed my advice. I tried to move on with

my boring retired routine: short walks around the pool, newspaper, radio, TV, Rita, Emilia, restaurants on week-ends, doctor's appointments, but I couldn't get the damn list out of my mind. I decided to investigate.

# Chapter 39

*São Paulo, March, 1993:*

Valentina opened the door and I was relieved that she didn't seem upset, after all.

I placed a kiss on her left cheek. "So do you work from home now?"

"Sometimes. Come on in. Sit down."

The chocolate brown sofa was still at the same place. Relief again. I sat down. She offered me coffee.

"Sure," I said.

"Do you know I got this amazing coffee machine for Christmas? It comes with a special device to make milk froth, like in cappuccino bars."

"So, let me try a cappuccino then."

That's when I remembered I'd already had two at the place in front of her house. But it was too late to go back. She was already frothing the milk and explaining how the machine worked. I got up, walked to the kitchen, and stood by the door, watching her move around, barefoot on the tile floor, wearing jeans and a pale blue shirt. What would have happened if we were married?

"So, you were not upset because of…you know….because of what happened in the cab the other day?" I asked.

"No."

"So why did you never call me?"

"Why did *you* never call too? You could have."

"I told you. I thought you were upset, I didn't know what to say."

"Why did you call me today?"

"To say I'm sorry."

"Why you didn't say I'm sorry two months ago?"

My voice got louder. "I don't know. I was confused."

"Well, I was not upset, or offended, don't worry about that. Let's forget the incident and keep going."

There was something strange in her voice, something that didn't sound true.

"Did you feel anything when I kissed you?"

"Why are you asking me?"

"Did you? You say you were not upset, so why did you stop calling me as well?"

"Because I was afraid."

"Afraid of what?"

"Afraid that it would happen again. It can't happen again, you are married."

Then I understood. And I couldn't think anymore. The next minute, we were kissing on the rug. I was not just rediscovering her, but also the feeling, the easy erection, the heartbeat. Everything reappeared as in magic. Her kisses tasted the same honey strawberry mix as I remembered from so many years ago. Her tongue did the same hungry movements inside my mouth, the same rhythm, the same way of hugging my waist with her legs. I got lost inside her, as I never could dream it would happen.

We woke up in the middle of the night, the glass door was open and a fresh breeze got into our bones.

Valentina wrapped herself in a throw that lay close to the sofa, closed the door, and went to the kitchen. She came back with two cups of coffee and chocolate cookies.

"You are not on the diabetes watch yet, are you?" she said while letting all her weight collapse on the couch.

"Not that I know about. And even if I was I wouldn't miss those cookies."

"Well, I don't drink chocolate milk anymore," she said.

"Coffee is better."

I sat beside her, I didn't want to leave. I thought about what was going to happen when I got home. In a flash, I brushed the problem away from my brain as soon as I sipped the black, strong, unsweetened coffee. She sat beside me and pulled half of the throw to my side. I felt a bit embarrassed. My body shape was not as skinny and flexible as hers. I noticed my belly, my legs seemed to be getting thinner. My toenails needed a trim.

"I think I need a bigger blanket, do you have one?"

"Sure."

She disappeared into the corridor and came back with a colorful comforter, three times the size of the throw she had around her body. Before she gave it to me she was careful to stop by the glass balcony door and pull out the blinds completely.

She then turned around, stopped right in front of me and dropped the small blanket on the floor. She unfolded the comforter, put it around herself and sat on my lap, making me feel dizzy with her perfume. She wrapped the comforter around the two of us together.

"Do you think the big one would be just for you?"

"I wouldn't dream of being so selfish."

We started all over again and stopped when it was almost noon.

"I have to go to work, Felipe. I am sorry." She kissed my lips, stood up, and ran to the bathroom.

I could hear the shower and confusion finally sat on

my mind: what I was going to tell Emilia? The truth? An excuse? I had been in a few romps over my married years, but normally after a drinking celebration with good friends and mostly with prostitutes. Emilia never asked too many questions. Maybe she didn't want to know. But at this point of my life I knew women had a special sense for serious fucking and not ordinary-meaningless-just-for-fun fucking. I knew I wouldn't fool her for long.

# CHAPTER 40

*São Paulo, January 8, 1994*:

São Paulo was not a pleasant place to be in hot summers, but there was something about the humid smell of January afternoons that always hit me—a mix of jasmine, dust, and chlorine from the pool on your skin and the inevitable approach of the tropical storms. I used to be afraid of them when I was a child, but now it was something that I loved to watch as a sublime show of nature's power, the same as the sea vastness or a lion's roar. Almost every end of a hot day was crowned by heavy rain, wind, and lightning. And floods. But the real *espetáculo* for me was the changing of the sky before the water started to descend.

If you could enjoy a late lunch, you would notice the change of the wind when you walked out of the restaurant around three in the afternoon. It blew on a different direction and its smell was fresh and clean. Clouds started to pile up, covering the sun and the sky changed color dramatically. It was not the washed gray of cloudy days. It was a bluish, intense gray that became dense and dark as lead, almost navy blue. As the city was so large, sometimes we had a huge storm in the south side and not a drop of water in the north. If the storm was forming far away, you could just watch the scary changing of the sky, the darkness and heaviness of clouds getting ready to break. And you heard thunder.

On that day in January, I watched the storm approach. I was at the balcony when the first large drops covered the walls and the windowsill. They were rapidly absorbed by the hot and thirsty cement, but the rain won in the end and soon walls were soaked, water was covering every surface: cars, buses, sidewalks, balconies, plants. Suddenly we were in a cloud and the noise of a gigantic shower took over. Summer storms didn't last long, just enough time to create damage, traffic, and floods but also freshness and the smell of wet dirt. On that day the rain also made me think for a long time of Valentina and the road we were taking. We had been lovers for almost a year.

I dreamed of her many nights and I was afraid of mentioning her name during my sleep. I hope Emilia didn't hear or notice anything. I know she would pretend to herself she didn't notice any changes in my behavior. But the situation was escalating. It was not a fling or a fall into the past. A few hours before the rain, Valentina cornered me against the wall, after a night spent together, and after I lied to Emilia in the morning on the phone:

"Felipe, this is going too far. Where are we headed to?"

The streets were now washed by the rain and smelled of wet bricks. It was almost dark and I was still at the balcony thinking about what she said. Flashes of moments we had together came to my mind, and I felt I was in a different plane of existence where time made little sense.

"Do you love your wife?" She always repeated the same question. The answer was also the same, so obvious.

"I love her, but it's different from what we have."

"Men always say that."

And I tried to mend it. "I found her at a time when my friends were married and my siblings were out of the house. She was perfect. She is perfect. I truly fell in love with her."

"Why she is too perfect? Isn't it good to be married to the perfect woman?"

"Yes, it is, but there was something missing, and now I understand what it is. Even before, when you and I were so young, there was a magnet that pulled us toward each other. With her I always felt it was just a good match: no issues, no big disagreements, but no magical magnet. It's good for the long term, though."

She kept quiet for a minute.

I broke the silence. "For many years I thought you were a whore, I thought you never loved me but you just wanted a stupid simple-minded boy to marry you and give you a respectable name. I thought you wanted to fuck everybody and make a fool out of me."

"Do you still think the same?"

"No. Now I see that you were just different from most of the girls. You were ahead of time."

"And now you want to go to bed with that girl you couldn't have in the past?"

"I would love you even if we never go to bed again."

"So, I got redeemed."

"Do you regret what happened that night on New Year's Eve at the beach?"

"I never regret anything. There's no way we can go back in time and change—It would be easy if it was possible."

"Did you ever think of what would have been if we ever got married?"

"No. Do you?"

"Sometimes."

"And? How would it be?"

"It could be wonderful or we could be divorced without speaking to each other now. Who knows? But if we were married, maybe I would have kids. That could have been nice."

"Sorry, I didn't want to touch this issue when I asked."

"No, no, it's fine. I have my niece. We love her and raised her as a daughter. When she came into our lives, left by her parents, I understood why Emilia and I never had kids. We were meant to stay with her. I couldn't have a better child."

"I am happy for you. But, listen, I think we are not going anywhere here. You have a family you love. Everything was in place for you before we met again on the day of the street riots. Now Collor has abdicated, we have another president, and I think we deserve new chances too. Felipe, I don't want to be the other woman anymore. We need to spend time apart."

She was fierce. She didn't want to discuss it. She left for work and I slowly got dressed and walked home. Emilia was on a trip with Mariana, so I was by myself and I could spend as much time as I wanted, looking at the rain-washed streets from this balcony. Even cry if I feel like.

Two days later, I bought two tickets for a weekend in Buenos Aires and I begged Valentina to join me. I would be off from my radio program and we would travel separately and meet at a hotel at Recoleta, as we did some afternoons in São Paulo after the end of my morning broadcast. We used have lunch and later the afternoon for ourselves: new soft sheets, sunlight coming through white blinds and a newfound wave of middle age sensuality we both had never experienced. But around five o'clock we wouldn't need to shower and kiss goodbye. I wouldn't need to go to my own apartment where my whole life was waiting for me as a pendulum clock waking me up from a dream.

On Friday evening, we met at Recoleta. We walked the busy streets and went for dinner afterward. While we waited for the *parrillada*, Valentina spilled the beans again:

"Felipe, we can't go on like this. Even if I love you more than anything and would stay with you, we have to end this affair. It's wonderful but it's wrong."

"I saw this coming—"

"So, that's what you have to say?"

"Do we have to discuss this here, on our honeymoon vacation?"

"We are not in a honeymoon, we are not married."

There was no way out. The romantic evening was over. I'd better talk to her about it, or the whole trip would be ruined.

"I don't know, Valentina. Sometimes I think about coming clean with Emilia, tell her everything, apologize, and pack my bags. Nowadays I don't see any other option. I don't want to break up with you, and Emilia doesn't deserve an affair."

"Why have you never talked about it, Felipe?"

"I always thought we wouldn't last that long. But the more we stay together, the more I don't want to go back to my house. And, as I said, I knew you were going to speak up sooner or later."

She didn't say anything else but for the rest of the weekend there was a bubble between us. On the next day, from the moment my plane landed at Guarulhos Airport the clock started ticking. I had to come clean with Emilia. This time, I definitely wouldn't ask for my brother's advice. I thought about how nice it would be if I could talk to somebody about it, sharing the pain, the wonder, and the guilt. Maria, my oldest sister, had died a few months after Valentina and I reconnected. At the time I thought it was a sign. It felt so right to live that moment with her, to let it finally happen as life was flowing fast through my fingers, no time to waste. Lana had moved to California because of her husband's job. They lived in San Diego, her son was about to marry a blonde American girl and there was no possibility in sight of a return to Brazil. They always invited me to visit. I always promised I would go. I missed my sister.

As soon as I got home from the airport, bad news. I opened the apartment door to find Emilia on the sofa, so shrunk and dejected I was sure she'd found out everything about my affair. I jet of freezing blood went through my spine.:

"I tried to call your hotel but you had already left," she muttered. "Why did you have to go to Buenos Aires?"

I tried to be in control and play it cool. "Well, you and Mariana were supposed to come back just on Tuesday, so I wanted to do something different on my own. What's the problem with that? And why you and Mariana are back earlier? What's going on?

"It's Decio."

"What?"

"He is in hospital. He had a heart attack. Elvira called just this morning. You should contact her, I was waiting for you so we can go together."

"But I have to go to work this afternoon, I have a meeting—"

"They also called from the radio. They said your meeting today is canceled but they have to talk to you about a few changes tomorrow."

I smelled something fishy. But I didn't have time to think about it. Fifteen minutes later, I was in the back of the car again side by side with my wife on the way to *Sirio* Hospital. It was odd looking at her and thinking

that, just a few hours earlier, it was Valentina in the back
of a taxi with me, the car cutting traffic off in the streets
of Buenos Aires. The weekend didn't end up well, but we
were still holding hands, anticipating our separation.

I looked at Emilia one more time, and I felt the trip to
Buenos Aires was something I had read in a magazine, a
life that was not my own, that I was a character of myself
in some other distant existence.

At the hospital, I found my sister-in-law in tears, concerned doctors, and no sign of Decio's son. I felt for Elvira who had already lost her oldest son, going through a
hard time again.

The doctor said we had to wait. Decio had to undergo
bypass surgery. I sat down in the waiting room that
looked more like a five star hotel. Emilia came with a cup
of coffee, handed it to me, and didn't say a word. I
looked into her dark eyes and I sensed it. She knew. I
muttered a thank you. She lowered her eyes and went
back to her seat.

We waited for a long time. His situation was delicate.
The night was deep dark when we left and gave Elvira a
ride. We were silent and solemn as in a funeral procession.

My brother didn't last long. After the surgery he spent
a few days in Intensive care but never opened his eyes or
spoke again. His heart was too weak and, one morning,
he just stopped breathing. Like a bird that gets tired of
flying and suddenly lets go and plunges into the sea.
Simple and straightforward. It suited him.

We were not close, but his death shook me. I just had
two siblings left now, one that I barely spoke to and another who I adored but was thousands of miles away. After Decio's funeral, as it happens after somebody dies, I
made a lot of decisions based on the fact that life is short.
One of them was to visit Lana and the other was to come

clean with Emilia.

Before I executed the latest, I had another major event to deal with. Right after the funeral, I was called for a board meeting at Alvorada. All the directors were there and unpleasant news was expected.

"Felipe, you know your program is a mark and you are not to be replaced. But your audience is massively older than forty and we need some people of younger age to fill our sponsors' expectations and keep afloat. So we are considering moving your program to the afternoon slot and cutting it to just one hour a day. We will give the morning hours to Aldo Rey, the guy from Jovem Pan we just hired. We presume you've met him, right?"

Aldo Rey was an idiotic twenty-two-year-old, with purple hair that seemed to be cut by himself. He barely could articulate one proper sentence without repeating the same slang three or four times. But people like Mariana loved him, he was so *funny*. He had stupid opinions about everything, and he was not embarrassed to vent them on air. People thought he was so *authentic*. I said to myself that this country is really going down the drains, but put on a smile and had a sip of water before giving my polite reply to the people sitting around the large over polished table:

"Well, I can't complain about my long run here. It's been wonderful, and I owe you everything in my career. Don't forget that I started here as a messenger and came all the way to the top. But what I am really sensing here is the start of my retirement plan."

"Please, Felipe, don't get us wrong," said the chief of operations. "It's just an adjustment. We never considered your retirement. You are a brand, not just a radio host."

Some of them followed the comment with more *sala-maleques*, lots of polite and flattening bullshit words with empty meanings. I could feel my old Spanish blood starting to boil. I counted to ten and let them talk.

"Gentlemen, I presume you can give me a few days to settle all this information in my brain, right? May I give you an answer next Friday?"

"Felipe, you don't understand."

"What?"

"It's not an option—we mean—for you to take the afternoon slot. We already signed the contract with Aldo Rey's people…and…"

"So, you didn't even mention that to me when you brought the guy to my studio a few weeks ago? You were actually showing him his new workplace and his new time slot. Am I the last one to be informed about it? "

"You are not paid to participate on these type of decisions, Felipe, I'm sorry, but it is what it is."

"Yes, I guess you are right. But a little respect for all my decades of work here wouldn't hurt, Mr. Cruz."

"Felipe, this meeting is the proof of our respect. We want you to continue and to keep your audience, your fans."

"Until the sponsors consider me too old even for my own fans, I presume."

"Felipe, let's give ourselves a few days to cool down and let's discuss the terms of this new time slot soon."

"I think it's a good idea, because even I don't see anything else I can do or say today. Thanks for having me here, gentlemen."

I got up and left them at the meeting room, all facing each other around that expensive wooden table.

It was still mid-afternoon but I called Valentina and asked her to meet me at her apartment. I was glad she could leave work early. I bought flowers on the corner and let myself in at the gates. At that point, I was well known by the doormen.

Valentina had a cup of fresh coffee in her hands when

she opened the door. The smell of coffee was warm, and it took away the anger. I gave her the bouquet of pink roses and a long kiss.

"I am going to leave Emilia today. I just wanted to tell you, I want you to be the first to know."

She didn't seem over the moon when she heard it.

"Are you happy?" I asked.

"It's hard to say that I am super happy. I am happy to win you back, but I know there will be somebody suffering because of it. I feel guilty too, especially because we have been hiding for all these months."

"I know, I know. It will be over soon. It's official."

I had a few sips of her coffee and left. I told her I was coming back with a suitcase.

"I won't mind if you stay for a few days."

It was a warm spring afternoon. The five o'clock sun was lowering and tinted everything with a glow. I passed by a few bars and could smell empanadas and fresh bread from the street, I imagined their taste mixed with the flavor of coffee I still had in my mouth. I walked that path so many times from her place to mine but that was the sweetest stroll of all. I was at peace.

# CHAPTER 41

*São Paulo, November 10, 2009, the day of the blackout*:

I carried on three weeks of research about Boscobino's list without telling anyone. Almost twenty-five years after the end of the military dictatorship, we could dig out a lot of information about *Anos de Chumbo,* the lead years, the dark times. Books had been published in the late 1980s and all throughout the 1990s. It was a closure process that was beginning to fade at that point when the new generation hadn't heard about it as much as the people who were born under the regime and grew up with a patches in both eyes about what was going on. Libraries and museums had mountains of paper and gigabites of names, faces, and journeys. But still no sign of Sebastião, the man whose destiny I changed and whose loop was closing up around me.

On the morning of November tenth, I was so tired of looking for a clue that I woke up thinking about giving up, about not chasing this stupid hint, the stupid list. Would it change the fact that Mariana was in trouble and the bus hijackers were in jail but maybe not for too long? Would it change the fact we were the prisoners in our gated communities and bulletproof cars and the criminals had the world to themselves? I spent the day with these thoughts dancing all over my mind. The long blackout changed everything.

A few minutes after ten p.m., the lights went off in the blink of an eye, as if somebody had the power to make them disappear by waving a magic wand. Since I had been a child, my first instinct when it happened was always to look through the window and figure out who was in the dark and who was not, where I could see lights glowing. Sometimes I could reach their pale shine just on the other side of the road. Some other times lights were far at a distance.

On that day, I was playing cards at my friend Roberto's apartment, not far from mine. We did it every week, our old group of radio and TV retired men. When the power went out, I slowly walked toward the window to see how far the darkness reached. This time, all I could see through the glass was a deep black hole, as if a dark blanket had been thrown over the buildings, streets, and traffic lights. Later, we would know there was a massive circuit failure at the Itaipu hydroelectric system and half of the country and part of Paraguai was in the dark for not less than four hours that night.

As we had no TV or radio and most of cell phones were down, I decided to head back home. We still didn't know what was going on, and we all thought it was a minor power failure. We said our goodbyes and I got into my car, the driver always waiting for me in my friend's garage. When he turned the first corner at the beginning of our short journey, we hit complete chaos. With no traffic lights and an army of crazy drivers trying to get everywhere, we ended up in a car crash just a few blocks from home. We all left the cars parked and headed to the police station, a few steps from the mess, and the same precinct I entered a few weeks before with Mariana to recognize her captors. Nobody but the same *delegado* was there, monitoring the confusion and noise with a couple of candles, flashlights, and his powerful glance, teamed with a high baritone voice in full blast to set people in their places. When it was our turn to document the crash, he recognized me immediately through the flickering candles:

"I don't even need to see you well, Mr. Navarra, your voice is always the same!"

He greeted me as an old friend and I loved it at a time like that. It took two hours for him to settle down the story of our stupid crash due to the lack of traffic lights and four cars trying to move fast. As the night hours advanced, the precinct got more crowded with more accidents. Later, the biggest problems were robberies and lootings. After I signed a few papers, Mr. Soares invited me for a second cup of coffee. He was so relaxed in his office, he made the police station seem a kind of spa, apart from the noise and the smell of humidity which seemed even worse in the dark.

Before having my coffee with the man, I sent the driver home on foot to calm down Emilia and Mariana and decided to stay and not give up my research. The crazy blackout that brought me to him was destiny, a sign. I made up a story with a lot of appeal for him. "Do you know, Mr. Soares, I am making a special report for the radio, every now and then they ask me for a small thing just to pull me out from the anonymity of retirement. I think you could help me with that. And of course I will give you the credits."

I could see his dangerous eyes inflating with pride.

"Oh, what an honor! It will be my pleasure, Mr. Navarra. Anything you need. Anything!"

"Well, I am helping out at a special report about how people were arrested during the military dictatorship. I remember you mentioned a certain list of names who led to Sebastião Jr.'s father, you told me the whole story when I was here the first time—"

"Right, right, I remember."

"So, I was wondering if you have any clue that would lead me to this man. I thought the story was so interesting and has such an appeal for today's criminal situation, don't you think?"

He thought for a few seconds while he piled up sheets of paper on his desk. "Mr. Navarra, I would have to ask around. I have the son's files now, and I have to see if they can lead us to some document from that time. You have to remember that a lot of that might have been destroyed."

"I know. But I am ready to help you. I think this can be a major story."

He didn't seem too sure. There was something behind his eyes.

I insisted. "Here, between the two of us, it can be very good to your own career, the police chief seeking for justice, who looks at what's behind crime and criminals."

"Mr. Navarra, I am not sure about that but I will try to help you anyway. Who wouldn't help the incorruptible Mr. Diretas Já?"

I nodded and drank the rest of my cold coffee.

The blackout lasted many hours, and I ended up staying in the police station, chatting to the misfortunate creatures arriving from the darkness, each one with a different issue: a robbery, a broken car, aggression, traffic accident. It was chaos but I had nothing better to do at home, and I couldn't walk there anyway. I bet not even Jesus Christ could get a taxi that night. Mariana and Dominic called me on my cell phone. It finally started to work again. They were stuck at *Sé* subway station until the trains started to move again. I was happy Dominic was around. I would have been dead worried if she happened to be alone somewhere in the city during the blackout. Emilia was safe at home, praying, surrounded by maids and candles.

A few days later, when we recovered from the scare and the press was busy blaming everyone for the power failure, *delegado* Soares called me at home. "Mr. Navarra, I think I have a clue for your research. Can you come here this afternoon?"

"Sure."

One hour later, I was sitting in front of him with a cup of hot light coffee in my hands. It was more like a cup of what we used to call *chafé*, a crossover between tea and coffee. It slighted tasted like coffee but it had the color and the consistency of tea. Disgusting.

"If I believed in faith, I would say we were meant to find out this story together."

"So, don't you believe in faith?" I asked.

"Not actually. I believe we build our own destiny when we make decisions."

I started wondering if he knew too much about the list, more than I wanted him to know. "So, I guess you have good news, Mr. Soares—"

"I think I do. I called an old friend's father, who is retired now but who worked very closely to the *political police* in the seventies. He doesn't talk about it at all, he never did, but he told me a professor from the University of São Paulo, Olivia DomBosco, contacted him a year ago, and she was collecting documents for a new archive in the History Department she runs at the university. It's her pet project and she is well respected, the kind of professor who is always on TV. The archive is all about the resistance and apparently she collected a lot of stuff. My father's friend gave me her email. You should talk to her."

"Wow, this is great...I can't thank you enough."

"Take me to lunch, let's have a *feijoada* together someday."

"Of course, of couse. It will be my pleasure!"

I would be happy to take him to lunch but I hoped he would enjoy my *Rubayat* steak and salad, I hadn't had a *feijoada* in a long time, cholesterol had been skyrocketing for years.

I left the police station with a phone number written on a yellow piece of paper and went straight to the computer at home. I wrote Olivia DomBosco an email and kept checking the inbox every five minutes.

# CHAPTER 42

*São Paulo, 1994*:

The bomb exploded and scattered debris for miles. I walked back home that evening, sat down with Emilia, and told her everything. I had decided to come clean and I wanted to do it soon, before I lost my courage. I said I was in love with another woman, and I was moving out, that she would be taken care of financially and, of course, she would stay with the apartment etc., etc. Tears and anger happened as I predicted but the long-term damage was hard to envision. All I had in mind was to be true to myself, leave all the lies behind, and admit that I wanted to be happy.

I packed a small bag, remembering the last verses from a song from Francis Hime, *"Trocando em Miúdos"*

*"Eu bato o portão sem fazer alarde, eu levo a carteira*
*de identidade, uma saideira, muita saudade,*
*a leve impressão de que já vou tarde."*
(Shut the gate without making noise, I take the ID
card, one for the road, so much nostalgia,
slight impression I leave too late.)

I grabbed some books, my favorite CDs from my old

Brazilian idols, who I interviewed and played so much
during my radio days. I shut the door behind me as the
guy from the song does. I left Emilia crying and cursing
in the bedroom, swearing not to set eyes on me ever
again. I hoped she could forgive me one day. I felt a knot
in my stomach when I got into the elevator, leaving the
apartment of my dreams, the home we spent years setting
up to perfection with its heavy curtains and modern art
work on the walls. I felt bad for Emilia but not as bad as I
felt when I was lying to her every day. I went down to the
garage and ordered the driver to go to Valentina's apartment. From now on that would be my address and that
was my only luxury, to keep the driver.

I left my bags in the apartment and went to pick up
Mariana at a friend's house. I knew that was going to be
the most challenging part of my decision. She was just a
little girl. I took her for lunch and when two flans were
placed in front of us at dessert time I spilled it out:

"Mariana, I have something to tell you and it's very
important."

"What?"

"Well, I...how can I say this? I am going to move out
of the apartment. You know, your aunt and I are not...it
seems we get along well but, in fact, we don't. It's hard
to explain it to somebody who has never been married."

"All married people talk like that."

"I know." I felt dumb. "Mariana, I am just going to
live a few blocks away from you. You and I are still going to be the same, do you understand?"

Could I be more cliché?

"And why are you moving out if you and aunt Emilia
are not fighting?"

"Well, maybe we would be better off if we fought.
Sometimes disagreements keep things alive, shake them
up."

"I don't get it."

"I don't think I love her anymore."

"What about her?"

"I don't know."

"Did you ask?"

"No, but this is not the point."

"Well, maybe if you knew she still loves you, you would make an effort."

"Mariana, it's not that simple. There's more involved in the matter."

"What more?"

"You won't like it but I will tell you the truth. I—I am in love with somebody else. Please try not to judge me. I—"

"Who?"

"You don't know her."

"I want to know her name."

"What difference does it make? You will meet her soon."

"All the difference. People have names."

"Her name is Valentina."

"Does aunt Emilia know about it?"

"Yes. Obviously, she is not happy about it, but sometimes we have to make choices. All I want you to keep in mind is that I will always love you the same way, and I will never leave you alone. And Emilia feels the same. You have the two of us, always. Can you take care of her for me? She is a bit upset at the moment, and it's normal. She will need you.

She didn't answer. I ordered an espresso.

"Do you want a cappuccino, a hot chocolate?"

"No thanks."

We left and I dropped her off at home, strange to see that tall white building as my ex-apartment, strange to leave Mariana and go to a different place. But when I got there and saw Valentina everything changed and nothing seemed to matter anymore. We were living in a dream bubble, always trying to leave everything else outside of our magic door. But soon my problems would become large enough to break the lockers and spread themselves out in the living room.

Two weeks after my meeting at the radio, when they let me know I was being replaced after more than twenty years on the same time slot, I decided not to take their pity offer and offered my resignation.

"Valentina, you don't understand, Alvorada has always been my dream and I always thought I was going to be there until I dropped dead. I actually had dreams of dying while I was live, on air, like in an opera."

"Well, life is not an opera, my dear, even when we try to create one out of the ordinary."

She turned her back to me on the bed and filled a glass with water from a jug on the bedside table. Then she slowly arranged the pillows behind her and sat again, drinking the water. Valentina's face was peaceful in contrast with my despair.

"What am I going to do?"

"Felipe, wake up, have more self-esteem, *caramba!*"

"I am almost sixty years old! Do you think *Globo TV* will hire me to do the eight o'clock news tomorrow?"

"And since when you want to work on *Globo*?"

"You know what I am talking about. I am done. Retired."

"Do you really think nobody will ask you to work, that you will disappear?"

"At my age? Forget about it All these years, all the effort, and all I did to get there. And now they make me leave through the back door. This is what's killing me."

"This is life, that's the way it is. Now you sound like a soap opera. Think outside of the box: you still can create a program and sell it, you can be a music commentator, you can be so many things. Just don't be afraid, move on!"

I stayed silent and awake that night. I realized my fate was already decided. I gave the board a resignation letter during a meeting a few days later. In a month, I would be presenting my last program. During the following weeks, I went through a mix of euphoria, depression, and fear. And the last broadcast of Felipe Navarra in *Morning with the Stars* finally came. Fifteen minutes before it went on air, I got into the studio and sat on the swivel chair, looked at my papers, the screen in front of me with the music selection, the producer on the other side of the glass ready to lift his hand when the sign *On Air* appeared on a red light above. While I could hear the last commercials before the start, I looked around and realized how small that studio was, it was smaller than my own bathroom, the walls covered till the top with brown soundproof material. For the first time in many years I feared a voice failure. But talking with invisible listeners was like autopilot for me, it came from somewhere I didn't understand but once the red light was on, it was as if something possessed me and I just let go:

"*Bom dia ouvintes de todo o país,* Good Morning, listeners from all over the country, this is one more edition of *Morning with the Stars* and today I prepared a special selection to tell the story of our program, the last twenty years of Brazilian music from the past and present. There will be also branches of our best interviews with the greatest singers and songwriters of our time. We start with the singer who brought me inside Radio Alvorada so many years ago, Angela Maria."

The song "Lábios de Mel" started.

During the next two hours, I was on the verge of crying a couple of times and I could see my producer and assistant on the other side of the glass doing the same. I ended the program with one of my favorite modern songs, "O, Quereres" from Caetano Veloso.

"This is a song about what we have and what we want, about contrasts. I have been a fortunate man for many years, no contradictions between wanting and having, I was where I wanted to be, sitting here and talking to you every single day. But everything has an end, and I just want to thank my faithful audience. I won't say goodbye, but see you soon. Good evening, São Paulo. Thank you."

The red lights were off. Caetano Veloso's voice was the background and even if I loved that song, I couldn't hear it. I felt like I was underwater, listening to a distant drum. The knot in my throat lasted for a few days, and it ended up becoming a laryngitis. I was in bed for the rest of the month.

# CHAPTER 43

*São Paulo, 2000*:

In the next five years, I lived through the best and the worst. I knock on wood three times because I know the worst can always go deeper. Valentina and I decided not to officially get married, and I never bothered asking Emilia for a divorce. I was too busy feeling like a teenager again.

My ex-wife didn't speak to me for two years after I left the apartment but at least she didn't work on turning Mariana against me. As she knew me so well, I imagine she had her revenge with the loss of my job at Alvorada. She knew how important it was for me. In the first months after my last program, I was numb. I spent my days watching TV, reading newspapers, and playing bocce in the penthouse garden with old chaps from the neighborhood. I had several beers every afternoon, my belly grew bigger, I didn't care about getting dressed anymore and wore shorts and flip-flops all day long. I ignored the calls from other radio stations, the invitations to host parties and events. My name was still out there but I didn't care. Valentina was not happy about it.

"This is not the man I fell in love twice in my life. We didn't go through so much trouble to be together and now

I have a *desajustado* sitting in my apartment every day, doing nothing."

"Oh, it's *your* apartment now. The old unemployed man can't even buy us a place, right?"

I was a bit drunk that afternoon when she came back from work and fighting seemed to be the most exciting thing I could do all day long.

"What? Hosting *quinzeneras* balls for rich girls in *Morumbi?* So they can tell there was somebody famous at their party? Come on, Valentina, give me a break! I hosted one of the biggest audiences in São Paulo's radio for years."

"Well, you host*ed*…That's past. Move on, look forward. Think about something you want to do, something you never did. Life is short, Felipe, don't waste time."

"All I wanted to do was work at Alvorada and kiss you every night of my life. I had both, there's nothing else I wish for."

"If you want to sleep with me, you better take care of yourself, Felipe. And find something to do."

She left for the bedroom, furious, locked the door, and didn't leave until the morning. I fell asleep on the brown sofa as I did so many times those days.

I kept wasting myself in late night drinks with friends, bocce, restaurants, and weekly outings with Mariana, who was not as close to me as before but who never rejected me or took sides on my separation from Emilia. After one of these lunches, I dropped Mariana off at the end of the afternoon and decided to go to Guarujá and contemplate the sea. I sent the driver home and drove one hour down the mountains, the old road of Serra do Mar by myself. I hadn't paid attention to those roads in years: suddenly after a sharp curve you could see the white lines of foam from the waves down there, so far away, breaking in and disappearing in the blue water. The clear yel-

low stripe of sand was bright as the sun itself. Another
curve and a lean waterfall could be seen in between the
mountains. Groups of macaws and green parrots flew
over and crossed into the waterfall, screaming in chorus,
*crah, crah, crah.*

Getting away from the city and from the memories of
my life there made me feel better. I parked the car close
to the boardwalk, walked on the beach back and forth for
a long time. Then I sat in one of the *barracas*, the coastal
stalls where we drank fresh coconut water straight from
green coconuts with a long straw. It's funny how Brazili-
ans use coconut water for everything, from healing stomach pain to making your skin look better. I had two serv-
ings and decided to have a *caipirinha.* The next thing I
remember was mixing them with a few bottles of beer. I
recall chatting, watching the sunset, and hugging everyone. Some of them even recognized me from the old
times, from the *Diretas Já* campaign and all. I felt I still
could hold on to something. I woke up in a hospital the
next morning with a furious Valentina and an astonished
Mariana by my side. Through the half open door I could
see Emilia outside talking to a policeman. Even Emilia
came—and police. What I did was definitely serious. I
slowly opened my eyes and adjusted to the bright lights
in the room. At that point, it looked more like a wake
room to me.

"Where Am I?"

"Santos, Santa Casa de Misericórdia," said Mariana
with no emotion or sweetness in her voice.

It worried me. Before I could ask what happened Valentina spoke:

"Do you remember anything?"

"I remember sitting on the beach stall with some locals and—"

"You got drunk and tried to drive your car. You were

going back to São Paulo but before you reached the outskirts of Guarujá, you ran over two people and crashed.
What a mess, Felipe."

She sounded tired, more tired than angry or disappointed. I felt embarrassed and for one second I wished I
had died in the accident. My heart accelerated.

"The people I ran over—Did—did they die?"

"No, but they are in bad condition here. Internal bleed-
ing, broken bones in one of them. Serious concussion for
the other. Two young bikers. We still don't know if they
are going to make it. Oh God—"

She gave a long sigh and avoided eye contact.

I was paralyzed for a few seconds. I closed my eyes
and saw the image of a huge mirror, broken in hundreds
of small pieces, and in each piece I could see a deformed
image of my own face. Valentina's voice took me away
from it:

"You rest now. The policeman wants to talk to you
soon. He will come in a few minutes."

She left without kissing me, without a smile. She
didn't even hold my hand.

After a few days of expectation, when I thought I was
going to leave the hospital I had the stroke. Nobody could
say if it was a missed clot from the accident or if excesses
and disappointments caused it. I would say it was a combination of all. After it happened, I lost track of time. All
I thought about was dying. I still had frequent dreams
about the broken mirror showing tiny images of myself,
most of them distorted by the shape of the glass. In some
I had enlarged eyes or ears, in others I had a Franken-
stein's front head. For the first time in many years I
missed Mother to the point of tears. She would never
have let this happen to me.

# Chapter 44

*São Paulo, 2002*:

I walked through the door, feeling like I was thirty years old. Life was throwing an opportunity into my lap again, even if my legs where not as firm as before and I kept my head up while holding my fancy cane. The stroke hit me hard. I started to take medication as I drank *cafezinhos* before, many times a day. My left leg was never the same and I moved around like a ninety-year-old, even if I was just reaching my seventieth birthday.

When I stopped to be photographed by security cameras at the lobby I remembered the day I got into the elevator with Angela Maria and her fans, my first day at Radio Alvorada. Instead of the narrow entrance of an old building downtown, this was one of the new *intelligent buildings* that were popping up all over the southern side of the city. They had even voice recognition in the elevators. After getting clearance at security desk I carefully walked to the elevator. A smiling security guard was holding it for me for a time that I perceive as eternity. I tried not to be embarrassed and said "thank you" with a smile. When I felt the fluffy navy carpet under my shoes inside the box all I had to do was say "Forty" and the doors closed in a quiet *swoosh*.

The offices and studios were on the fortieth floor and the ride was too fast for my pace. An air bubble formed instantly inside my ears when it started going up. As the spaceship ride started, the voice of a woman who seemed to be in bed with you gave the headlines of the day's news and the forecast for the next hour. I wondered who was that woman behind the voice and a wave of bitterness came to my stomach when I realized a lot of people might have had that same thought about me for so many years: who is the face behind that voice coming from the magical box?

I looked around to distract myself from the memories: the box was all stainless steel and glass, it could take at least fifteen people up and down. The ceiling was a large mirror and also the wall on the opposite side of the door. Buttons were blue lights popping up from the panel on the wall. I wondered where the old *ascensoristas* had gone, people who were tight brown suits and sat on a tall stool all day inside elevators, greeting passengers and pressing the buttons with an eternal air of servitude.

I reached the fortieth floor in scary few seconds. Doors opened, *swoosh* again. They opened right into the offices of Rádio Independência, in the middle of action. There was no lobby or a special place to wait while all the fun happens behind doors and walls. Now everything was in front of your face, like in a movie: producers with walkie talkies moved fast, always with a few sheets of paper in their hands, dead worried as if a live program malfunction was the end of the world. Two maids in uniform carried trays with little coffee cups in opposite directions.

People talked and there were desks scattered around, no division, no cubicles, except for the bosses' offices, small aquariums close to the walls, with the privilege of city views behind them. Differently from my early days on Alvorada, when the noisy *tac tac tac* of typewriters was the soundtrack of our afternoons and the cigarette smoke was mandatory for atmosphere, now everything was robotic and disinfected, TVs hanging from the ceiling on silent mode, the rumor of computer typing, and the low ringing of phones.

The table in the middle of the room looked like a spaceship. Behind it, the young receptionist looked like a small dot, seeming a bit lost. I approached the silver shiny counter.

"Good afternoon, I came to talk to Mr. Santos Lima, the director. I am Felipe Navarra."

"Mr. Navarra, he is waiting for you. You can go in straight away. It's the second door on that side."

She pointed to an office with her right hand and I followed the direction of her index finger after thanking her and the heavens for not letting me stand there too long with my cane.

Before I reached his office, I couldn't help noticing a coffee corner set along the wall. Two ladies talked and laughed while sipping black coffee. There was no cigarette smoking anymore and a cybernetic coffee machine the size of a vault was placed on the table instead of the thermos with labels for *coffee* and *milk*. But it still made me feel at home.

I knocked on the glass door and he, Mr. Santos Lima, was on the phone. He made a sign for me to sit down and wait. When I placed my cane by the side of the chair, a flash came to me on these last two years: the long months of physiotherapy, the pain, readjustment, and court, the process against me for driving drunk and hitting people. I liked to think that Mother, wherever she was, put her hands on their stomachs and heads and didn't let those two boys die. She thought I deserved a chance to recover. I still dreamed about mirrors and I saw her sometimes in my dreams. I feared my death was coming soon. But there was nothing I could do about it except keep going.

"They will bring the contract in a minute," Mr. Santos Lima said when he hung up the phone. "So, are you ready to start next week?"

"I was born ready!"

"Good. Well, Mr. Navarra, even if we are so honored to have you working with us here as a music special commentator and critic, I hope you understand this is an experimental trial period. We have to see how the audience reacts to your participation in our programs, if it can propel some new advertisements too."

"I know, I know…I remember how this business works. Don't worry, I am sure there will be dozens of new ad people knocking on your door."

"I hope so. And, please, Mr. Navarra, no mention at all about your, hum….negative period. I know papers published notes about your drunk driving incident, but I hope this will never be mentioned, and it will never be a topic on your broadcast."

"I don't see how commenting on new CDs will take me to talk about an accident from a few years ago. It's all behind me now. Except for my cane here, this is the sole reminder of those times."

"Good, good! Welcome to Radio Independência! Make yourself at home.

"Thanks, I will."

# CHAPTER 45

*São Paulo, 2009*:

I had nightmares for days about the list. It couldn't be me. But what if I found out I caused all these arrests and deaths? Would they arrest me at this point? I thought what was happening to Mariana was enough revenge, but once a storm started...

Weeks went by, and I realized I would feel better not to know the truth than being punished by what I did. I was getting old and weaker anyway, with a stroke under my belt, and moving slower every day. Jail or death didn't bother me that much anymore. Bad sign. I went to talk to the woman, Mr. Soares mentioned, but she had little information to provide, nothing more than what I already knew.

So I decided to look for some people myself. I knew the old radio director who signed my contract was dead and so were most of the people from that era. I contacted their families anyway and started to get some clues. I told them I had an incident with my niece and finding out about that list would help me solve the case.

It was not a lie and at that point I didn't care what people thought. Weeks later, I decided to hire a private detective. I couldn't even believe they existed. I thought it was something out of a *telenovela*. His name was Artur Molina. I went to his office downtown, close to the crowded Páteo do Colégio, the oldest building in São Paulo, a school built by Jesuits in 1554. The *edifício* was old and there was no elevator. I called Molina downstairs and offered him a cup of coffee at a place nearby.

"We can't start by the list. We have to follow the son's steps and then get to the father and how he really died."

"Is it all confidential, *Senhor* Artur?"

"Yes, for sure."

And he was hired. In one month, he called me again. This time, I invited him to come to my place. He arrived on a rainy Tuesday afternoon and was worried about sitting on my fancy sofa wearing his wet clothes.

"Don't worry, when I die I won't take any of these with me. Make yourself comfortable." I turned my head to the kitchen to call the maid. "Rita, can you bring two coffees here?"

"Yes, Seu Felipe," she answered from the other side.

When she came with coffee cups and the *bule* on a tray, Molina was telling me how confident he was. I saw him smile for the first time, even if he tried to keep a neutral tone:

"I have good news. Well, more good than bad—"

"Okay, good news first."

"I am getting close to a confirmation that Sebastião was found thanks to the list you provided to the police in the seventies. I looked for his son's police files that just government can access, I have my contacts in the police."

"But how can you prove it was my list? Maybe there were others, who knows?"

"Going back to other arrests that happened at the same time and were executed by the same agents, we can figure it out. That's what I am working on right now."

"So I killed this guy's father and fucked up his own

life and his family. And God knows how many more people I messed up with. This is the bad news right?"

"I'm afraid so."

"Damn it!"

After he left I thought the bad news was to realize I was the one who started the chain who messed up my niece's life. How crazy was that?

I waited three more months in agony and anxiety just to find out the horrible truth, proving that six degrees of separation are a painful reality. Molina had an amazing network of contacts and informants inside police and by pulling a few strings here and there he could confirm our suspicion. It was also painful to realize how people could be efficient inside the police department when so many cases of violence were unsolved in São Paulo.

On his last visit to my apartment, after several meetings and many cups of Rita's strong black coffee, Molina gave me an envelope, not very different from the one that contained the list years ago.

"The original list was destroyed for sure but these are copies of the police files that could be opened recently. They detail the search for *terroristas* and there were easy clues to find fourteen of them in just one week and that was very unusual. The dates match the time where you found the envelope, just a few weeks after the guy— Boscobino Bandeira—died. Also, there are certain connections between Boscobino and some names there: transcriptions of phone calls and addresses found in his house after he died. Most of the group survived jail, one girl left the country after she was released, and three other guys are accounted as *desaparecidos*. No one has heard of them after their arrest. We presume they died in jail and their bodies might have been taken in small planes and dropped into the sea far from the coast where sharks could eat them. It was a usual practice at the time."

I felt queasy but didn't say anything. I greeted him by the elevator door and stayed there, with the envelope in my hands for a few minutes. I went to my bedroom, locked myself in, and opened the middle closet door. Behind the lower shelf there was a safe, invisible to anyone who didn't know about it. I counted the floor planks and under one of them I picked a small key. As I opened the safe I remembered the magazine pages that covered Boscobino's locker and the moment I found the envelope behind them. I pulled a passport cover from the safe but inside it there was no passport, just a regular sheet of paper taken from a college ruled notebook many years ago. Even if I didn't know what I was doing at the time I had the idea of copying the names on the list on a sheet of paper, maybe I could later put a face on each of those names.

In a game with my own fear and conscience, I never looked back to those names but now it was the right time. I placed the papers Molina gave to me side by side with the old sheet, with my own handwriting, on the bed and sat down in front of them. Name by name, letter by letter, they were all the same, including Sebastião. I never told anyone about this copy and I decided to tell Molina I could remember a few names and the list was probably the right one.

I carefully placed the lists inside the passport cover, put them back in the safe, and unlocked my bedroom. In the kitchen I called Wilson, the driver, and asked him to take me to Capão Redondo, in the far outskirts of the city.

"*Seu* Felipe, *pelo amor de Deus,* for the love of God, we might not come back," Wilson said, his eyes translating the panic. "A car like yours won't cross that area without being attacked, without getting the wrong attention. People can kill for a Mercedes, you know? Why do you have to go to a place like that?"

"I just want to see it, just want to get out of this bubble."

"At least let's go in my old Volksvagen, we can pass as locals or at least as poor people."

"If you think it's necessary. Okay, it's a deal. I will pay for a full tank of gas, though."

"God bless you, Seu Felipe."

Half an hour later, we were in his noisy old car, I was sitting in the front beside Wilson, as if we were old pals. He seemed nervous and made me promise we were not going to stop anywhere in Capão Redondo, just drive through.

"And I will bring you back home before it gets dark."

"Okay, Wilson, I didn't know I had a nanny," I said.

He was still serious.

The trip was like a surgery in the city tissue: first we cut a perfect skin to reach muscles, veins and organs, going deep into the entrails until you find the tumor, hairy and odd shaped, smelling of death, growing, spreading until it took over, transforming the body into a decaying gray mass.

We left our garage with four car spaces for each apartment and turned the corner at Haddock Lobo Street, passing the Max Mara and the Armani shop, restaurants with glass ceilings and internal gardens, the café *Paraíso,* that got three stars on the *Veja* gourmet guide. Wilson's car was old and noisy but not slow. In five minutes, we were reaching another neighborhood and zooming by the long fence of a private club.

We went down on Marginal Pinheiros, the long and messy river drive, where the harmony of the Garden District dissolves into sewage smell coming from the Tietê, giving place to factories, smoke and a sad view of the river which has no sign of frogs anymore. Traffic was slow and it took us a long time to reach the exit where life held its breath. Houses got smaller until they were just shacks, built with blocks and metal foil with no finishing or painting. Streets were narrow and were paved on the year pitch was invented. A few kids ran around, a few men stood on a corner doing nothing, wearing discolored long shorts, T-shirts and *havaianas*. The place smelled of garbage and wasted time.

"Wilson, let's take one of these back streets."

"With all due respect Seu Felipe, are you crazy? Forgive me but I can't do it. They don't know us, they might think we are watching them, some guys here can be dangerous."

"Look, you have kids running around, you can see grocery shops, butchers, women going to places holding their children's hands. There are even a few decent houses amid the shacks. It can't be that bad."

"They know who's from here and who's not. Most of people who live here are hard-working, honest guys. But there are drug dealers hiding behind them and they can be powerful, maybe more powerful than any politician here. It doesn't look dangerous but if you do the wrong thing or take the wrong turn you can be in trouble."

"You seem to know a lot about it. "

"When you grow up in one of these bad suburbs, you develop a radar for life, Seu Felipe."

"Where did you grow up?"

"Not far from here, sir, in Taboão. "

"Does your family still live there?"

"My mother does. My brothers and I wanted her to move to a better place but she likes there. She knows everyone. She says she wants to die surrounded by friends and not alone in a nicer neighborhood."

"Well, I don't blame her. My mother did the same and the whole community went to her funeral years ago. It was nice to see it. In a way it's good to stay where you belong. What about your brothers, where are they?"

"The oldest is a pastor in an evangelical church some-where in the countryside, I don't even know where he lives now. He moves around a lot. The other lives close to my mother and he is a taxi driver. The younger one is in jail."

"And why?"

"Drugs."

"Sorry to hear that. How old is he?"

"Twenty-four. It's the second time he is involved in trafficking. I think he will never get out of it."

"You never know…"

"Well…we grew up very poor with no father. Mom was strict, there was not too much opportunity to study but we knew we would be decent. Not little brother, though, he was embarrassed by our condition. He always talked about making money, moving to a nice area, buy-ing a cool car, a motorcycle, sunglasses, this kind of thing. More than rich, he wanted to have the power, you know? But he quickly realized people like us have a tiny chance of moving that far up. You have to be okay with what you are or you will be very frustrated, angry. My brother was always angry. He was angry with people like you. The kind of stuff we see at war, you know what I mean?"

"Well, I grew up poor too. And I changed the game, I worked hard—"

"With all due respect, Seu Felipe, those were old times. Being poor nowadays is more humiliating."

I kept silent and thought about Coroa Street. I hadn't been there in many years, since Mother died. I looked outside and saw the back of a small house. There was a woman washing something on a *tanque,* an outdoor stone sink, and two kids sitting close to her and playing with a stray dog. The kids were not older than five and I thought what would happen to them when they reached fifteen. Would they be angry? Would they work at a paper factory?

"Seu Felipe, it's almost getting dark. Do you mind if I drive back to your place?"

"No, Wilson, not at all. Let's go back."

# CHAPTER 46

*São Paulo, 2007*:

Valentina died on the day I decided to retire. I was getting bored. My audiences were not bad at Independência, but I felt I was not the same, and I didn't want my fans to call me a dinosaur. Also, I wanted to spend more time with her before we both got too old. I secretly made the decision on a Thursday afternoon, the day she left for work and never got back home.

She had a brain aneurysm. She was still active, volunteering at a children's hospital after she retired from her practice. She drove to the hospital in the morning and parked the car in the garage, but before she could reach the elevator, she fell to the ground. A janitor found her and she was taken upstairs to the ER, but she was already dead. Fast as blowing a kiss. Gone.

When they called me from the hospital, before I felt my legs becoming jelly, I thought about Mariana and her panic attacks, her fear of life. Life was a sequence of suffering and let go.

A week later, after Valentina's burial, when I still couldn't open a closet in our apartment and see her dresses hanging there, I received the news about Lana. She had died in the same week and by the same cause as my girlfriend. And I never made it to California to see her. Damn it. What kind of life I was living? I thought it couldn't be a coincidence. A circle was closing up around me.

That's when a little voice inside told me to go see Rá, who was still living in Coroa Street in our old two-storied house. We all had bought it years earlier as a present to Mother. Rá retired and moved there before Mother's death. After that, when she found herself on her own, she executed a curious plan. None of us ever gave any credit to the weird sister, who barely knew how to sign her name and made a humble career at a public hospital. I never quite understood how she saved so much money. Thousands. She had a live-by-the-paycheck salary. She helped Mother with the smallest amount of money compared to the other siblings, always making clear that she was very poor:

"Gilda might be in a worse situation, but at least she has a husband to take care of her, I am alone in the world, if Mother was not here I wouldn't have a home." She winged about that every year when we decided how much money we would give to Mother. But I couldn't believe what I saw when I stopped in front of my old house, stepping out of a cab—I didn't want to arrive there with a *chauffeur*.

I barely recognized the façade and also the place next door, which had been bought and incorporated to it. Everything was painted white, but not redone in a proper way. The wall that separated both houses was destroyed and a passage had been built to connect the two places. It looked like a miniature hospital with passages from a ward to the next. Iron grids protected windows from burglars. The front gate was now eight feet tall, and walls around the house were the same height. Large pieces of broken glass were glued to the wall cement on the top, forming a deadly border to avoid intruders.

I rang the bell and she came fast to the front door, wearing an *aventail* similar to those Mother used to have over the nightgown.

"Felipe? What a surprise."

She took a long time to open the door.

"Hey, how long are you going to leave me standing here?"

"I have three lockers, just a minute."

"Don't you think it would be easier if you sell this place and go to an apartment?"

"I like it here, that's where we belong. Come in, but— I was not expecting anyone, so it's a bit messy and—"

"Rá, do you think I came here to check on your housekeeping?"

I got in and kissed her cheeks. I rarely kissed her. She didn't kiss me back, just stood there, shy. She didn't invite me to sit on the couch in the living room. She walked straight to the kitchen and I followed her.

"Coffee?"

"Yeah, of course."

The house inside hadn't changed much from the 1970s: same furniture, a new coat of sad beige on the walls, the old *cristaleira* still on the same corner. Inside it, replacing Mother's cups and jars, there was a collection of ugly bric-a-bracs: small dolls, glass figurines, little souvenirs from parties and free samplers. The walls were bare, Mother's images of saints, the photos of Getúlio Vargas and our few family shots were all taken away. Our real memories were not visible anymore. When we walked, a loud noise of old rotten wood came from the planks.

"Rá, you must have termites here, you should check. Some planks seem to be hollow."

She didn't answer. I thought she might be a little deaf.

And I was about to be surprised in the kitchen: our old demolition wood table was still there on the same place along the tiled wall. Instead of our hardwood, uncomfortable chairs, there were now three ordinary plastic chairs around the table. They had nothing to do with that majestic piece, made decades earlier with wood left behind in a construction site. My uncle's weathered hands gave it a regal quality. It was a dignified art work that survived poverty, tears, and loss; saw presidents rise and fall; held Christmas dinners with chicken, *panettone,* and wine; and days when all we had was black beans and bananas or Mother's corn war cakes. There were multiple round marks of hot cups and a few accidental knife carvings on the wood. I felt a punch in my heart when I saw myself sitting there with Valentina, having *café com leite* and cake when we were teenagers.

"I didn't know you had the table, Rá. It looks like a valuable antique now."

"Do you think I can make any money out of it?" Her eyes sparkled among the wrinkles and freckles.

"Listen, do not sell it, even if somebody offers a lot of money. I can buy it if you don't want it anymore."

"I will think about a price, but you are right, it should stay in the family."

Rá would always be Rá.

"Nobody thought you—especially you—would be interested in anything coming from our years of poverty, Felipe. These are all *velharias.* "

I ignored her.

"Do you remember this kitchen with the wood charcoal stove? Remember that Mother placed the radio always on the table so the cable could reach the plug on the wall? We did all our cooking and our meals listening to the musical programs and *radionovelas.*"

"Yes, Mother used to cook dinner listening to *O*

*Direito de Nascer* and sometimes she stopped stirring the sauce when there was suspense."

"When the food was ruined she got so upset and yelled that she would never listen to *novelas* again—"

"But on the next day she was there with the radio on at the same time."

"Yes, I forgot about that. I was out of the house most of the time though. I used to come home every other weekend."

"Do you remember the program with *Padre Donizetti?* The priest who blessed the glass of water placed in front of the radio?

"Oh yes. I drank the priest's water every day at the hospital. Everyone listened to his broadcast and at the end there were at least twelve cups of water around the radio."

"What happened to Padre Donizetti?"

"He died a long time ago, but people still talk about his blessings. I heard they want him to be canonized."

I pulled one of the plastic chairs and sat down. She came with the hot *bule* with the coffee, and placed in on the table, a little drop fell on the wood. Then she opened one of the two cabinets on the wall and took two cups with no saucer, a sugar bowl and spoons. I could smell hot milk.

"Rá, milk is boiling on the stove."

"*Ai,* Felipe, no!"

In one second the milk boiled over, spilling white foam on the stovetop.

Rá was old, she moved much slower than me. It looked like she was shrinking, her body so skinny and frail she could break in pieces any minute. She picked a cloth from the sink and started to wipe the stove.

"Leave it there, I'll help you later. Come and drink your *café com leite* before it gets cold."

She came to the table and pulled out a chair:

"I heard about your lover. Are you sad?"

"Devastated would be a better word. And she was not my *lover.*"

"You slept together for years without being married, she was your lover. What other name you have for it?"

"I loved her very much and I didn't come here to discuss what she was."

"So why are you here? You never pay me a visit...Did you bring me something special?"

"I brought myself." I was not going to pick a fight, I was too numb. "You don't look bad, Rá. You will probably close the gates of the family."

"Felipe, do you really think I look good?"

"Well, if you spent some money in new clothes you would look better."

I looked her up and down. *Havaianas* with socks, a discolored black skirt under the *avental.*

"Why spend money for clothes? I don't go anywhere."

"You would look healthier. You don't seem to eat well. I don't see any food here. Do you spend any money on food?

"I like my *café com leite* and sandwiches. I don't do warm meals, too much work. At night I have a Knorr soup."

"Every night?"

"Yes, they are very tasty."

"Well, I have back pain, diabetes, high blood pressure. And you live on Knorr soup...I really don't know who will close the family gates."

"Whoever stays longer takes the kitchen table."

"It's a deal."

We drank our coffee in silence. I was itching to talk about the money and the house next door.

"Rá, how did you get money to buy the house next door and to renovate ours like you did?

"Well, I saved. I saved all my life. While you were going out to restaurants, buying good clothes, I was working at the hospital and wearing hand-me-downs."

"You were always whining, saying you had nothing, how did you have money to save?

She had a devious smile on her face. "I didn't have money because I saved it."

"So, what you mean is that all this time you had money to help Mother, to bring food for Christmas, but you never did, isn't it?"

"You all had more than I could ever dream. Mother didn't need my pennies."

"Rá, it's so unfair! Think about Gilda, who died in deep poverty. She didn't even have a house of her own."

"Well, it's not my fault that she married that frog! Look, I can be an old fool, a weirdo, but I don't judge people. People always judge me. Mother judged me. She humiliated me. I wanted to have money of my own and this house for myself. I deserve it. I was the only one who ended up alone."

"We are both alone." My heart sank as I said it out loud. I took a deep breath. I didn't have energy to keep going on a discussion with my sister. What for? "Rá, I came here to tell you something.

She straightened herself on the chair like a child who's reprimanded for sitting in a bad position. I told her the whole story about the list, about how I got my radio program, about the connection of what was going on with Mariana, chapter by chapter, as in a *radionovela,* missing no detail.

I talked and she poured the coffee. We drank many cups of it. She made good coffee, not too strong, not too light. When I finished, she was silent for a while. Then she started talking about coffee and how many cups she used to drink every day. I felt relieved, even if I knew I couldn't love her.

I got up: "I have to go home. I am packing Valentina's stuff with Mariana. I better do it at once, as painful as it is."

"Come back for more coffee sometime."

"I will."

I never did. That was the last time I saw her alive. She died weeks later.

# CHAPTER 47

For a week I didn't want to talk or leave the house. Mariana was the only person I saw. We went through Valentina's clothes, jewelry, and papers. I was boxing most of it and sending to her sons, who would come to visit me in a few days. I also promised I would give them the apartment. I didn't want to be living there anymore, even if they insisted. We had a good relationship and the boys, all married with children, came to visit often from Rio.

Months later, I painfully finished going through the last box. I didn't do all at once, and I felt that every piece of me was going away every time I touched something that belonged to her. I finally told Mariana I was going to live in a hotel.

"Why?"

"I am tired of getting attached to things."

"You should go back to our apartment."

"Are you crazy? Emilia would never take me back."

"It's not a question of taking you back. We are still family."

"Mariana, she's barely spoken to me since the day I left. I understand I have hurt her and I don't deny it. So I want her to have a good life but I am not part of it anymore. I made my choice years ago."

The next morning, Emilia rang the bell. I opened the door in pajamas with disheveled hair and dark circles around my eyes. I was surprised to see she hadn't changed a bit—the same sad eyes with light make up, her honey-colored hair in a bun, her hips rounder than what they should be, her conservative dress in pastel blue.

"You look miserable," she said.

"My best days are behind me, for sure."

"Mariana wants to invite you for dinner tonight."

"Why did she send you to do the talking?"

"Well, I want you to come for dinner. We want you to come and eat with us. Rita is still cooking and she misses your complaints about the food. We would love to see you dressed, shaved, and clean at eight o'clock."

"Emilia, I don't know…"

"We insist. You have no choice."

"Thank you." I raised my head to look into her eyes but she had already turned her back and walked toward the elevator. I realized I never invited her to come in.

Later that day, I went for dinner with them and felt a strange comfort being in my old apartment, even if it was embarrassing and brought me so much guilt. Everything looked the same. A sixty-inch flat-screen TV was the only new detail I noticed.

After the three of us had dessert in the balcony, I got up to leave, but Mariana and Emilia insisted I stayed.

"This was your house for a long time. You stay here tonight," Emilia said.

She still had her angelic manners but her voice was imperious now.

I stayed and never left. She never asked any questions. We slowly picked up an old friendship and silently promised to take care of each other.

# CHAPTER 49

*São Paulo, 2009*:

In April, the swine flu was taking over the country and all I wanted was to stay at home for the whole month. TVs showed crowded hospitals, masked faces in the subway, and all the inevitable talk about viruses and symptoms. I felt sick, just looking at the images, and it made me think how afraid we are of dying, of disappearing. Every cause of death seems foolish to me, not good enough to take me away forever. I still felt a sting in my heart when I remembered Valentina and the way she disappeared, taken by a purple wind that just blew, messing up with her hair and taking her away. Mariana was still taking photographs all over, and I was terrified for her, even if I couldn't say anything.

"You should wear masks when you go out."

"Uncle Fe, you need to go back to work again. You are becoming too scared with the news, it's not that bad."

Well, that was a good sign of recovery coming from Mariana. I said nothing. She was actually getting better with those photos. She could even consider doing it for a living. But soon I realized this was not part of her immediate plans. Her thing with Dominic was going stronger and, during one Sunday lunch, he dropped the bomb:

"Seu Felipe, Mariana and I are thinking about getting married."

"Well, this is good news! I am very happy for you and—"

"Thank you, I am happy you approve...but we are considering...well, after the wedding we would maybe..."

"What? Are you pregnant Mariana?

"No, Uncle Fe!"

"So, what?"

"Uncle Fe, Dominic wants to go back to New York after the wedding."

"For how long?"

She paused. "Maybe for good."

I stopped with the fork and knife, my fingers got suddenly rigid. I could feel a flush of cold blood all over me. I decided not to meet Emilia's eyes. I knew she would be holding her tears and our lunch could end badly.

"But why? You seemed so happy here, Dominic."

"Yes, I am. But I have a family business there. It's better to manage it than finding a job here as a swimming instructor. That's the only thing I know how to do besides my family business. And it won't be enough to support a family. Also, there is also Mariana's problem..."

"Uncle Fe, what Dominic means is that my fears will disappear if we move to New York and start fresh, I will be able to leave all the trauma behind."

"I am sorry. I don't agree with that, you will not leave the trauma behind, you will hide from it. When you come back to visit it will be there. You won't solve the problem, I am sorry to be so blunt but that's what I think. Well, I mean *if* you consider coming back for a visit."

"Do you really think you will never see me again?"

"Well, we never know."

"I promise to come as much as I can. And you can come and visit us too."

I looked at Emilia and she seemed to be under control. We smiled at each other.

"So, you don't approve of our decision?"

"I don't have to approve anything, Mariana, you are old enough. I don't agree that it will make the scar disappear, but all we want is to see you guys happy." I extended my hand and touched Dominic's shoulder. "Welcome to this crazy family, I wish you luck."

"Thank you, *obrigado.*"

Emilia finally opened her mouth. "I will organize a great party to celebrate."

They started talking about all that *lero-lero* of dresses, invitations, venues, and I felt a rush: the list, the kidnapping—She had to know what I had found out, what I did. I couldn't let her go without telling her.

"I hope she forgive me." I told to myself before I cut my steak and joined the happy conversation again.

# CHAPTER 50

A few days later, Mariana was called for a confrontation at the police station and I thought it was time to tell her the truth. I came to her bedroom with a cup of coffee in the morning, it was a school vacation and she slept until late.

"Good morning my dear. Big day!"

"I know."

"Are you afraid of going through it all over?"

"I would prefer not to think about it anymore, ever."

"Well, you have to close the door, think through it before you let go."

She clutched the cup and lowered her head.

"There is something I have to tell you."

"U-oh...you and Auntie Emilia are splitting up again?"

"Noooo! We are fine."

"So what?"

"It's about one of the guys who kidnapped you. In a way we have a connection to him."

"*What*?"

"I will explain. It's difficult for me but I hope you understand it and forgive me."

"Why should I forgive you? This is getting confusing."

She placed the cup still half full on the bedside table and sat straight, looking right into my eyes. Mariana could be intimidating. Her green eyes were like darts when she was inquisitive. She would make a good lawyer.

I told her everything in detail: from my dream to work on radio, our difficulties during my childhood, how I found the list by chance and also, how I was so ignorant at the time I didn't fully realized what was going on with the political arrests and the hunt for *terroristas*. She barely moved, her eyes were just sucking all the information from me. Finally I got into Sebastião's story and the spectacular circle that has closed itself around us.

"Life is all interconnected," she said.

"Yes, Mariana, every little grain of sand."

As I expected, she didn't say too much after our conversation. Mariana's thoughts were never out there.

The confrontation was at three in the afternoon. We took her to the station, and Dominic was waiting at the entrance. He held her hand:

"Are you ready?" he asked.

I didn't know if she had told him about our conversation.

"I think so."

We entered the place again, the same smell of urine and humidity, the same anxious atmosphere, the same worried people sitting in the waiting room. We also waited for a while and they called Mariana to another room. They said she could take one person with her to help out. She looked at me. I stood up slowly, grabbed my cane, and held her hand.

The room was all gray and soundproof. It reminded me of an old recording studio. A young man offered me a chair along the wall and he placed Mariana in another seat, in the center of a room facing a large mirror. I knew that the suspects were behind that wall and there was an interrogation going on in the other side. A woman came in and introduced herself as a *delegada,* one of Mr. Soares's substitutes in charge.

"I am Doutora Assis, nice to meet you."

She looked briefly at us and started asking Mariana questions about the day on the bus, questions she had answered many times already. But I noticed something different, I noticed Mariana had an anxiety to talk, differently from other occasions at the precinct when she blocked all the memories of that day.

"After they pulled you out of the bus, what happened?"

I knew she was going to start saying *I don't remember.*

"They shoved me into the back seat of a car. It smelled of cigarettes and marijuana inside. One of them was in the back seat and pointed a gun at my head. They told me to be quiet or I would die."

I started to feel my hands cold and I feared I'd get sick.

"Who was the man sitting in the back with you?"

They turned on some sort of light and now we could see the three of them on the other side of the glass but they still couldn't see us. She pointed to Sebastião.

"Where did they take you?"

"I don't remember how long we were in the car, but a few minutes after I got in they covered my head. I was so scared that I didn't pay attention to what they were saying, I just prayed because I thought I was going to die. Then the car stopped, they pulled me out and we went inside a place I couldn't see."

"What happened then?" The *delegada* was very fast and I thought it would make Mariana nervous. She lowered her head and rubbed her hands.

"Do you recall what happened inside the house?"

"I...don't' remember much. I remember them talking about splitting the money, somebody was asking about the crack stone. I was afraid of saying anything. I was there for a long time before somebody came with a glass of water. My eyes were covered, I don't know who was the person. But I was thirsty and I thanked him."

"Did he say anything?'

"No. He smelled of cigarettes, that's all I can remember."

"Where were you sitting?"

"On the floor. It was probably tile floor, it was very cold."

"Could you see anything in the place?"

"No."

"How did you get out?"

"I remember one of them was very angry. He wanted to beat me. The others said they should let me go. He said *she looks rich, she should die, all rich people should die.* But the other two men said they would be in trouble if I died. They played this for a long time. The man who wanted to kill me spent hours by my side pointing the gun at me and saying that he was going to shoot. He even played *Russian roulette.* I was so scared that I started hearing a noise in my ear. I think I didn't want to hear anything anymore. After a long time, maybe a day or two, they dragged me to the car again, drove for about fifteen minutes and left me on a street I've never been on before. I just had two glasses of water during all that time."

"Did they say anything when they left you?"

"No, just to wait five minutes to uncover my eyes. I heard gunshots but that's what I did. I was afraid."

That was the last time Mariana spoke about it. We were still waiting for procedures and public court. The process was very slow. She might have to come from the US later for deposition. They say they will get a few years in jail but they can get out earlier if they have good behavior. I felt so disappointed with justice being so sluggish that I decided to organize a small charity to help poor kids with education. I made Emilia promise she would continue this job after I couldn't do it anymore. We inaugurated the charity months later at Mariana's wedding, a ceremony followed by a nice dinner in our apartment. After the party she gave me a box with all her photos of São Paulo.

"I want you to keep this. When I look at them I see so much about this city and I see more beauty than tragedy. This is your city, your place. I will soon adopt another home."

" I'm sure you will leave in between, always divided, like a person with two lovers."

"At least you can love two cities, it's less complicated than loving two men."

I smiled.

"And what about your plans to become a photographer? Do you still think about it?"

"I actually enrolled myself at a photography course in New York, starting in one month. I am on my way, Uncle Fe!"

"I am so proud of you!"

"And I am proud of you too!"

# EPILOGUE

*São Paulo, December of 2009*:

It was almost dark when Rá's funeral ended. We were heading to the restaurant, Mariana by my side in the car, rushed from the US a few days earlier for the wake. Our car finally left the Araçá cemetery and went down the hill, which gently embraces Pacaembu soccer stadium, drawing curves on the road. The driver went so fast I am sure the four tires were all suspended in the air for one second when we reached the top and started the descend. I was silent, just looking at the city lights dissolving into the evening fog. The lights in São Paulo always fascinated me. They were the first detail I noticed when I moved here, almost seventy years ago. I always liked to imagine there's a person living inside every bulb, small universes coexisting in chaotic and fascinating synchronicity.

I wished I was on a plane, taking off, when you see all the infinity of those shining gems getting smaller, when you have the idea of how immense this city is, when you don't see the end of the sea of lights for a few minutes. I thought about my dead sister and I made a mental note to pick up our demolition table in her house. It was intact, after all. I closed my eyes and thought about the plane taking off again. I saw Rá as a small bird, free at last, looking down at each of us inside our bulbs of light.

The End

## About the Author

Ines Rodrigues is a Brazilian journalist who worked in newspapers, magazines, and hosted radio programs. She moved to New York years ago to become a fiction writer and is a mother of two. In 2010, she started attending writing courses at The Writing Institute at Sarah Lawrence College, where she now teaches a Fiction Writing Workshop. She is one of the creators of the Scarsdale Salon, a literary event that happens three times a year in Scarsdale, NY.

Rodrigues lived in Italy and London before landing in New York. She is also a certified Italian teacher and has a deep interest in multicultural issues.

CPSIA information can be obtained
at www.ICGtesting.com
Printed in the USA
BVOW06s0249161017
497767BV00015B/82/P